Ghost Dancing

JAMES MAGNUSON

Doubleday
New York   London   Toronto   Sydney   Auckland

Ghost Dancing

Published by Doubleday, a division of Bantam Doubleday Dell Publishing Group, Inc.,
666 Fifth Avenue, New York, New York 10103
Doubleday and the portrayal of an anchor with a dolphin are trademarks of Doubleday, a
division of Bantam Doubleday Dell Publishing Group, Inc.

Library of Congress Cataloging-in-Publication Data

Magnuson, James.
  Ghost dancing / by James Magnuson.—1st ed.
    p. cm.
  I. Title.
PS3563.A352G46 1989   88-16144
813'.54—dc19

ISBN 0-385-23041-9

April 1989
First Edition

BG

For Billy and Martha

All have to come from under and through a dead layer.
—William Carlos Williams

But when he was yet a great way off, his father saw him.
—Luke 15:20

Ghost Dancing

One

GAGE WOKE to the sound of runaway horses. It seemed almost close enough to be in the room with him. He swung his feet to the floor, sure that the animals had broken free and were streaming past the house. He yanked the shade to one side and peered out.

There had been a frost during the night and the pasture was silver. The horses chased one another in long, thundering figure eights from fence line to fence line, still contained. They kicked and reared, made frisky by the chill October air.

Sounds carried in the cold. Everything seemed closer than it was. The Sangre de Cristos, ten miles away, were dusted with new snow. The faucets on the lawn were wrapped with rags.

It was early for a freeze, the ninth of October, Peter's birthday. It had been seventeen years since his son had died. Ragged layers of fog lifted off the mesa beyond the barn. Everything seemed closer than it was. Gage let the shade drop.

From the distant kitchen he heard running water, the slam of the refrigerator, Jody's six-year-old complaints about how she wanted only girls at her party, not boys.

He told Amy at breakfast that he was going into Santa Fe to run errands. She let it pass. It was understood that this was a day Gage spent alone. Some things were not shared easily; Peter was his, not hers.

Gage tied up the garbage bag while Amy put the breakfast dishes in the sink. Jody worked busily on her invitations, writing the names in big block letters and chatting away. She didn't want to invite Casey, Casey was her enemy.

It had always seemed funny to Gage how often in a family the birthdays bunched up within a few days of one another. Peter was born on the ninth, Jody on the twelfth, a son from one life and a daughter from the other who would never know anything of one another.

Amy fumbled through her purse, looking for her keys. Silence worked between them like a wedge. Jody called from the hallway that she couldn't find her mittens. Amy turned instantly at the sound of her daughter's voice. Amy, with her auburn hair, dancer's carriage and huge gray-green eyes, seemed so young to Gage just then. He was sixty, she was thirty-five. Some people considered it a scandal; what it felt like at the moment was a gulf.

It was the first time he'd gone into Santa Fe in almost a month and the drive, with the slick roads, took almost forty-five minutes. He dropped off a pair of saddles to be repaired and picked up a half dozen bags of sweet feed at the feed store.

He browsed at a downtown newsstand, but ducked out in time to avoid a Tesuque matriarch who'd been trying to corral Gage for years. He had gone to just one of her dinner parties and vowed never to attend another after she'd introduced him to a

2

visiting Tibetan priest as "the most notorious of our American film directors, why he and his actors throw Bowie knives at one another just for fun. This is a *very* dangerous man."

Safely out in the street, Gage decided to check out the downtown video store to see if his film *The Outriders* had shown up on the shelves. He pushed through the turnstile and strode beneath the battery of electric eyes into the world of pink and blue neon.

Everything in the place seemed to be marked down: albums, workout tapes, obscure brands of soda. Cardboard cut-out gorillas advertised the newest release. A spiky-haired clerk at the cash register gossiped with her pudgy girlfriend. A rosy middle-aged couple in matching baby-blue running suits stood in front of the television, holding hands and watching *Swingtime.*

Gage moved down the aisles. The place felt as alien as the moon. When he looked up at the curved surface of a huge surveillance mirror what he saw looking back at him was a foreshortened, burned-out cowboy, bandy-legged and leathery, wisps of thinning hair flying in all directions. He did not look like a man who could ever have been a danger to anyone.

He scanned the film titles and recognized less than half of them. He edged down the alphabet, past *Howard the Duck* and *Last Tango in Paris,* past *Monkey Business* and *Night Moves.* Finally he spotted *The Outriders,* announcing itself by the famous shot of Crow and Eloi with their pistols drawn, making their doomed dash for freedom.

Gage picked up the cassette and flipped it over. On the back were two stills, one of the terrified townspeople caught between the bounty hunters and the gang, the other the shot of Roy Eagle, his eyebrows and beard glistening with ice, peering out of the slit and steaming carcass of a steer in the blizzard scene. Underneath the stills was the Stanley Kauffman quote: "A savage masterpiece from the master of cinematic violence."

Gage tried to figure out if he was pleased. If his agent wasn't lying to him, they would be re-releasing four of the other films in

3

cassette in the next year. It would be a regular Gage revival and there could be real money in it.

But somehow Gage was less than pleased. Maybe it was the cheap, milky-white plastic box it came in; it looked like the kind of container you'd use to keep your leftovers from rotting. Gage felt no connection to any of it. Thirty years he'd spent creating these images and it had cost him plenty. If you believed some people, it had cost him his son's life.

Gage felt someone watching him. He glanced over at a punked-out hulk squatting at the far end of the aisle. The kid quickly looked away.

He was dressed all in black, with torn sleeves and a silver-studded leather wristband. He had a dirty green book bag over his shoulder and his head seemed almost too big for his body, like André the Giant, but the most amazing thing about him was his boots. They looked as if they weighed five pounds apiece, adorned with chains and dirty red ribbons.

Gage did not like the idea of being caught admiring his own work. He put the cassette back on the shelf, feigning indifference, then moved to the other side of the aisle and began flipping through a stack of old Danny Kaye films.

Maybe a minute later Gage looked back and saw that the punk kid had picked up *The Outriders* and was turning it over in his ham hands. Gage gave a half smile; he might have been beyond many things, but he wasn't beyond flattery. The kid stared at the back of the cassette for an awfully long time. He didn't look as if he was that swift a reader.

The kid glanced up at the big overhead mirror, then looked back to see if anyone was watching him. The clerk was still laughing and talking to her girlfriend. Gage kept his head down. The kid quickly slid *The Outriders* into his shoulder bag.

Gage was too astonished to do anything at first. He watched the kid clop up the next aisle, sounding like a Clydesdale, stop for a while to gawk at Fred and Ginger gliding across the TV screen.

4

So now they're stealing me, Gage thought. He wasn't exactly mad and he wasn't exactly proud, but he was curious. He wanted to see if the kid could get away with it.

He watched the kid mosey up to the spiky-haired clerk and flirt with her for a minute, the dirty green book bag slung over his shoulder. He showed her the metal studs on his black leather wristband, then took off the band as if to give it to her. She laughed and waved him away.

The kid thudded off through the rows of record albums, stopping once to shout something back to the two girls, then pushed through the turnstile at the front of the store. Gage followed.

A crowd had gathered on the sidewalk; at first the fact did not strike Gage as extraordinary. He pushed his way through, focusing only on the hulking kid, who had already crossed to the far curb.

Gage stepped out into the street. He was halfway across before it dawned on him that something might be wrong. He looked up.

The sidewalks had been cordoned off and policemen leaned against sawhorses. On the plaza people were packed four and five deep. Some of the faces Gage recognized: a solemn bookshelver from the library eating nachos out of a Fritos bag, the Indian who sold jewelry in the La Fonda lobby; Simon Huerta, the small-time contractor Gage had used to reroof his garage, was there in tie and ill-fitting suit.

They all stared at him as if he had made some terrible error. For one crazed moment it occurred to him that it might be a practical joke, a trap, a monstrous surprise party.

Then he heard the hooves. He turned and saw the team of four white horses trotting down the street toward him. They pulled a wagon on which sat a simple wooden coffin. Behind the coffin a procession filled the streets. A Hispanic policeman hustled toward Gage, waving him off.

Gage moved quickly to the far sidewalk. He heard the bells of the cathedral. This had nothing to do with him. It was incredible that he could have forgotten. The story had made headlines in every paper in the state.

Father Ortiz had gotten a call in the middle of the night from someone who pleaded with him to come deliver the last rites to a dying man. The priest was given directions to a remote rest stop in the desert, fifty miles from Santa Fe. He left the cathedral sometime after midnight on a Sunday. His body was found two days later. He had been shot three times, once in the stomach and twice in the head. His abandoned car was found halfway across the state. Still missing were his wallet and the bag carrying the sacraments.

On the evening news a grim-faced police chief vowed vengeance. Both *The New Mexican* and *The Albuquerque Journal* carried page after page of testimonials to the priest's kindness, his selflessness. He was a man without enemies, that's what everybody said; he had died the death of a martyr. All the police leads had quickly evaporated. In the coffee shops the rumors were of Satanists and motorcycle gangs and escaped convicts. When a man without enemies was killed, all that was left was speculation about pure malevolence and the random exercise of evil.

Just another spectator now, Gage watched the coffin pass. The priest's mother, in black dress and veil, walked directly behind the wagon. She was a frail woman, probably in her seventies, and she had a son and a daughter on either arm.

Behind the priest's family stretched an endless line of mourners: Catholic women's groups, teenagers costumed as conquistadores, a uniformed mariachi band and what looked like every nun and priest in the state of New Mexico. Some sang softly, the chanting moving up and down the line.

Gage studied the gaunt, wind-burned face of a sandaled monk, saw the barely suppressed pride in the way he carried himself. The death of Father Ortiz had justified all of their vows, made sense of how they had chosen to lead their lives.

6

Gage jostled through the crowd. A large young black woman in an I LOVE THE BIG APPLE sweatshirt stood weeping on the curb; no one was immune to the intensity of emotion. A group of red-jacketed busboys huddled together in front of The Base Camp, whispering in Spanish. They looked Central American. Simon Huerta, the least pious of men, crossed himself as the casket approached. Something ancient was asserting itself, blowing tourist Santa Fe right off the street.

The procession came to a momentary halt. The brown wooden casket sat on the open hearse, five feet away. The impatient horses snorted and stamped their feet. Pigeons strutted unafraid beneath them, scavenging for scraps of food.

Peter had never had a casket. There had been nothing left to bury. No prayers, no procession, no one would have dared.

Gage felt his eyes shine with tears. He had to turn away. The lantern-jawed young thief leaned against a parking meter seven or eight feet away, sure that he was safe. He took the cassette from his book bag, fondling his prize, examining the pictures on the back.

It was all the trigger Gage needed. He was suddenly furious. It seemed, at the moment, as if his life had been nothing but thieves and pirates and rip-off artists. It was impossible to hold on to anything. You wake up one morning and reach out for the hand that was always there and it's gone. The sons of bitches would steal you blind if you let them.

The kid sensed that he was being watched and looked up. His eyes widened; he recognized Gage from the store.

"You got a problem, man?" One of the horses shook in its harness as chanting began far down the line.

"No problem," Gage said. "But that movie you've got there, it's mine."

"Yours?" The lantern-jawed kid was incredulous. He scratched at his pitted face. "You crazy, mister?" He took a couple of nervous glances to the left and the right, checking for an escape route, but the crowd was packed in tight behind him.

Gage came forward a couple of steps. A white and gold silk banner snapped in the breeze above the massed, waiting line of mourners. "Want me to prove it to you?" Some of the people on the sidewalk were aware of the disturbance; Gage didn't need to look to feel their disapproval.

The hulking young thief frowned. Gage was forty years older and thirty pounds lighter than the kid, but there was no sign that Gage was bluffing.

The kid turned, intending to split, but came up short. Gage had gotten help from an unlikely source. The young thief had turned in to Simon Huerta, who had a restraining hand in the middle of the kid's chest.

The young shoplifter swung an elbow, trying to get Huerta off him. Huerta did not back off. Even in his too-snug Sunday suit, Huerta was not without menace. The kid knew he was trapped.

"You don't have to prove nothing to me, mister. You say it's yours, it's yours."

The kid tossed the cassette out into the street. It skated under the horses, rebounded off a hoof, skittered under one of the wooden wheels. The hearse lurched forward, shattering the plastic cassette. Startled pigeons took quick flight, whirling up like scavenging angels.

A murmur of disapproval rose from the onlookers. A policeman hustled forward, too late; the young thief had already broken through the crowd and plunged across the bank parking lot in his seven-league boots.

It was Huerta who played the Good Samaritan, stepping out into the street, going down on one knee to reach under the belly of the coffin to gather up the plastic shards and tangled spools of tape.

Gage still had not moved. He had made a fool of himself and for no good reason. When Huerta brought him the snarled remains of the cassette, Gage gathered it in with cupped hands.

The procession had begun to move again. Gage stuffed the

unraveling tape into his jacket pocket, ignoring the stares of those around him.

Huerta straightened his tie. "So what was that about?" Huerta, even freshly scrubbed, still had the smell of cheap roofing jobs.

Gage shook his head; he'd already given enough away.

Huerta was silent for several seconds, growing melancholy. The chanted reassurances of eternal life swelled up and down the line. "I'll tell you," he said. "It's getting hard to know what you can believe in anymore."

Two

T̲HE BLACK CAST-IRON RAM, a hundred yards off, seemed to tremble against the sandy bunker with a palsied life of its own. Gage let out his breath evenly, trying to get the gunsight to settle in the chest of the silhouette.

He was dimly aware of the pop of shots to the left and right of him, dimly aware of heavy metal targets tumbling far out on the range. Rig Jensen stood as silent as a valet at Gage's shoulder, frowning at the scorecard.

Gage pulled off the shot. Sand sprayed up just beyond the target.

"Tad high," Rig said.

"You sure?" Gage disengaged the chamber of his pistol and stepped back off the line an unhappy man. On the handle of his revolver were etched the faces of Crow and Eloi, the two side-

10

kicks in *The Outriders*. It was a gift from the finest gun manufac-
turer in the world. Every person in the gun club would have
given his eyeteeth for a pistol like that and Gage couldn't hit the
broadside of the barn with it.

"I think that shot went right through the curl in the horn, I
really do," Gage said.

"You never know."

Gage glanced back at Rig, who looked more worried than he
should have. Rig was in his mid-fifties, still as lanky and fit as a
twenty-year-old, still flying patrols for the Fish and Game Department.

"Am I doing something wrong? Tell me."

"No, you're doing fine," Rig said. These damn Scandinavians,
Gage thought, they'll drive you crazy, being nice.

Gage jerked off his heavy metal earmuffs. "That's the problem
with these store-bought bullets. Too much kick to 'em. That's
what you get for not taking the time to pack your own."

Rig folded up the scorecard and jammed it in the pocket of his
red flannel shirt. "You want some coffee?" he said. "I need to
talk to you about something. And I've got something to show
you too."

Gage followed Rig through the maze of haphazardly parked
cars and pickups. A German shepherd leaped, barking at the
window of a stock truck as they passed. At his back Gage could
hear the continuing pistol shots, the ping of metal chickens, rams
and pigs taking hits. Above the tawny mesas near the river, a pair
of hawks floated high up, playing off the thermals.

Rig had driven Gage out there once, showed him the skeletons
of the old doper trucks along the La Bajada highway. Rig had
explained how it worked: one plane would file a flight plan in El
Paso and, as he took off, his partner waiting on the Mexican side
would take off too, rising quickly to meet him. They would fly
wing tip to wing tip all the way up so that on any radar screen
they appeared as a single dot. Then, as they approached the
Santa Fe airport, the plane with the dope would drop down onto

the desolate back road, where a truck would be waiting. Sometimes they made it and sometimes they didn't.

Rig slid open the camper's panel door and there was instant scrambling inside. Gage peered in and saw the startled fawn, no more than a few days old, peering back.

"Good God," Gage said.

"What do you think?"

The fawn got her feet tangled in the old sleeping bag Rig had fixed up for her bed, slipped to her knees, skittered up again.

"When did you find her?" Gage asked.

"This morning. Early. I was on my way over here when I saw something hopping out in one of the fields." Rig extended the back of his hand and the fawn took a cautious step forward to sniff at it. There was a flurry of shots out on the shooting range, as if someone had thrown a string of firecrackers off a roof. "Her mother must have been hit by one of the logging trucks. Who knows how long this little one had been hiding in the grass. No way she was going to make it on her own, so I caught her, brought her along. Go on, get in, I'll make you some coffee."

The two men crouched on the narrow leather seats of Rig's camper. Gage fed the fawn out of a bottle. The tiny animal nursed greedily at the rubber nipple; Gage had to hold on with both hands to keep her from sucking it off. The milky-white calf formula ran down his wrists.

"So what are you going to do with her?" Gage asked.

"I don't know," Rig said. He sipped coffee from a Styrofoam cup, and took a white donut from its cellophane wrapper. "I can always call one of the zoos, but I thought I'd see if you were interested. I was thinking about your little girl. She's what now?"

"Six . . . well, actually seven today. I've got to go into town right after this to pick her up a present."

"This is perfect. She couldn't have a better birthday present."

"I don't think so, Rig. She'd love it, I know. But it never seems fair, keeping wild animals penned up. You know what I mean?"

"She would love it."

"I know that." Gage wrested the bottle free. "But we'd have to keep her in a horse trailer, keep her away from the dogs."

"You aren't even tempted?"

"Oh, I'm tempted all right. But I'm not going to do it." Rig puffed up his cheeks, staring out the windows at the distant mesas. "But this isn't what you really wanted to talk to me about, is it?"

"Not really, no." Rig pressed his long fingers together. The ring on his left hand was so impossibly blue it looked more like Ty-D-Bol than turquoise.

"So if you've got something to say, say it." The fawn pushed forward against Gage's knees, its tiny hooves skittering on the slick floor, its nose in the air, searching for more food.

"You know how a person is always hearing things."

The man is the Dag Hammarskjöld of game wardens, Gage thought. "So what is it you've heard?"

"You know about the priest who was killed?"

"Sure. I ran into the funeral procession a few days ago."

"You can imagine how gung ho the cops have gotten over solving that one."

Gage ran his hand over the fawn's back, over the ragged white spots. The tiny animal shivered. "I can imagine."

Rig wouldn't look at him. There was a faint droning of a plane. Rig crumpled up one of the cellophane wrappers. Somewhere outside, the scorekeeper announced the winners. "Your son's name came up."

Gage stared at him. It was an impossibly sick joke. Rig had a trace of white under his lower lip. "You've got powdered sugar on your chin," Gage said.

Rig tried to wipe it off, coloring red. "I didn't know if I should tell you or not."

"I have no son," Gage said. The fawn butted her wet, black nose into Gage's hand, demanding mother's milk. "My son is dead."

13

Rig looked up, his light blue Nordic eyes locking in with Gage's; they were flying wing tip to wing tip. "I know that," Rig said.

Gage pushed open the door to the detective's office and caught Captain Trevino about to bite into a sticky bun. The gimpy-armed clerk at Gage's shoulder tried to wedge his way in.

"Captain Trevino, I'm sorry. I told him he'd have to wait, but he wouldn't listen. I don't know who the hell he thinks he is."

"My name's Jeremiah Gage."

The detective's soft brown eyes seemed to swell with interest and he quickly brushed the sugar from his neat mustache with a napkin. He was a small, spidery man and even in uniform he looked more like a librarian than a cop.

"Come in, please." The detective's gesture to Gage was courtly. He motioned reassuringly to the anxious clerk, who clutched a bottle of Liquid Paper correction fluid in his good hand. "If you could just hold my calls for fifteen minutes. Thanks." The clerk resisted for a couple of beats and then vanished.

The detective picked up his coffee cup, the product of some children's pottery workshop. "Sit down, Mr. Gage, please." Gage clearly did not want to sit down. 'Tell me what I can do for you."

It was a cheery corner office, with more yellow in it than you could expect at a police station, with big windows and, on the wall, family pictures: a wedding, a sheep shearing, a darkly handsome nineteen-year-old in his army uniform.

"I was at the Caja del Rio gun club this morning," Gage said.

"The one out by the dump, sure. I've shot there myself." The murmur of young voices rose in the hallway; it sounded like a troupe of second-graders on a field trip.

"And someone said that my son's name had come up." Trevino frowned and set down his coffee cup. "I know cops," Gage continued. "I like cops. And I know that nobody likes a good

14

cops-and-robbers story more than cops. But if anybody tries to drag what happened to my kid into this Father Ortiz business, just to get themselves a little ink, I'll have his ass in court so fast it'll make your head spin."

Captain Trevino walked over and gently closed the office door. "Sit down, Mr. Gage, please. I want to show you something."

He went to his file cabinet and began to search through it. Gage begrudgingly lowered himself into a ladderback chair. Captain Trevino finally found a yellowing newspaper at the back of the second drawer and presented it to Gage.

It was *The Fargo Forum*. The name of the paper wasn't what mattered. What mattered was the date: May 14, 1970. The lead was the same as the lead of every paper in the country that day: THREE DIE IN MUNITIONS PLANT BLAST. Next to it was the wire service photo of the firemen still spraying water over the smoking ruins. Just below the big photo were smaller pictures of the three who had died, the night watchman, the twenty-year-old farm kid, and Peter, except where Peter's face should have been, someone had taken a felt-tip pen and blacked it out.

Gage stared at it for several seconds and then looked up at Captain Trevino. "Who scratched the face out?"

"I don't know."

"Where did you find this?"

"In the trunk of Father Ortiz's car."

Gage stared out the window, too stung to think. A young lawyer in a blue blazer locked his ten-speed into the bike rack, metal clips still on the cuffs of his trousers.

"You ever been to Fargo, North Dakota?" Captain Trevino asked.

"No," Gage said.

"Neither have I. Neither had Father Ortiz, as far as I can tell. You have no idea what this means?"

"No."

"Neither do I." Gage folded the newspaper and set it on the detective's desk, on top of a stack of flyers about dog poisonings.

"Why would someone, seventeen years after the fact, scratch out your son's face?"

"How many people know about this?"

"Just a couple of the officers. It was unfortunate anything was said. Don't worry. We'll make sure the talk stops."

The detective leaned against the windowsill. Yellow flecks of newspaper still clung to the sleeve of his blue uniform. Trevino, a fastidious man, flicked them away.

When Gage finally spoke, the words came out of him like a cry. "I just don't think you can possibly know . . ."

"Know what?"

"Nothing. Nothing . . ."

"And then again." The detective pushed away from the windowsill. "If we're talking about pictures of our kids." He tapped at the color photo of the young dark-haired soldier. "Americo. Named after my grandfather. But he liked everyone to call him Rick. All-state miler in high school. Killed walking point in a mine-sweeping operation outside of Da Nang. He was nineteen years old. There's a bridge name for him north of Española."

Trevino picked the newspaper off the desk and stared at the headlines again. "Those were hard times for everybody. All those Anglo kids came here running from the war and all our kids headed the other way, going to serve. They thought it was their duty, they owed their country that much." He slapped the folded newspaper against his thigh. "But there's no solving that. Why my son died. Or yours. That's not what we're after. What we want to know is what happened to Father Ortiz, right?" He tossed the newspaper back onto the desk. "Something like this, what's important is keeping your eye on the target."

16

Three

FIFTEEN MILES north of Santa Fe, Gage turned off the main highway. The country road wove through golden cottonwoods, following the course of the river, nearly dry now in the second week in October. A battered pickup with mismatched doors sat on the rocks of a riverbed and three teenagers skipped stones over the shallows.

Gage was incapable of thinking it all through. Who would keep a newspaper, *that newspaper,* for seventeen years? Only someone whose life had been marked by that explosion. Gage didn't know anyone like that, not here, not anyone who could possibly have known Father Ortiz. The whole thing made him feel stupid and simpleminded, like a child incapable of tracing lines between numbered dots.

There had been so many times in the past when he would have

17

given everything for the scene in Trevino's office, when he would have worked it up into the most insane kind of hope. But not now. He had a life now. He bumped through a dusty arroyo, past the slender white pole set in the rust-colored bank. It was a water gauge, absurd-looking on a day like this, but during flash-flood weather it served its purpose, warning travelers when to turn back.

He drove past his neighbor Orlando Cantu's place, where chickens scavenged among rusting farm equipment. He passed the field of sunflowers and as he crossed the fast-flowing irrigation ditch, the high stone walls of home came into view.

There were a half dozen cars lined up along the road: a couple of Suburbans, a dusty Ford station wagon, a new Volvo. His instinctive reaction was that something terrible had happened, but then he realized. It was his daughter's birthday party and he had forgotten.

He parked outside the open gate. As he stepped down from the pickup the dogs slunk out to greet him, tails flailing happily. He moved toward the house, his heart filled with dread. This was a major screwup. A saddled horse rested at the pasture fence, reins looped around a post. Amy had probably already given all the kids rides.

He paused for a second at the top of the steps, listening to the children's laughter inside, and finally punched open the latch.

Amy bent over the kitchen table, lighting the candles on the birthday cake. She paused for a second to lick some white frosting from her knuckle. The other mothers surrounded her. Gage knew most of them. Ona had on one of the peaked birthday hats and fiddled with the rubber band under her chin.

Ona saw him first and threw her hands wide in mock surprise. "Wel-l-l, look who's here."

Amy glanced up. A strand of auburn hair fell across her forehead and she brushed it aside. She looked flushed and frantic.

"Are you okay?" she said.

"Yeah, I'm fine," he said. He felt all the other mothers' eyes on him, disapproving. He could hear Jody holding forth in the other room; she tended to get bossy when she was having a good time.

"I'm really sorry, Amy," Gage said. A plastic garbage bag next to the refrigerator bulged with party cups, torn wrapping paper and ketchup-stained napkins. "Something came up."

"We can talk about it later," she said. He could hear the hurt in her voice. The other mothers were silent as jurors. Gage turned to them, trying to recoup.

"Hey, Ona. Hey, Janis, how you doin'?" Gage leaned over to give Janis a peck on the cheek. "I see where Whit got his picture in the paper the other day."

"Why don't you hit the lights in the dining room?" Amy said.

"Sure, hon, sure." He put a hand on Amy's back and kissed her softly on the hair. She was concentrating on lighting the last of the seven candles and did not look up.

As Gage entered the room Jody was entertaining the tableful of girls by holding her nose with her fingers and blowing bubbles in her ginger ale through a straw.

"Daddy! Daddy!" She bounced up in her chair. Gage gave her a hug; there was at least one person in the world who wasn't mad at him. "Daddy, look what Mercedes gave me. A Barbie Doll pool house!" She clung to his sleeve; with his free hand Gage batted away a drifting green balloon. "Where were you, Daddy? We needed you to give us horseback rides!"

"Darlin', I'm sorry. But the best is coming, you just hold on."

He pulled the curtains across the living room windows to shut out the afternoon sun, then snapped off the light switch. All the girls let out a big "O-o-o-w-w-w!" and Amy appeared in the doorway bearing the cake and the singing began.

Amy set the cake in front of Jody. The children's and mothers' voices rose and Gage joined in, the only male voice in the room. Jody sat with her face basking in the glow of the candles—she knew how to be cherubic when she chose to—and Ona got down on one knee to take pictures. Gage's voice trailed off as he stared at the candlelight flickering in his daughter's sweet face. It was

19

suddenly Peter's face he was thinking of, the face inked out in that newspaper, that face in the searing light of the explosion seventeen years before.

He looked across at Amy and, after a second, reached across and squeezed her hand. Amy smiled gamely, trying hard not to hold a grudge.

"Blow out the candles!" the girls shouted. "Blow out the candles!"

"Wait a minute!" Ona had her hand up. "I want to get one more picture."

"I was worried about you," Amy said softly.

"It was a real mess-up, Amy, I'm sorry."

"Mercedes! Ginger!" Ona waved for the girls to move in closer. "Squeeze in a little bit. I don't want to leave anyone out!"

"I called Rig," Amy said. "He said the gun meet ended three hours ago. I thought maybe you'd had an accident."

"No accident."

"Say cheese everybody!" Ona said.

"So what was it?" Amy said. Gage looked quickly at her. He realized that he was not going to tell her.

Someone banged on the table with a spoon. "Blow out the candles!"

"Remember to make your wish first!"

"I'll tell you later," Gage said.

Jody rose up, taking a huge breath. Amy moved away from Gage, genuinely upset now and trying not to show it. She was a southern aristocrat, of the country liberal variety, and she didn't believe in making scenes in public.

Jody blew hard and long, her face almost in the candles, and she blew out every one. The girls all clapped and Jody waved her fists in the air as if she had just been named heavyweight champion of the world, but, even as she turned to ask her mother something, one of the candles sputtered back to life.

Mercedes hooted; Ginger shrieked. Jody's mouth dropped open and she looked up at Amy in protest.

20

"Mom-my!"

"You didn't blow them all out! Ha-ha-ha-ha-ha-ha!" taunted a chubby girl in a frilly blue dress.

Jody tried to be a good sport about it. She got up on her knees on her chair and blew the candle out a second time and a third. Each time it flamed up again, the funnier the first-graders thought it was.

Jody wasn't sure it was funny and Gage wasn't either. Part of him was still back in Trevino's office; there was something perverse and unnatural about what had happened. A man's life was not intended to be a trick candle that could be snuffed out and then sputter back into flame.

"You didn't blow them all out! That means you don't get your wish!" sassed the cruel girl in the frilly dress.

"Dad-dy!" Jody was in distress. The stubborn candle was down to a stub, bleeding a tiny pool of pink wax onto the white frosting. "It's not fair."

"It's just a joke, darlin'," Gage said.

"It doesn't mean I don't get my wish, does it?"

"No, darlin', it doesn't mean that." Gage wet his fingers, leaned over and pinched out the candle. He sucked at the burn at the tip of his forefinger. "All you have to do is remember to keep your wish to yourself."

That night, as penance, Gage spent an hour assembling Barbie's pool house and then read his daughter three books instead of two and lay down with her until she was asleep. Before leaving he pulled the quilt up to her nose. Nights were getting cold now.

Amy sat at the kitchen table, the sleeves of her bulky Irish sweater pushed up to the elbows, phone propped between ear and shoulder. She was lining up volunteers for the carnival at Jody's school. Amy believed in being a good citizen; tonight he wasn't going to tease her about it.

He came up behind her while she was still on the phone and

put his hands on her neck, trying to massage away the tension. She tolerated it for maybe a minute and then gently brushed his hands away.

When she hung up she did not look at him at first.

"You all right?" he said.

"Yes."

"Are we going to be able to get over this?"

"Of course." Now she looked up. "But how could you forget about your daughter's birthday party? We talked about it this morning. . . ." He said nothing, drifting toward the sink. "It's not as if this were just one isolated incident. It seems to me it's happening more and more, your forgetting things."

"So maybe I'm getting old. A little senile."

"No, I don't think it's that. I think forgetting is a hostile act. I think you're just not that emotionally involved with us right now."

"Amy, you know that's not true."

"Okay. Maybe I've got it all wrong. Let's just not discuss it, then, all right? I need to make these phone calls. I just need a little time to myself."

Gage put another log on the fire and watched a few minutes of *Magnum, P.I.*, but when it failed to hold his attention, he padded off to put the dogs outside. The night was clear and full of stars. He turned on the lawn-sprinkling system, pulled the gate shut and locked it.

His obsession with security still exasperated Amy. She had never had to face what was out there in the dark; he had. After Peter's death there had been threats, unsigned letters, anonymous phone calls. There had been none for several years. Still, Gage had always been a kind of lightning rod; the nature of his reputation drew the attention of the bizarre, the hostile. Granted, a stone wall wouldn't keep them all out, but there was nothing so crazy about the locks, the alarm systems, the electronic eye mounted on the garage wall, the gun in the back of the bedroom closet. It was just facing facts.

22

When he came back inside, Amy had gone to bed. He got a glass of milk and a piece of birthday cake and wandered through the house, turning off lights. When he came to his study, he paused for a second, then flicked the light on.

There could be no connection between Peter and the murdered priest. It was just one of those freak things. Nothing to be done: there was no other line he could take. He tried to remember the name of the girl Peter had been living with before he disappeared. It was Joan, but Joan what? He knew he had to have the name somewhere.

He stood on a chair so he could reach the highest shelves in the closet, where his address books were stored. He pushed aside the scarves and winter caps, carefully unstacking the worn boxes of Monopoly and Wuzzles.

He wasn't careful enough. A shoebox slid free. Gage grabbed, but couldn't hold it. The box tumbled off the back of the chair, the rubber band snapped, pictures showered across the floor. The past lay scattered on the Navajo rug like so many loose tiles.

Gage got down from the chair, cursing, and began to gather the old pictures. He tossed them back into the shoebox almost thoughtlessly at first, as if what had happened was no more than a clumsy mistake, stubbornly refusing to treat it as a sign. Then he came to the picture of Peter in his high school football uniform, face flushed and grinning above shoulder pads, a child's face.

He stared at it a second, then turned the desk lamp up a notch and held the photo under the intense circle of light. When he set it aside he stood listening for any sound in the house; the only thing he heard was the dogs thumping against the wall outside.

He began to go through the pictures one by one. He might have been there, kneeling on the floor of the study, for an hour, he had no sense of it. He found the picture of Peter in Guatemala, standing on the plaza with two Indian weavers. He found the snapshot of Peter and Nina and himself huddled together at the top of the Empire State Building, the wind in their faces, the

23

city in mist below them. They looked happy. They had been a real family then.

Gage began to sob. He grimaced, trying to pinch it off, fighting against it. It was weak, corrupt, he had no right to these tears.

He threw the last of the pictures into the shoebox, snuffling, disgusted with himself, and hid the box at the back of the top shelf, burying it beneath scarves and mittens.

He stopped again in his daughter's room. She had kicked off her quilt. Gage carefully lifted her legs to work the quilt free and pulled it over her again. He rested his hand against her cheek for several seconds.

He tiptoed into the bedroom and undressed silently, and slipped into bed. At first he thought Amy was asleep, then realized she was only being quiet. Neither of them spoke. He pushed up close to her and rested his hand on her hip and after several seconds her hand came up to cover his. Amy was wrong; the problem wasn't his forgetting; the problem was that he remembered all too well.

Four

THE SECOND UNIT DIRECTOR signaled frantically from the riverbank. Gage was on a raft with the dynamite man and two cameramen, scheming how to blow up the bridge above them. It was the spring of '69 and they were in the second week of shooting *The Outriders*. Gage ignored the desperate wavings from the shore at first; it was impossible to hear even the loudest shouts above the rush of muddy water and Gage did not take kindly to interruptions. Things never turned out to be the major crises that second unit directors thought they were. This time was the exception.

Peter had been arrested for assaulting a police officer in a riot in Madison, Wisconsin. The dean of students at the university had called the studio, but it was Sunday morning and the message just sat there until Monday. Peter had been in jail for two nights, his bail set at fifty thousand dollars, well beyond the reach of any student bail fund.

Gage dropped everything, sketching out the next day's shooting schedule with the assistant director on the way to the airport. He caught a middle-of-the-night flight out of Phoenix. He had six hours alone to get himself worked up; by the time he arrived in Madison he was ready to wring his kid's neck.

He picked up a paper at the airport newsstand. The headline read, YOUTHS, POLICE STAGE 3RD NIGHT OF CLASHES. The pictures were of a long line of riot-equipped cops guarding the City-County Building, a student pinned to the ground by police nightsticks.

Waiting for car keys at the Avis counter, Gage scanned the newspaper accounts. In three nights of tear gas and burning barricades there had been a hundred and ten arrests, forty people hospitalized, all of it triggered by police trying to break up an unauthorized block party. Gage had trouble focusing. There was something he wasn't getting here. After missing a night's sleep he found reading almost impossible; the letters seemed to lift off, swarming and dancing on the page.

Father and son tripped down the steps of the Detention Center in grim silence. Peter's right eye was swollen and he cradled his left arm as if it gave him pain.

"The car's over here," Gage said.

Peter got in on the passenger side, wincing as he slid down into his seat. Gage got in, pulled his door shut, engulfing them in new-car smell.

"So you must be pretty happy with yourself," Gage said.

"Why should I be happy?" Peter snapped his seat-belt buckle into place.

"I guess you just proved what a tough dude you are, beating up a cop."

Peter's eyes had a wounded, uneasy flicker. "Don't start."

Gage tried to fit the key in the ignition, but it wouldn't go. He groped along the steering wheel for a button to push. "Who's starting? I didn't start anything." Gage finally got the key to fit and the motor turned.

A ponytailed juggler in whiteface and baggy sweatpants strolled past, wooden pins under his arm. Gage hated jugglers. Mimes. Street musicians. The list could go on. He wheeled the car into traffic without looking. There was a loud screeching of brakes. Gage glanced into the rearview mirror and saw the driver of a city bus waving his arms.

"You go left at the corner," Peter said. Gage did as he was told. For a block neither of them spoke. "What about your movie?" Peter said. "You're not done shooting."

"No, I'm not done shooting." They were circling the domed capitol where a half dozen children raced and tumbled on sloping green lawns. "I've got sixty actors and a crew sitting out there in the middle of the desert twiddling their thumbs so I could come bail you out."

"I'm sorry to cause you so much trouble." Peter's voice suddenly took on an edge. "I'll tell you what. Why don't you go back now? No, I'm serious. I'll get out right here and you can just turn around and go back out to the airport; they've got flights to Chicago every couple hours. . . ."

The sudden hiss of rushing air made Gage look across. Peter had the car door open and his face was livid with anger.

"Shut the door," Gage said. Peter made no move to obey. Gage slammed on the brakes. "I said shut the door!" For several more seconds Peter did nothing, his chest rising and falling like someone who'd just finished a long run. Then, quickly, he pulled the door shut. A woman on the sidewalk with a shopping cart stared at them. Two or three car horns sounded from behind. Gage reached across and tousled his son's hair.

"Aww, hell. The only thing that matters is that you're all right."

Peter gave directions as they drove through the elm-lined streets. They passed a food co-op with a broken and boarded-up

27

front window. A red flag rippled from the balcony of a rooming house. The fence surrounding a construction site bristled with slogans: ROLL YOUR OWN REALITY . . . A REVOLUTION WITHOUT JOY IS SCARCELY WORTH THE TROUBLE.

There didn't seem to be much joy around. Grim-faced students lined the porches, slumped along the sidewalks like inmates in an exercise yard, looking up sharply to check out each passing car. The sting of tear gas was still in the air. Battered trashcans and charred boards were still in the streets. Gage had never seen anything like it and it threw him. A patrol car, its windows taped, cruised slowly past them.

Peter leaned forward to turn on the radio but pulled back suddenly as if stung.

"That shoulder's giving you trouble," Gage said.

"It's just a bruise."

"We should get it looked at. That's the same old shoulder, right?"

"There's something I should tell you," Peter said.

Gage rolled his window back up, his eyes smarting from the tear gas. "What's that?"

"I'm living with someone. Her name's Joan."

"What are you looking so worried for?"

"I didn't know what you'd think."

"Long as they're not arresting people for it, I don't think it matters what I think."

"It's the second yellow house," Peter said.

Gage pulled the car to the curb. A tall girl with thick blond hair swung off her bike and lifted a violin case and an armful of sheet music from the wire basket. When Peter opened the car door the sound made her turn. A hand went to her mouth and sheet music slithered to the ground. As Peter maneuvered stiffly out of the car she quickly lay the bike against the yellow house and ran to him.

As they embraced Gage stared at the dashboard for several

seconds, then looked up. A light breeze rolled sheet music across patchy lawns and broken sidewalks as if it was tumbleweeds.

Gage got out of the car finally and retrieved his soft leather suitcase from the backseat. He glanced at the girl; she seemed lovely, long-limbed and alive with urgency. She ran her fingers across Peter's puffy eye. Peter was embarrassed by the intensity of it and she didn't fully understand why.

"Joan," Peter said. He took hold of her hands. "I want you to meet someone."

She turned to face Gage. She was stone-faced suddenly, her blue-gray eyes changing to slate. It was a look reserved for the enemy. It was clear to Gage that she thought he was some sort of probation officer.

"This is my father."

She was astonished. She looked quickly back at Peter to see if he was kidding and realized that he wasn't. Her face began to color.

As Gage moved up onto the lawn he stepped on a little pocket of tear gas trapped in the grass. His eyes watered. "Nice to meet you," he said.

"It's nice to meet you," she said. She extended her hand. Her fingers were cold. Gage liked the fact that she had manners.

Gage began to sniffle, wiping the corners of his eyes with the back of his wrist. "Wow, this stuff is strong, isn't it? We better get inside before we all start weeping like something out of the end of a Victorian novel."

Joan went off shopping for dinner and Gage roamed the apartment while Peter took a shower. The floor of the small two-bedroom walk-up listed heavily to the west. Mounted above the kitchen table was the poster of the Vietnamese girl running and screaming down the road, aflame with napalm. The furniture was all St. Vincent De Paul and an old beanbag chair in the corner was beginning to spill its beans. The only thing Gage recognized was a shaman's mask mounted above the brick and

29

board bookcase, a grotesque black and red head with deer horns that Peter had picked up during his year in Guatemala.

Gage snooped a bit, but all he came up with were two half-smoked joints, a Christmas card from Joan's parents in Winnipeg, and some pressed flowers that tumbled out of the pages of *One-Dimensional Man.* It was a warm May afternoon and all the windows were open. The sounds of a harmonica and a tambourine drifted up from below.

He put water on for coffee and tried to read *The Daily Cardinal* accounts of the riots, but when he got to the quotes about the United States being a disease and how the students were here to perform surgery on that disease, he threw the paper away.

He heard the shower go off, then the creak of Peter moving around in the bedroom. He waited a minute and then knocked tentatively.

"Can I come in?"

"Sure."

Peter stood drying his hair with a faded beach towel. Gage hadn't seen his son naked in years. Peter tried not to look embarrassed, but the trace of crimson in his cheeks gave him away.

He'd filled out in the arms and shoulders, but he still looked like a boy with his pink skin, the small, delicate mouth, the hair sticking up in all directions. The knot on his collarbone, souvenir of high school linebacking, had grown to the size of a baseball. As Peter stepped stiffly into his underwear Gage saw the long purplish welts on his back and legs.

"Looks like they worked you over pretty good," Gage said.

"Looks like."

Peter rummaged through his dresser and found a faded blue workshirt. When he tried to put it on, he couldn't; he wasn't able to reach back far enough with his injured shoulder.

"Let me help," Gage said.

Gage untangled the shirt and held it so that Peter could wriggle into it. Gage buttoned the buttons one by one, Peter silently letting him.

"I probably haven't done this for fifteen years, have I?" Gage said.

"Thanks," Peter said.

Gage picked the wet towel off the floor and folded it. Peter stepped into his jeans. "Listen, I know you're probably edgy about getting back," Peter said. "There's no real reason for you to stay."

"No. It's all right. Actors need to get used to waiting. I like Joan. She seems like a substantial-type person." Gage went to the closet and opened it.

"What are you doing?" Peter said.

Gage slid the winter coats with hangers to one side, thumbed through the plaid shirts and turtlenecks. A couple of belts slithered to the floor. "I want to see if you have a decent suit to wear. You go in front of a judge, I don't want you looking like some Haight-Ashbury refugee."

A stained down jacket separated Peter's clothes from Joan's. Gage fingered one of the dresses, a filmy flowered print. He could feel Peter's disapproval without looking back. The kettle shrieked in the kitchen. Gage let the silky fabric drop and checked the label.

"Bergdorf Goodman. Nice to know you young revolutionaries are doing all right for yourselves."

Peter swatted at the brass bedpost. "Listen, you don't have a clue to what's going on here. You'd be a lot better off not saying anything, you know?" Peter turned on his heel and left the room.

Gage followed. The lid of the teakettle rattled and water hissed in the flames. Peter turned off the burner and the shrill whistle sank and died.

"You know where I was?" Peter said. "The afternoon before I was arrested?"

"No."

"At the navy recruiting office."

"Doing what? Pouring blood on the files?"

"No."

"You were trying to *join?*" Gage said. Peter found a jar of instant coffee in the cupboard and slid it down the counter toward his father. "This is supposed to make me feel better? Two years ago you're teaching Guatemalan Indians how to read and all I hear from you is how U.S. imperialism is keeping three quarters of the world in poverty. You better figure out what side you're on, boy."

"It doesn't matter what side you're on anymore. For two years I went on the marches, I passed out the leaflets. Lot of good it did, right? I got knocked around in the Dow demonstrations along with everybody else. In February they had a machine gun mounted on Bascom Hill. Carloads of high school football players showing up to take on striking black students. The whole thing is out of control." Peter stopped talking for a second to watch his father drop a spoonful of coffee into a mug. "John Lennon has a line about living in the back of your head. For a moment, walking into that recruiter's office, I thought I could do that. Not let anyone know what I thought about anything. Just disconnect a few of the wires in my head. The recruiter asked me if I was interested in aviation, computers, it was just like the TV ads."

"But what were you thinking?" Gage asked.

"Just that I wanted a way out." Peter moved to the refrigerator, took a couple of the pink phone messages down, read them, crumpled them. "Sure, it was crazy. Maybe I just wanted to see what it would feel like. But I'm just trying to let you know."

"And so what happened?" Gage asked. "After you saw this recruiter?"

"I ran into Joan on State Street. She was all upset. She said the cops had busted up the block party on Mifflin Street and that a lot of people had been arrested, a lot of people hurt. I wanted to go see. Joan didn't, she was scared, so I went on my own. It was almost dark. People were building barricades in the streets, using garbage cans and lumber and dirt, whatever they could get their hands on. Then the cop cars would go roaring through at

32

forty miles an hour, plow through the barricades, everybody would scatter. It just kept building. People started throwing rocks. Some high school kids in an Impala rolled their window down right in front of me and shouted, 'Get the Jews out, cops, we're on your side.' "

Peter ran a hand through his still-wet hair, his fingers trembling. Gage still had not poured the water into his coffee.

"But why did you stay?"

"I'm not sure. But once you were in it, it was impossible to get out. Patrol cars would cruise by with the back doors open so they could drop tear gas cannisters in the street. Somebody would shout an obscenity from a porch and the cops would charge into the house, swinging clubs at anyone they could get their hands on. Some kid riding through on his bike, they pulled him down and beat him bloody. It got so there was a big white cloud of tear gas hanging over the street, people ran through the darkness with bandanas soaked in vinegar covering their faces. Some of the barricades were on fire. It was truly amazing. A bunch of kids shoved a truck into the middle of the street and they were all hollering, 'Paris Lives!' "

The phone rang but Peter made no move to answer it. After four or five rings it stopped. Peter turned to face his father. The meaning of what his son was saying eluded Gage, it was like sand slipping through his fingers.

"I was with seven or eight people. Someone threw something off the roof and the cops charged us. One of them waved a big fogger. Everybody took off. I ran into a gardening shed alongside one of the rooming houses and pulled the door shut.

"I could hear the fighting going on, glass breaking, sirens. After a while the sounds seemed to move off. I opened the door. Ten, twelve feet away in front of me was a cop, leaning over the hood of a car. He had his gun drawn, both hands on it, aiming across the street at this kid who was smashing the windows of an empty police car with a rubber hammer. I saw the cop's thumb jerk when he took the safety off. He can't do this, I was thinking,

33

it's against the law, but then I realized there was no law here. Everyone was on their own."

"And so you jumped him?"

"Yeah." Peter screwed the top back on the coffee container. "What would you have done?"

"I would have jumped him. But then I've done a lot of stupid things in my life."

The apartment trembled with the sound of feet on the stairs. The door swung open and Joan, arms filled with Kroger's bags, stepped into the room. Her face was shining, but as she looked from father to son, the brightness faded. She sensed that she had walked into something. When she set the bags down an artichoke fell and rolled across the counter; her reflexes were good enough for her to catch it before it hit the floor.

By late afternoon exhaustion caught up with him and Gage went into the bedroom for a nap. When he awoke, Joan and Peter were making dinner.

Gage was at his most charming at dinner, telling stories, keeping everyone entertained. When Joan made the mistake of asking him if his new movie was another period piece, Gage made a big deal out of it, taking mock offense. Once he got them laughing he was on a roll. Period piece. Hell, sooner or later everything and everybody would end up as a period piece—Vietnam, hippies, New Wave cinema, it would all end up on the pile with the buffalo and the passenger pigeon. They finished off a second bottle of wine and everyone seemed to be having a fine time. Pale streamers of spring light angled through the windows.

After dinner Peter switched on the local news. There was footage of campus ministers and faculty with white arm bands walking through the riot area interviewing students. A ten-second clip showed an alderman pointing out blood on the walls and holes burned in the carpet of a rooming house. The police chief displayed some of the weapons used against his men: a meat cleaver, an iron, a long switchblade knife. Halfway through the mayor's plea for an end to the violence, Joan snapped the set off.

"I've got ice cream in the freezer," she said. "Any takers?"

There were none. They were all silent, careful again. It was as if someone had just pulled the shutters on their evening.

Peter went to the bathroom to take some aspirin. When he returned he looked pale and on edge. He thought he would turn in. At the bedroom door he looked back for a second, put his hand to his neck. "I'm glad you came," he said.

Joan and Gage talked for a while, but after a half hour Joan went in to see how Peter was and Gage was alone. He pulled out the couch in the living room and put on sheets, but he was nowhere near sleep. Talk and the smell of dope drifted up through the open windows. A distant siren rose and then quickly died away.

He went to the telephone and after a half-dozen attempts he finally got hold of the assistant director in Arizona, a man on the brink of hysteria. They were in the middle of shooting the big battle scene and people were dying too fast. Wardrobe couldn't keep up. Counting all the takes there were three thousand deaths and they were out of uniforms.

Gage made him get Wardrobe on the line and the three of them hammered out a new strategy. While they talked, Gage fished around in his luggage until he found the airline's complimentary bottle of tequila and used it to wash down his vitamin pills.

With the aid of alcohol the answers came quickly. They would get some big blowers, mix up new paint, set up an assembly line. When one of the soldiers bit the dust, they'd hose him down, tear out his special-effects wires, run him through the blowers, repaint and rewire him, have him back in action in no time.

Someone had Dylan's new *Nashville Skyline* album on full-blast next door. The Guatemalan shaman's mask grinned from the wall.

"So when are you coming back?" the assistant director wanted to know.

"Tomorrow," Gage said. He yanked off one of his boots and tipped it upside down. Sonoran desert sand disappeared into the worn midwestern rug. "I'll give you a call."

"The studio phoned this afternoon. They seemed quite distraught about the situation."

"I'm a little distraught myself, to tell you the truth." A breeze rippled the poster of the Vietnamese girl. "You just get those damn blowers set up."

He slammed the phone down, finished off the bottle of tequila and tossed it toward the wastebasket. He missed.

He heard a heavy whomping sound, like a motorboat, but overhead. He went to the window in time to see a National Guard helicopter sweep above the trees. A couple of freaks sitting on the stoop stood up and screamed at it. Gage stared down at them. He was a little drunk. He thought about hosing them down and rewiring their circuits. He slammed the window shut.

He got the script out and lay on the pull-out couch. He thumbed through the marked-up pages, not really able to read. Now and then he heard the murmur of voices from the bedroom, but it was impossible to make out distinct words. Peter was telling her everything, everything he was too proud to tell his own father.

Gage tossed the script aside and snapped off the light. He lay still for a while. A pale fan of car lights flickered across stained wallpaper, across the shaman's mask. Far off was the sound of a train coupling and uncoupling.

When he was little, Peter had been afraid of the dark. A couple of times a night he would pad into Gage and Nina's bedroom and Gage would carry him back, show him there weren't any bogeymen in the corners, scratch his back until he fell asleep.

He had been the gentlest child. Some mornings Nina would drive Gage to the studio, and Peter, strapped in the backseat, would be perfectly content inventing battles with tiny green and

36

red plastic cowboys and Indians on the padded armrest. Before Gage could get out of the car Peter would grab Gage's hand and hold it to his cheek for a second and kiss his father's knuckles. He was four then, or four and a half, as he liked to announce. As Gage walked away, Peter would call out, every time, it was their ritual, "Have a good day at work."

He was a kid who had to be trained to keep his hands up. He seemed to be a child devoid of anger, as if Gage had used up the family allotment and there wasn't any left over for Peter. The friends Peter brought home were always the cripples and the strays. Gage worried that his son was too soft and made attempts to toughen him up: boxing lessons in the basement and a disastrous summer on a ranch in Wyoming.

For a long time Peter seemed magically protected from the growing tension between his parents. After Nina and Gage separated, Peter lived with his mother for a while, but Nina was in no shape to care for a fourteen-year-old boy. After six months Peter was sent to boarding school.

Urged on by Gage, Peter finally went out for high school football. It was a revelation. He turned out to be a dynamite hundred-and-sixty-pound linebacker, a natural, so quick and aggressive he would be in the quarterback's face with the snap. The boy Gage had worried about being too soft now played with a controlled fury. He shone until the sixth game, when he broke his collarbone and the injury never healed right.

The year after Nina died, Peter left college and went to Guatemala to work for the Friends Service Committee. Gage was dubious, but held his tongue. His producer advised him not to make a big issue out of it; it was Peter's way of working out his mother's death, they said.

When Gage visited him in the Guatemalan highlands Peter was living in an adobe hut Gage would have been ashamed to raise chickens in and he was as gaunt as one of the Desert Fathers.

They got into it the very first night. Peter was trying to explain

37

how difficult it was to make any impact. You could go to almost any stream in the highlands and when you scooped up a handful of water you could see worms wriggling in it. How could you teach kids to read when they were too weak to hold up their heads? Gage got mad. Was Peter trying to blame that on Lyndon Johnson too, bad water in Guatemala? It turned out that he was.

They went at it for three hours, huddled around a low charcoal fire while rain beat on the tin roof. They disagreed about everything, from United Fruit to Eleanor Roosevelt to genocide. Gage had never had the patience for closely reasoned argument. Peter had a wagonload of facts, all right, but he was taking everything too far. Peter tried to argue that everything was political, everything was connected, the exploitation of Central America, the bombing of Vietnam, the wiping out of the American Indian, the poisoning of the streams, it was one long death trip.

That kind of talk made Gage crazy. He finally couldn't take it anymore. "I'll tell you what I think. It's not America that's the problem. It's not Johnson or capitalism or the system you keep talking about. The problem is, man is a killer. He's never been anything else. Bottom line. And none of your do-gooder schemes for land reform are going to touch that." It was then that Peter got up and walked out of the dim, smoky hut.

Now Gage lay on the pull-out couch, the script open on his belly, staring at the shadowed shaman's mask, the animal's horns, the red tongue protruding from the black mouth. Maybe there was something to all the shouting; maybe it was Vietnam; maybe Vietnam was killing them all. He didn't know. He was out of his depth. He didn't really get it: history. He was out in the middle of the desert doing his period pieces; how could anyone expect him to have the answers? He had come here ready to take the kid's head off and suddenly found he had no more fight left in him. He was boxing with shadows.

He wasn't sure what the ticking was at first, faint and rhythmic, but it grew more intense, more distinct, and he realized it was

38

bedsprings creaking in the bedroom. It was Peter and Joan making love and he was the one locked out, alone in the dark with the bogeymen.

The next morning on the way to the doctor's they listened to the radio. There had been no violence during the night, just a lot of name-calling and a couple of walkouts at the city council meeting. Nothing apparently was as bad it seemed. At the doctor's office the X rays came back negative: the only thing wrong with Peter's shoulder was a bad bruise.

They spent an hour with the lawyer, a ruddy-faced bear of a man named Art Radke who listened carefully to Peter's story, rolling his ursine head sympathetically, making low grunts and an occasional note.

"Let me ask you something," Gage said. "Fifty thousand dollars. That's a lot of bail."

"Yes, it is," Radke said.

"You think they're trying to make an example out of Peter?"

"Not necessarily." Radke leaned back and propped a massive wing-tip shoe on his desk.

"If Peter's father had been Joe Blow from Oconomowoc, it wouldn't have been fifty thousand dollars."

"No. But we can't choose who our fathers are, can we?" Radke swung forward in his chair. "Let me ask you something," he said to Gage. "Wasn't there an article, a couple of years ago, about your punching out a photographer or threatening him with a knife—"

"That has nothing to do with this."

"Of course not. But refresh my memory."

"I threw a bowie knife into my producer's door."

Radke pressed his hands together, frowning. His fingers were thick-knuckled, like an old catcher's. "But there were other incidents too. . . ."

"This is irrelevant." They could hear the whine of a drill from the dentist's office next door.

"Of course. But the first thing I like to do in a case is circle the herd, see what we're dealing with, so to speak. You never know what a D.A.'s liable to try to drag into this."

"It's your job to keep him from doing that."

"That's right."

Peter seemed cowed and younger than he really was, as if he'd been called into the principal's office. The room was decorated with ceramic mallards. Over Radke's desk a team picture of the 1957 Milwaukee Braves nestled in among framed diplomas.

"I could always go hire a big-name lawyer," Gage said.

"I'm sure you could." Radke rose from his chair and clapped Peter on the upper arm. "You look like a ball player."

"I was. Till I got hurt."

"I've got something to show you." Radke yanked open the lowest drawer in his desk and pulled out a baseball. He tossed it lightly to Peter, who caught it one-handed. "Take a look at that."

Peter turned the ball over slowly. Gage could make out a faded signature between the seams.

"That's right," Radke said. "Warren Spahn. He signed it for me, the fourth game of the 1957 World Series."

"You watch the Brewers now?" Peter asked.

"No. I was a Braves fan, all the way. When they left for Atlanta it left a bitter taste in my mouth. Seemed to me it was a very cynical kind of betrayal. In my mind, that's when it all started to go downhill, the Braves left Milwaukee, then comes Vietnam. You couldn't trust what anybody said about anything."

Peter handed the baseball back. Highway traffic hissed through the open window.

"What happened here, son, is that you were caught up in the heat of the moment. Like a lot of other kids. This is not a special case. It has nothing to do with your father." Radke slipped the autographed baseball into the pocket of his suit jacket. "To be frank, your father's reputation is a tar baby we don't want to be stuck with and the farther he stays away from this case the better off we'll be. I do not want this to come to trial. We're going to try

40

and get the charges dropped. If you could bring yourself to issue an apology, publicly or privately, it would help."

Gage looked quickly over at his son and saw there was no way in the world Peter would do it. Whatever Peter was, he wasn't a bootlicker. Radke saw it too.

"That's just one rabbit trail to explore, there are plenty of others. If any of these reporters call, you let me handle it. Keep your nose clean, you know what I'm saying?" He leaned forward to cuff the back of Peter's neck.

He glanced at Gage; Gage clearly was not his favorite. "We'll take good care of him, don't you worry. Really, I never thought I'd live to see what I've seen, the past three days. I remember when I was a kid growing up, you wanted to block off the street for sledding or a soapbox derby, you just called up the Traffic Department and they'd *bring* the barricades out. All you had to do was promise to take 'em down when you were done."

Gage and Peter shook Radke's hand and left his office. Outside, mud-splattered trucks thundered up the Beltline. On the far side of the highway was a decaying miniature golf course and a U-Haul lot. Where there had once been cornfields there were now insurance buildings and new churches that looked like insurance buildings.

"That didn't hurt as much as you thought, did it?" Gage said. He scanned the half-dozen silver-gray cars in the parking lot, then glanced at his Avis key ring to be sure of the license number. "We're over here. You know, I like that guy. I think he's what you want. Low-key. Noncontroversial. America's Dairyland. You like him?"

Peter walked to the far side of the car. Gage could read his son's suppressed emotion in the tightness around the eyes, the slightly pursed lips. "He's all right."

"You know what I think the best thing would be?" Gage said. Peter ran his fingertips along the car's antenna, waiting for his father to unlock the doors. "You should come back with me."

"Back where, Dad? You're making a movie."

41

"So? A little desert heat would do you some good. It would be a nice break for you."

Neither of them was on home ground. They could have been anywhere: the gravel lot, the chain link fence, the hiss of tires on the wet highway, behind them a horseshoe of low brick offices for doctors and lawyers and dentists. There was even an animal hospital.

"You can fly back for the trial. Or whenever you need to. But I think you and I need to spend a little time together."

"You were the one who taught me never to run from a fight."

"You wouldn't be running. If things are as bad as you say they are, anyplace would be better."

"So maybe I exaggerated."

Gage leaned on the roof of the car. Another truck thundered by, plastered with the license plates of fourteen states. He felt out of joint, incomplete. Had they really solved anything? It was all slipping away too fast.

"I want you to know something," Gage said. "Your mother and I loved each other. Maybe we weren't always so great for one another, I think you picked up on that part of it, but we did love each other. And having you was the best thing we ever did."

Peter looked as if he'd just been hit in the face. He turned away, kicked softly at the chain link fence. The two men stared across the highway at the distant statues on the miniature golf course, Peter Pan and Captain Hook and the Mad Hatter, the huge, badly painted ruins of childhood.

"What time is your flight?"

Gage looked at his watch. "In no time at all."

The flight had already been announced. They rushed down the long glass tunnel, sidestepping mothers and their strollers, skipping past toupeed fertilizer salesmen trudging under Valpacks.

"What gate, did you hear?" Gage said.

Peter swung his father's tan leather bag at his side. "I think it's right up here."

Most of the passengers had already boarded; three or four still negotiated with the flight attendant at the gate. A mother shepherded a pair of toddlers across the runway, stopped at the steps of the plane to turn them back and have them wave to their grandparents. A baggage tractor scooted toward the terminal.

"Last call, Flight Eight-fifteen, direct service to O'Hare."

Gage patted his jacket, looking for his ticket. "Now, you call me. As soon as you know anything."

"I will," Peter said.

"And I'm serious about your buying that suit. Blue blazer. Something nice. I left my credit card on your kitchen table."

Gage opened his briefcase and shook it, still looking for his ticket. Peter had turned away. There would be a forty-five-minute layover in Chicago; Gage could call Arizona then and make sure someone would be at the Phoenix airport to meet him. God knew what sort of messes lurked in wait. He spied the corner of the ticket sticking out of one of the scripts. He pulled it free, looked up, relieved, and saw that Peter was bawling.

For a second Gage was too dismayed to do anything. He looked down at his shoes, then set his briefcase on the floor, plastic-jacketed scripts slithering free. Peter tried to hold it all in, one hand to the side of his face, but it wasn't working.

"Come here," Gage murmured, "come here."

There was no sign that Peter heard him and Gage finally pulled his son to him, held him close. Peter's head rested on Gage's shoulder. It had been so many years since he had held Peter like this: it felt odd, his boy in this huge man's frame.

People around them discreetly tried to look without really looking, all except a seven-year-old boy in a Braves hat who didn't know any better and stared dumbfounded until his mother yanked him away.

Peter made a short chucking sound, self-disgusted, and pulled

43

back. He puffed out his cheeks and stared out the windows at the last scurrying passengers.

"You miss your mother, don't you?" Gage said. "I miss her too. I still dream about her all the time."

Peter's eyes darkened; he thought his father was lying.

"Come with me," Gage said. "Come on. It's not too late. I'll buy you a ticket right now."

"No."

"Why not? I can't leave you like this. Come on. Even for a couple of days. You're the only family I've got left, kid. I don't want to mess that up too."

For a second Peter considered it, but then looked up at the sound of the grim-faced flight attendant pulling the metal door shut.

"You go on," Peter said.

"Peter, they can hold the goddamned flight for five minutes. Miss . . ."

"I'll be all right, Dad. Come on."

Gage said nothing. He knew his son. Peter didn't want to cause a ruckus. He could jump on a cop's back but he was mortified at the idea of inconveniencing a stewardess. Gage bent down and shoveled the loose scripts back into his briefcase.

"When this is over, we're going to go someplace," Gage said. "You promise me. We'll go up to the Wind River, rent horses, just like we did two summers ago."

The flight attendant leaned cynically against the half-opened door; she had dealt with his type before. Peter smiled and punched his father lightly on the shoulder. "Sure. Don't worry about me. You just go back there and knock their socks off."

Gage finished *The Outriders* two weeks late and a million and a half over budget. He had fired twelve crew members, banished three reporters from the set, and shipped his best stuntman off to the hospital with second-degree gunpowder burns.

Through it all he was on the phone with Peter at least twice a

44

week. They talked more easily than they had in years. Gage was convinced his trip to Madison was some kind of breakthrough. Peter seemed positively chatty: he was working on his Orwell paper, Joan was playing in the orchestra for a student production of *Abduction from the Seraglio,* they had gone to Spring Green for a picnic. Radke's motion for a dismissal had been denied, but everyone was optimistic.

Two days before the trial it all blew up. Gage was drinking gin in the Paramount office with two film editors and a vice-president. The rough cut looked terrific and everything was forgiven. Someone snapped on the evening news.

Walter Cronkite had an update on the black students' takeover at Cornell, there was a clip of the Harvard strike, and, one cut later, Peter was on the screen, addressing a rally on the library mall.

At first Gage was too stunned to hear what Peter was saying. Peter leaned forward to read from his notes, flanked by a solemn work-shirted council. Spray from the fountain blew in gusts behind him. A techie gnome crept past, holding a microphone aloft.

The studio vice-president sucked on his swizzle stick. One of the film editors glanced at Gage, as if waiting for some signal, but there was no way they were going to cut this footage short. The only sound in the room was the soft clink of ice in glasses.

Peter's face burned, his voice was tremulous. He forgot his notes, raised his eyes to the crowd. "When I was a kid," Peter said, "my father tried to tell me that men were killers before they were anything else. He tried to teach me that when somebody hits you, you better hit them back, hard. I didn't like those rules. And I refused to play by them. But when I look around at what's going down . . ." His voice caught for a minute and nearly broke. "I'm here to tell you that I'm learning. I'm here to tell you that I am my father's child." He raised his fist in the Black Power salute, and Gage thought he saw a feeble smile. The gesture was

45

answered by the crowd's roar and the camera panned across a sea of raised fists.

Gage raced down the hallway to his office, called Peter's apartment and, when there was no answer there, called the lawyer, Radke.

"Yes, yes, I just saw it," Radke said. "Of course you're upset, I don't blame you. I did talk to him. He left here about an hour ago. Try to understand, the boy has been under a lot of pressure."

"I'm under a lot of pressure! That doesn't mean I go commit hara-kiri on the goddamn television!" Gage paced the cream-colored carpet, winding himself into the phone cord. Twenty stories below, L.A. gleamed and blinked in rush-hour haze. "What did he say to you?"

"None of this was premeditated. It was one of those spur-of-the-moment things. Some friend of his had been beaten up. The kid was hitchhiking and got picked up by three high school wrestler types who didn't like the length of his hair, so they knocked him around and then dumped him out of the car, gave the kid a concussion."

Gage sat down in one of the blue leather armchairs, stared at the framed picture of D. W. Griffith on the oak-paneled wall. Gage's hands were trembling. "I'm flying out there."

"I think it would be better if you didn't. It might only add fuel to the fire."

"What am I, some kind of leper? He's my son."

"I think everyone's amply aware of that. It wouldn't be a help, take my word for it."

He tried to take Radke's advice. For a day he sat tight. He kept calling Peter's apartment. For five hours there was no answer and after that all he got was a busy signal; someone must have taken the phone off the hook.

The next day the afternoon papers ran a syndicated column by

Wendell Hare, a conservative Washington columnist. The piece
was entitled

SON OF THE ENFANT TERRIBLE

What's in a name? At first we thought it was
just more of the same; a highly strung young
man, about to go on trial for assaulting a police
officer, raising his fist in a Black Power salute and
making the usual emunctory noises about revo-
lutionary violence.

Only when we caught the name did we realize
this was something special: Peter Gage. Son of
America's most violent film director. The para-
ble would be neat enough if you stopped right
there, but that's only half the story.

In Washington in the mid-fifties I had a chance
to meet Peter's mother, Nina, through a bleeding-heart liberal journalist friend of mine. Nina
was there to lend her father moral support during his appearance before the McCarthy hearings. For those of you with an abbreviated histor-
ical sense, let me refresh your memory. Leon
Friedman was the émigré physicist whose guilt
over being one of the A-bomb architects was so
great he spent the last fifteen years of his life in
bleating recantations on behalf of various
peacenik and Communist-front organizations.

Need we ask any longer where the anarchic
fuse has been lit? For years we've been blud-
geoned by the liberal press into treating Jeremiah Gage's Western luridities as high art, but
do we really have to put up with the sight of his
son celebrating the spilling of American blood in
Vietnam?

Gage knew he couldn't wait any longer. He put down the
paper, called the airlines and made a reservation for the first
flight to Madison.

He drove home, spent twenty minutes throwing clothes into a
suitcase and, just as he was walking out the door, decided to
check his answering service one last time. There was a message
from Joan to call immediately.

Joan picked up on the first ring. Her voice was shaky and

hostile. "I was just wondering if you'd heard from Peter," she said.

"Why would I have heard from Peter?" Gage said. "I've been calling every two hours and no one answers the damn phone. If you wouldn't mind, I'd like to speak to my son."

She didn't answer at first. He thought he heard her crying. "I don't know where he is."

"What do you mean?" The front door was still open. Gage could see the Mexican gardener hauling hoses across the bright lawn.

"I haven't seen him since yesterday afternoon. He went to talk to Radke and no one's seen him since. I've called all our friends. I thought maybe he'd contacted you. I'm afraid to call the police."

"Don't call anybody!" Gage said. "Don't do anything! I'm on my way to the airport now."

Radke tried to stall the judge, but the request for a continuance was denied. An arrest warrant was issued and bond forfeited. A mob of reporters trailed Gage and Radke down the courthouse steps. On campus, leaflets sprang up overnight. Peter was hailed as a new hero of the underground. Like Ho Chi Minh, Che, Geronimo and Billy the Kid, he swam free in the Sea of the People.

Gage didn't believe it. He couldn't have miscalculated his son that badly. Peter must have been mugged, shot, kidnapped. But it took just one phone call to discover that Peter had emptied out his bank account the afternoon he disappeared. Two days later the police found, in a trash can, the half-burned remains of Peter's identification: driver's license, university fee receipt, his father's credit card.

Gage was furious at Radke and Joan, and though, in his worst moments, he suspected them of conspiring against him, it was clear they knew no more than he did.

The only one he talked to who might have known something

was Neal Sprinker, the organizer of the rally. Sprinker held court in the dark recesses of the Rathskellar, attended by a trio of dance majors and a shrimp-shouldered melancholic studying Introductory Chinese. Sprinker leaned back in his motorcycle jacket, threading a roll of caps through a toy pistol.

He let Gage do most of the talking at first, content to play cat and mouse, but he warmed up in time, delivering free-form lectures about everything from the Tupamaros to the Nuremberg Trials to the injustice of pay toilets. Gage held his tongue. Obedience was a disease, Sprinker said, but the seeds of liberation had been planted; there would soon be two, three, many Vietnams.

Sprinker slid his cap pistol across the table and took a carton of yogurt from one of the dancers. "So what do you think about this?"

"You already know what I think about it. I think it's all bullshit."

The shrimp-shouldered melancholic looked up from his book. Sprinker dug for the fruit at the bottom of his yogurt. "But your son doesn't think it's bullshit, does he?"

"I don't know what he thinks."

On the walls around them were faded murals of castles on the Rhine, monks exhorting a mob. Two of the dance majors drifted off toward the cafeteria.

"Well, I do know what he thinks," Sprinker said. "And I'm telling you, you didn't lose your kid the day before yesterday; you lost him a long time ago. Your boy's gone to join the Indians."

Gage's eyes met Sprinker's; neither man backed down. Sprinker licked the back of his spoon with a thick tongue.

"Did you put him up to this?" Gage said.

Four country-looking kids in letter jackets played bridge at the next table. Lunch traffic flowed around them. "If I had, what would you do?"

"I'd reach across the table and tear your heart out."

Sprinker began to laugh. "You're really hopeless, mister, you know that? And you want *me* to help *you?*" Gage said nothing. "And what is it you want me to do?"

"I want you to get a message to him. You think you can do that?"

"I'm not sure. Here. Write it on one of these." Sprinker took a napkin from the center of the table and tossed it to Gage. The long-haired girl in the leotard dunked her teabag into her cup of hot water, her eyes averted.

Gage hesitated, then took out his pen. Neal was just trying to make a fool out of him. After Gage left, they would all pass around whatever he had written and have a great laugh over it. He wrote anyway.

Nothing's changed. I'm still your father. You still owe me a trip to the Wind River. Let me know when.

Neal waited, hands clasped behind his head. Gage looked over what he'd written. The blue ink had already started to blot and spread on the soft paper. He folded it twice and handed it over.

"Whatever you can do," Gage said, "I'd appreciate it."

The *Enquirer* hired a photographer to follow him day and night. Peter wasn't the only one on the run; in order to dodge reporters Gage was forced to adopt a series of bizarre disguises: dyed hair, an exterminator uniform, a grisly-looking beard. He stayed for ten days in his producer's cabin in the redwoods, two weeks hiding out on the Mexican coast.

Friends tried to console him. He wasn't the only one whose kid had disappeared. It was just the times they were living in. The son of a director over at Disney took off one night on his bike, left a message on a tape telling his parents he was on his way to Austin, Texas, to make his fortune as a blues guitarist. The boy showed up a month later, perfectly all right.

Gage had many offers of help. He met with an FBI man from Chicago, a detective out of Kansas City whose specialty was recovering stolen art, a bubble-sleeved psychic from Malibu, a dope-dealing graduate student in Madison who boasted he knew the ins and outs of every radical cell. After several months Gage called them all off, afraid that even if they did come up with something, they would only drive Peter further away from him.

A half dozen times, late at night, Gage answered the phone only to have the caller hang up after three or four seconds of silence. For a time that gave Gage hope; he talked himself into believing the caller was Peter, but then the phone calls stopped.

Once, on the Venice boardwalk, his heart leaped when he saw someone he was convinced was Peter. He ran for three blocks before he caught up and saw the man full-face. It wasn't even close. The same thing happened at Heathrow Airport.

The idea of Peter underground was preposterous. Whatever Peter was, Gage knew he was not one of them, those mad vandals smashing windows in the streets of Chicago, not one of those novice bank robbers and saboteurs hiding out in New Hampshire cabins reading three-volume biographies of Trotsky. What was he, then? Gage couldn't even guess; he had lost all confidence in his ability to predict what his son might do next.

Gage tried to read the manifestos, tried to understand, but the rhetoric made him physically ill. He saw the pictures of student demonstrators drenched in animal blood, saw the loathing in those streaming faces. He wasn't a dope. He knew it was nothing but a sideshow, he knew where the real violence was coming from; it was from those reasonable-sounding politicians who talked law and order and rubber-stamped the daily bombing runs, but when he saw those children's faces glistening with blood it filled him with rage and terror. It wasn't even that what they were doing was that new; it seemed to him a kind of ghost dancing; a mad, messianic summoning up of ancestors, Crazy Horse or John Brown or Nat Turner, who would somehow render them impervious to the bullets of their enemies.

When Peter was six, Gage had taken him tubing on the San Marcos River in Texas. Peter sat in Gage's lap, laced in his red

51

and yellow life preserver. For an hour they had a wonderful time floating past huge cypress trees and elephant-ears, bumping through gentle rapids.

Then, after they had pushed their way through one of the shallowest sections of the river, a current caught them and swirled them into the bank. Gage tried to kick off the cypress roots, but they hit with too much force and overturned.

They both went under. For a few seconds Gage lost Peter. It was the most horrifying moment in Gage's life. He had visions of Peter caught and held under by those roots. He groped desperately in the foaming water, it was impossible to see. Suddenly he had hold of one of the life preserver straps and, in trying to keep his hold, pulled Peter further down. When they surfaced and Gage carried Peter to shore, the boy was hysterical and furious. He had seen a huge snake underwater, he said, and his Daddy had held him down. Trying not to lose him, Gage had only pushed him further from the surface.

The Outriders ran over four hours in first cut, and though editing removed a good hour, the studio wanted more. Some executives were appalled by the amount of blood and gore; the American public would never accept it.

Gage was tired of being treated like a patient. Work had rescued him before and it would rescue him now. He redubbed and rescored the entire film. He fought to keep the essential scenes in place.

He had a vague memory of days and then months passing. He was obscurely aware of Woodstock, of Hell's Angels killing someone at a concert in Altamont, of the trial of the Chicago Seven, of Fred Hampton shot by police, but he wasn't truly present to any of it. It was as if there was a brawl in the backseat and Gage couldn't afford to look back. He kept his eyes glued to those bright images flitting across the editing machine in the pitch-dark room.

After months of delay *The Outriders* was released. The film was vilified and acclaimed, debated in every newspaper in the country. By the time Nixon invaded Cambodia, the film had done thirty million at the box office. Every studio offered Gage projects. The day before the shootings at Kent State an article in *The Atlantic* called the tale of gunfighters on the run "an exorcism, a ceremony filled with the dark forces of the blood, the national myth laid bare."

Two days later Gage had lunch at the Russian Tea Room in New York City with a young actress and her agent. Afterward the three of them strolled down Fifty-seventh Street. They were close to a deal. Every eighth person seemed to recognize them.

The actress was on edge. It would be her first leading role in a film. Everything else she'd done had been stage, she was leery of Gage's reputation, and she would need someone to care for her two-year-old child during the shooting.

Gage tried to reassure her as they wended their way past the three-card monte games, jostled past the women in short fur coats coming out of galleries. The line Gage was pitching was that the stage was great training, but let's face it, motion pictures were where it was at. Cranes swung thirty stories above them.

A *New York Post* truck unloaded the afternoon edition at the corner. A crowd gathered at the newsstand. Gage wanted to pick up *Variety:* he excused himself and pushed his way in.

He was fishing for change when he saw the *Post* headline: THREE DIE IN MUNITIONS BLAST. He put *Variety* down and picked a *Post* off the stack. The horns of backed-up traffic echoed off the buildings and a drill started up, just a few feet away. Someone elbowed him in the back.

He stared at the photo of the smoking ruins, the three who had died. He heard the agent call his name, but moving pictures didn't matter anymore. He stared at the still photo of his son's blurred face.

53

Five

GAGE HATED TO SPOIL Father Higgins's fun. He stood silently in the doorway of the rectory office watching the priest pry a set of angel wings from an old costume box and shake out the tinseled straps. The New Mexico October sun streamed through the narrow window, illuminated the cleryman in a nice accident of light.

Gage's knock caught Father Higgins off guard. His head swiveled, his mouth formed a perfect O.

"I hope I'm not disturbing you," Gage said.

"No, no, come in."

"The secretary said—"

"Yes, of course. Sit down. Let me get these things out of your way." Father Higgins gathered up a patchy velvet robe from the back of one of the chairs, batted dust from it and lay it in the windowsill. "Sit down, please."

Gage did as he was told. It had been a long time since he'd been in a clergyman's office and it didn't feel real natural. Father Higgins pushed the costume box, bristling with swords and shields, to one side. The gnome of a priest seemed so Irish and unprepossessing he could have been the trainer for the Boston Celtics.

"You have to excuse me. You see, every year the children do a little play about David the shepherd boy and I always get to play Goliath. They seem to enjoy it. The trick always is finding the old costume. Now what can I do for you?"

"I just need to ask you a question."

"Yes, go ahead."

"I know you must all still be in shock." Father Higgins's face was blank; for a second he had no idea what Gage was talking about. "It was a great tragedy."

"Oh, yes, a great tragedy," Father Higgins said, recovering.

"But I need to ask if you've ever heard the name Peter Gage."

"No, I can't say that I have." Father Higgins leaned against his desk. He couldn't have been more than five-four. It was hard to imagine him playing a giant, unless it was for first- and second-graders.

"You've never heard any of the other priests mention—"

"No." Father Higgins unscrewed the top of a half-used tube of spirit gum and squeezed a bit onto his finger. "Does he attend this church? This Peter Gage?"

"No, he doesn't." Gage saw that there was no way for this to go, except into deeper water. "And you never heard Father Ortiz speak of him?"

Father Higgins screwed the top back on the tube of spirit gum. "Were they friends?"

"I don't know. But I think there was some connection." It was no time for finesse; he was waist deep in the swamp already. "When they found Father Ortiz's car, there was an old newspaper in the trunk. My son's picture was in that newspaper."

Father Higgins's face changed, all brightness gone. He pushed away from the desk. "Oh, yes. Someone did tell me, yes. But your son's dead."

"Yes."

"I guess I hadn't gotten that impression from the way you were talking." Higgins glanced toward the open door. It was easy enough to read his mind. Higgins was used to all kinds of nuts walking in off the street; it was one of the hazards of the job.

"I was hoping someone might be able to explain this to me."

"Of course. Perhaps you'd like to speak to one of my superiors." Father Higgins reached for the phone and Gage put out a hand to stop him.

"No," Gage said. The last thing he needed was for this to get back to Captain Trevino.

"Let me have a number, then, where I can reach you."

"No. It's no big deal." Father Higgins looked as if he were prepared to grab one of the wooden swords to fend Gage off. "I just wanted to know if you'd ever heard the name, that's all. No need to make a federal case out of it."

Gage stood up, took a step back and crunched a plastic shield. He picked it up and offered it to Father Higgins.

"Listen, good luck with your play. Just remember to tell them the whole story."

Red began to show around Father Higgins's temples. "What do you mean, the whole story?"

"I'm not exactly up on my Bible, but it doesn't end with killing Goliath, does it? The way I remember it, he ends up killing his own son."

"Absalom."

"That's right. And so maybe if he hadn't killed the one, maybe he wouldn't have killed the other."

"Well, I guess I've never heard anyone look at it that way before."

He stood in front of the cathedral, where a trio of tourists draped themselves around Bishop Lamy's statue, having their picture taken. Gage stared at them. Maybe he should have gone on and talked to someone else. For a second he considered going back and buzzing the rectory door, barging in. There had to be someone in there who could tell him something.

He wandered around to the side of the rectory and stared down the long wall with its shuttered windows. A sign on one of the doors read: CLOISTER: NO ADMITTANCE. Idly Gage tried the knob; it was locked. A small statue of Saint Francis stood with welcoming arms. Gage moved up and down the path outside the rectory, restless as a cat searching for a place to scale a fence.

A man who looked like a retired spook—dark glasses, shaved head, canvas shoes—entered the cathedral with his wife. On impulse Gage followed them.

It had been years since he'd been in a church. There were maybe a dozen tourists with cameras strapped around their necks and a school group whose tennis shoes squealed on polished stone floors, echoing through the vaulting space. A lone Hispanic man knelt in prayer in one of the pews. Gage stared at the flickering candles and the gentle, slightly vacant-faced saints in baby-blue robes. He felt the aversion he always felt—this was all for children.

He walked past the confessional booths, past the spook and his wife who, guidebooks in hand, craned their necks to examine the stained-glass windows. Gage carried himself with a studied casualness; no one would ever get the idea he was going to kneel to anything.

The Shrine of the Conquistadora was at the far side of the church, grillwork protecting the tiny saint in her velvet dress. The sign read: CANDLES 25¢ DO NOT PUT MATCHES OUT IN WAX. Gage stared into a dark window that led to the sacristy. There had to be someone to talk to. He walked down the long aisle toward the front of the church.

Everything in the cathedral—the flickering candles, the stained-glass saints with oxen or lions resting at their sandaled feet—said surrender. But Gage was not going to surrender. He was going to understand why his son's picture had been defaced, blotted out. It was a matter of will, but his will was baffled now, he did not know in what direction he could apply it.

He spied a lens cap under one of the pews. He picked it up and looked around. The only person nearby was a woman in a wide straw hat sitting in one of the front pews. Maybe it was just thirty years in the film business, but Gage had never considered losing a lens cap a laughing matter.

The woman was bent slightly forward, but it was clear that she wasn't praying. He took a couple of steps and saw that she was scribbling in a notebook.

"Excuse me," he said.

She looked up, genuinely hostile. She was a woman of maybe forty, dressed in black blouse and slacks and cowboy boots. A camera hung around her neck and a red and blue Guatemalan bag lay on the pew beside her.

"Someone dropped a lens cap back there," he said. She reminded him of someone, but it wasn't until she cracked a cynical, too knowing smile that he knew. "Tina?"

"Hey, Gage." She snapped her notebook shut and slipped it into her woven Guatemalan bag. She stood up and glanced at her camera. "I guess I did. Lose a lens cap." She took the cap from him and snapped it back on her camera.

"I don't believe it," he said.

"Why don't you believe it?"

"I thought you were dead."

"Dead? Christ, Gage, you really know how to make a girl feel good."

"No, I'm serious. Last thing I heard you and Cooter were driving across Mexico drinking Ever-Clear, looking for his kid that he'd left with some Mexican family and you got thrown in jail. . . ."

"Who told you that story? Gusty? That little bullshitter."

"Maybe it was. I don't remember."

"Dead? Hell, no wonder I have trouble getting work. Gage,

that story is ten years old." She stood with her hands on her hips, mulling it over. "This really upsets me, you know?" She looked at him, shook her head, snorted, then laughed.

Gage hadn't seen Tina Lancet in almost twenty years. She was full-faced now, but she still had big brown eyes and she still liked to play the tough lady.

A flashbulb flared at the far end of the cathedral. Tina gave a start, real alarm in her face.

"You waiting for somebody?" Gage said.

She looked at him as if she hadn't heard. "I'm supposed to shoot some pictures for an article on the cathedral."

"Who you doing it for?"

"Who? I'll give you one guess. *The New Mexican.* Only thing is, I'm supposed to meet one of the priests to get the official okay."

Tina Lancet had been the Queen of the Hippies. Gage met her in L.A. when she ran the Stone Palace, a rambling Victorian mansion where all the rock musicians stayed when they were in town. She cooked macrobiotic for Dylan, gave Stevie Wonder massages and if she caught anyone using white sugar she tossed it out the window.

Gage had hired Tina in '68 to round up a group of hippies and freaks for three or four scenes in *Savages*. It turned out to be a disaster. The hippies were impossible to direct. They wouldn't learn their lines, they wandered through the background of a half dozen good takes and two of the wranglers Gage had used on every film started dropping acid. Gage and Tina battled for a month. The only thing that came out of it was the bus that she and her tribe drove to New Mexico to begin America's most famous commune.

Gage never saw her after that, though every now and then he'd catch a glimpse of her onstage in some rock festival documentary. When he heard the wild story about her and Cooter getting lost in Mexico, Gage had no reason to doubt it. With Tina anything was possible.

"You're living up in the mountains, then?" he said.

"No, I moved back to town a couple of years ago. Strawberry Fields is fourteen years old now, can you believe that? I think I sent you a picture of her when she was born. And I've got an eight-year-old now too. The kids were taking the school bus twenty-five miles down the mountain every day and the tires had no tread because the superintendent had spent the appropriation on beer. I kept having visions of them plunging over the cliff. It just didn't seem fair to the kids. What are they going to tell people? 'I was raised by a river.' " She ran her hand over the smooth wood of the pew. "Gage, this is really great, but I should try to find this guy."

"But what about *the* bus?" Gage said.

"*The* bus? The one you paid for, you mean? It's still in my front yard, still has the rainbow over the window. The body's rusted out some, but as soon as I get a new distributor it'll be on the road again."

"Remember that speed freak with the long blond ponytail who used to drive for you? I forget his name."

"Lakota." She stared at the schoolchildren gathered at the altar listening to their teacher. Something melancholy and anxious had come over Tina.

"That's right."

"He's still around. He runs a flower delivery service. Still has the ponytail. And a little bit of a belly."

Gage smiled and she caught him at it.

"You think it's funny? Big joke, right? The ones who never got out of the sixties? What were we supposed to do? All go work for *People* magazine?"

A sullen old man in a Highlands sweatshirt shuffled past with a cardboard box of fresh candles.

"Oh, come on, Tina."

"Don't 'come on, Tina' me. Maybe it would have been more convenient if everybody had all died in Mexican jails or vaporized into the universe, but it didn't work out that way."

60

"So where is everybody, Tina?"

The man with the votive candles turned and shushed them. Tina continued, lowering her voice to a furious whisper.

"You want to know? Acid Alice is born again and living in Velarde with a motorcycle mechanic. Rattlesnake drives the fire truck for Rio Arriba County. Neal Sprinker has a flag shop down in Madrid."

"Madrid, New Mexico? Neal Sprinker?"

"Yeah."

"You know him?"

"We were lovers for two years. We didn't make love a lot, but we had a terrific relationship. I didn't know you knew him."

"I met him once. In Madison. After my son disappeared. Before Sprinker got famous." He hesitated just a beat. "He's there now? In Madrid?"

"Yeah. His place is called Airships."

She stared across the cathedral. Gage turned and saw a young priest in his robes poised between two pillars like a deer about to take flight.

"Ahh," she said. "That must be the fellow I'm supposed to see." She tried to sound casual, but her voice betrayed her. She stood up and hitched her woven bag securely on her shoulder. "Go on down and see him. You can't miss the place. Big stone house past the ballpark, up on the hill with all the flags flying. I'm sure Neal would be happy to see you."

"I'm not so sure," Gage said.

She extended a hand, waving good-bye. The priest had not moved. He was twenty-eight or twenty-nine, Hispanic with wavy, jet-black hair. A nice-looking kid. Gage really wouldn't put anything past her.

Gage watched Tina clomp across the cathedral in her cowboy boots, angling between pews. God bless her, Gage thought. She'd never believe it if I told her, but she's the answer to my prayers. The only question Gage had was, How was she going to shoot inside the dark church without a flash attachment?

Six

THE STATE PENITENTIARY was on the right side of the highway. Through the wire mesh fence Gage could see, still miles off, the dry, scarred hills of played-out mining country.

He passed two laboring bicyclists on a long incline, passed the town of Cerrillos, passed the jumble of trailers, collapsing corrals and rusted cars upended in sandy arroyos, and began the long, curving climb into Madrid.

Gage might have spent only a half hour with Neal Sprinker seventeen years ago, but the visit occupied a special place in his memory. Sprinker had been one of the few people in a position to help find Peter and he hadn't done it. Maybe he had tried, though Gage doubted it. When Sprinker shot into national prominence six months later with his bring-the-war-home speech at the big fall demo, dressed in warpaint and feathers, Gage remembered.

For a time Neal seemed to be everywhere at once: organizing teach-ins at high schools in Watts, blocking New York induction centers, climbing fences at Fort Dix.

He had a genius for publicity. He somehow snuck into the White House with a small red fox hidden under his coat. When he let the animal loose, photographers got a dozen good shots of guards chasing the terrified animal down hallways and under antique colonial tables in the Blue Room. When Neal was arrested he feigned innocence. "What did I do wrong? The American people voted the fox into the hen house, I was just carrying out the will of the people."

He seemed invulnerable. Charges continued to mount against him, but trials were postponed again and again. He was represented by a team of the most famous radical lawyers in the country. It wasn't until he was arrested on drug charges that he finally buckled and went underground.

But even being underground couldn't shut him up. Neal did clandestine radio interviews, published articles and a book in which he claimed he had been working as Nixon's houseboy. The book jacket photograph was of him leaning against the gates of San Clemente. For two years he mocked the government's attempts to catch him. It was then that Gage really began to hate him. Peter was dead and this kid was out there, unscathed, playing Robin Hood.

When Sprinker turned himself in, he spent a year and a half in a minimum security prison teaching the inmates creative writing. A couple of years later there was a smattering of articles about him finding a guru, marrying a wealthy young woman from Long Island and becoming a spokesman for some self-realization organization. Gage had read the article with grim acknowledgment. He had to give Neal credit; one way or the other, the boy was going to come out on top.

The notion of Neal making flags in Madrid didn't quite fit, but then with Neal, any transformation was possible.

One thing, though, Gage was certain of: Neal was the man he

was looking for. Neal had known Peter. Neal had been the advocate of insurrection, resistance, bringing the system down, any way you could. Who else could it even matter to, a seventeen-year-old newspaper story about the sabotage of a midwestern munitions plant? It probably came right out of Neal's scrapbook.

It made sense and it didn't. There was still something perverse and incomplete about it. It was not the same as a World War II veteran stashing away the D-Day edition of *Stars and Stripes* in the attic. It did not explain Peter's inked-out face.

Gage passed the old stone ballpark and drove slowly into Madrid. There were still slagheaps on the hillsides, but the rows of miners' shacks all seemed to be occupied now. Dogs trotted past an Allied Van Lines truck that blocked the narrow main street. Gage hadn't been down here for a couple of years and it seemed as if there was a sign on every other gate and picket fence announcing a new weaving shop or gallery.

Madrid had been a coal-mining town until no one needed its coal. For forty years it had been a ghost town, until squatters and drifters began occupying the ruins in the late sixties. The tipple where the ore cars had been unloaded still clung to the hillside, the remaining blackened beams in some precarious and logic-defying balance. Even with his pickup window rolled halfway up Gage could smell the coal dust. Madrid was a place America had spit out, had no further use for. It was an outlaw town, a place where people could grow dope or paint or make neon sculpture without being hassled. It was a place where you would be left alone.

The stone house sat across the arroyo, festooned with flags and banners and windsocks, a fury of color against the burned hillside.

Gage turned off the paved road, crunched along the streets of pulverized coal, bumped through the arroyo. Three kids with smudged faces and knives in sheaths at their belts ambled down the middle of the street. One of them carried a ghetto blaster and as Gage passed, the boy gave the pickup a thump with the flat of his hand.

A rosy-cheeked young mother in a long skirt squatted in the doorway of one of the shacks nursing her baby, watching Gage with the suspicion of an Afghan peasant. A dog rushed out to bark at Gage's truck. On both sides of the road were fences improvised out of scrap metal and cedar posts.

There were a half-dozen cars parked in front of the stone house. Gage swung down from his pickup.

The Airships' banner rustled and snapped above the front door, ropes banging against the metal poles. Trudging up the stairs, Gage could hear the hum of sewing machines and Janis Joplin singing "Me and Bobby McGee."

Inside it looked as if people were decorating for the world's hippest prom. Nylon kites designed to resemble parrots and ringed planets, dolphins and swallow-tailed dragons, butterflies and unicorns hung from the walls and ceiling.

Janis Joplin was turned up so loud no one heard Gage come in. There were a half-dozen women at work, ex-hippies with headbands, one Central American and an alcoholic desert rat. Three sat pushing long red nylon wings through their sewing machines. Two cut patterns at long work tables and the desert rat leaned against the ironing board pressing seams, tiny pins bristling from her mouth.

A man and a woman stood together at another work table. The woman was maybe fifty, handsome in an Angie Dickinson sort of way, wide-shouldered in cowboy boots and jeans. The man had his head down and Gage couldn't see his face. The top of his head was bald, desert leather. He wore a patchwork coat of many colors, black and lavender and red, with ribbons. He hovered over the blueprint of a kite, making a series of deft marks on the white nylon, his lips pursed as if he were explaining something that should have been obvious to anyone. Gage remembered the look.

"Me and Bobby McGee" came to its mournful end.

65

"You're going to have to slash that if you want to get the fold, you realize that," the man said.

"Neal?" Gage said.

The man looked up quickly, taken by surprise. He was wary, trying to figure out if Gage was a narc or a cop.

Gage wasn't finding it much easier. Neal had put on ten, fifteen pounds and lost a lot of hair, but there was something more. It took Gage a couple of seconds before it came to him. He had never seen Neal uncertain before. The massive confidence, the wise-guy grin, the coyote sassiness was no more.

"You remember me?" Gage said.

Neal's eyes widened. "Sure. Sure, I do. Gage, right? How about that?" He reached out to shake Gage's hand. "Wow," Neal ran his fingers through his thinning hair. "This really blows me away." Otis Redding came through the speakers with "(Sittin' on the) Dock of the Bay."

"So what's the deal, Neal, because it's a ghost town they only let you play dead singers?"

"I guess that's it, yeah," Neal said. He turned to the woman next to him. "Frances, this is Jeremiah Gage. You think I'm kidding? I'm not. The movie director."

She nodded hello, still not convinced that Neal wasn't putting her on.

Gage scanned the room. The women took discreet peeks at him above their sewing machines.

"Flags, huh?" Gage said.

"That's right."

"So you're not burning 'em anymore?" Neal acted as if he hadn't heard. "There's money in this?"

"Right now we got more business than we can handle. We did all the banners for the New Orleans World's Fair. We just opened a shop in Carmel. We're doing a thing out at Acrosanti over Christmas." He paused, gazed at Gage, still trying to get his bearings. "Wow. This is a little weird."

"The feeling's mutual," Gage said.

"You want a cup of coffee?"

"Sure."

Gage followed Neal into his narrow office, ducking to avoid the swaying wooden seagull that hung from the ceiling.

The office was a mess. Every available surface was blanketed with correspondence, bolts of nylon, Oriental box kites, heavy-duty shears. Cardboard boxes bristled with blueprints. There was a Mr. Coffee setup on the file cabinet. Neal poured two cups and glanced over his shoulder. "Cream?" If Neal was playing dumb he was doing a masterful job of it.

"Black is fine," Gage said.

Gage flipped open a promotional album sitting on the desk. It was filled with laminated newspaper and magazine articles, photos of Neal's work: New Orleans boulevards lined with banners, a crew installing Tibetan prayer wheels on an Arizona mesa.

Neal handed one of the cups of coffee to Gage and pointed to a picture of an American flag. What was different about it was that the stripes were all the colors of the rainbow.

"This is one of my favorites," Neal said. "I call it 'New Glory.' " Gage kept flipping pages. "One of the things we do is make personal flags for people. We work with them to choose their own private symbols. But it's not flags you're looking for."

"No."

"What is it, then?"

"Come on, Neal. You're a smart guy, you should be able to figure it out."

"Gage, I'm too tired to figure anything out. You're going to have to tell me."

Gage went over the story point by point. When he was finished Neal didn't say anything at first, fiddling with a ball of kite string, winding it around his fist. The phone rang a few times but Neal made no move to answer it.

"So?" Neal said. "What sort of trip are you trying to run on

67

me, man? You're gonna make me laugh. You think I was the guy . . ."

"You knew Peter."

"I met him *once*." He tried to yank his hand free of the kite string. It took three tries. "After he was arrested, I thought we could help him."

"Use him, you mean," Gage said.

"Neal." Frances stood in the doorway of the office, but Neal never turned to acknowledge her.

"Frances, I'm talking, all right?" He pointed at Gage. "You use whatever words you want. It was going to be a political trial, anyway it went down. Hell, his father was a big Hollywood director, his grandfather invented the damn A-bomb and you're trying to tell me the publicity was *my* fault?"

"Neal, this will only take a second," Frances said. Her face was scarlet. She wouldn't look at Gage. Her embarrassment seemed excessive for such a strong-looking woman. "That was the Folk Art Museum on the phone. They want to know if the polyurethane mesh comes in turquoise."

"No, just the five colors," Neal said. He batted the swaying wooden seagull lightly with his hand.

"I've got to leave early," she said.

"Since when?"

"I told you this morning. I'm supposed to pick up my car in Santa Fe."

"So go. I'll see you tomorrow." She took one quick guarded glance at Gage and disappeared.

Neal ran his hand over his high gleaming forehead. "What the hell do you think I am? You think I keep a *scrapbook*, for Christ's sake? Go around scratching people's faces out one by one like some voodoo doctor?"

"The only thing I know about you, Neal, is that you wouldn't help me find him."

"I didn't know where he was. Man, it wasn't like anybody had a directory or anything. All kinds of kids were going underground,

68

for all kinds of reasons. I didn't know one tenth of those people. . . ."

"But you didn't tell me that, did you? And you know why? Because you were enjoying yourself. I was the enemy, I was one of the pigs, and I had to come to you and you got to show off in front of all those pretty long-haired girls. I haven't forgotten that, Neal."

Neal sighed, fiddled with a giant pair of shears. He seemed grim and middle-aged suddenly, haunted. His beribboned jester's jacket seemed wildly out of place. Both men were silent. Neal turned to the window, stared out across the old miners' shacks. Rain clouds had begun to slide over the crest of the hill.

"So when are the cops coming out?" Neal said.

"They're not."

"But you talked to them about this, right?"

"Yeah. But your name didn't come up."

"I never preached violence."

"Come on, Neal. The revolution was at hand, that's what you were telling people."

Neal hit the desk with his fist. "I never told anybody to plant bombs, man! For fifteen years people have been trying to stick me with that, like I was some Pied Piper leading their kiddies into damnation. I was just trying to end a shitty war. People were angry, Gage. You gotta remember that was part of it. It was *their* anger, it wasn't just mine or yours, something was really wrong back there. . . ."

"But that was another time, right?"

"Yeah." Neal pitched his empty Styrofoam cup into the wastebasket. He was white-faced and spooked. "I make flags now. Everyone should follow their own flag, every man his own nation. You're right, Gage, that was another time. Except every few months someone like you will walk in. Or I'll get one of those funny phone calls."

"What kind of phone calls?"

The window shuddered. The wind had picked up, sweeping

down the slopes, cartwheeling loose sheets of tin into sagging fences.

"You've got a daughter, right?"

"How did you know that?" Gage said.

"There was a piece in the paper about you sometime last year. Here," he said. He yanked a slender package of folded red nylon from one of the shelves and handed it to Gage. "You give her this. It's a kite with a dragon on it. Kids love 'em."

"So you can't help me?" Gage said.

"I never could help you, Gage. That's the God's honest truth."

Neal walked Gage to the front door. Outside, the wind snapped flags, billowed banners, clanged ropes against metal poles.

"Flags are powerful things," Neal said. "You see one moving, what is it that's moving? The flag? The wind? Your mind?"

"Spare me, Neal."

Neal ran his hand over the fender of Gage's pickup. "You don't still have that newspaper, do you?" Neal said.

"No, the cops kept it." Gage tossed the kite through the front window of the truck.

"There's still a lot of weird shit out there," Neal said. "If I were you, I wouldn't go poking around in it. There's some folks I wouldn't want to get stirred up."

Driving back toward the main road, Gage was going too fast and the pickup bounced, scraped bottom as it crossed the arroyo. After all these years, Neal still got under his skin.

Gage lurched onto the pavement and headed back through Madrid. A couple of bikers leaned against their machines, drinking cartons of chocolate milk.

On the outskirts of town a woman walked by the side of the road. Gage was past her before he saw that it was Frances, the woman from the flag shop. She threw him a brief, fearful glance. Gage couldn't tell whether she had recognized him or not; the look might only have been pedestrian distrust.

A school bus blocked the road fifty yards ahead, its lights

blinking red and regular as Christmas tree lights. Gage stopped, watched the children leap out and run up the tawny hill.

He drummed his fingers on the steering wheel, then glanced in his rearview mirror. Frances still trudged along the highway, but only twenty yards behind him now.

He put the pickup into reverse and backed up, engine whining. When he leaned across to roll down the window she did not seem surprised.

"Can I give you a ride?"

"No, thanks." Her hand rested on the half-open door. She wouldn't meet his gaze directly. "I'm getting a lift from my neighbor, she lives right behind the ballpark."

"You're sure?"

She pursed her lips, distressed suddenly, watching the school bus wheeze over the hill. It made Gage angry. Did she think he was that hard up that he needed to pick up women on the highway?

"I couldn't help overhearing you and Neal," she said.

"It would have been hard not to," Gage said.

"You have a son."

"Had a son. He died. A while ago."

The remark totally stopped her. Her eyes widened; she wanted to back off. "Oh," she said. "Why?"

"No reason."

Gage turned off the engine. She hooked her thumbs in her belt and stared at the scuffed toes of her boots. Lightning flickered in the far distance.

"No reason," Gage repeated.

"It was just something that Neal said."

"What was that?"

Her glance was filled with dismay; this was not the conversation she'd had in mind. "I'm sorry. I shouldn't have brought it up."

"Tell me anyway. What was it that Neal said?"

"Something about his grandfather inventing the A-bomb."

71

"Yeah, well, that's true. Not my father. His mother's father."

"That seems like a funny thing to bring up."

A Hertz truck rumbled over the hill. Frances turned her back to the road, pressed herself to Gage's pickup as it passed. It was a bad place for a conversation, standing on a blind curve.

"Funny? What's funny about it?"

"Nothing, I guess. Except I've heard it before."

"When was that?"

She pushed herself away from the hood of the truck, buttoned her jeans jacket. "There was a kid who came through here in '73, '74 maybe. . . ."

"What was his name?"

"David."

"So what are you trying to say?"

"I'm not saying anything."

"Peter . . . my son . . . was killed in 1970." Gage pulled his keys out of the ignition and closed his fingers over them. "He and another boy tried to blow up a powder plant. They thought they could end the war that way. It was a pretty amateurish effort."

She moved away from the pickup. She had been thrown off track, like a needle bounced out of its groove by a sudden jarring. A flash of lightning made her look over her shoulder. "I really should go."

"Sure," he said.

He watched her cross the road and disappear down a path that led into the old ballpark. He sat for a couple of minutes, the keys clenched in his fist. She was only trying to be helpful. Or was she? He was provoked. People shouldn't be allowed to get away with stuff like that.

He pulled the pickup off the road, got out and slammed the door hard behind him. She was halfway across the ballfield. He jogged down the narrow path, lizards scurrying for cover in the rustling wheatgrass. As he came through the swaybacked grandstand there was an explosion of wings. Pigeons dove out of the rafters. The sound made Frances stop, just beyond second base.

"You got a minute?" Gage asked. She looked frightened. He stepped across the faded chalk that marked the foul line, strolled toward her, his hands in his pockets.

On both sides of the field were the stone walls and dugouts built by the Yugoslavian miners in the thirties, looking as if they might last another hundred years. Madrid had had great baseball teams then, playing against major league barnstormers when they came through.

Wind swirled dust across the eroded infield. They could see Neal's shop on the hillside with its rippling banners. "I'm sorry, but I said I'd pick up my car by five."

"I can drive you."

She said nothing. A strand of blond hair blew across her face and she brushed it away.

"This kid who said his grandfather invented the A-bomb. Who was he?"

"Just another kid." In deep left field was an attempt at a playground: half-buried tractor tires, a jungle gym, some empty metal swings that squealed and swayed in the wind as if rocked by ghost children. Towering poles, long since stripped of their lights, ringed the field. "There were so many of them coming through then, coming through here. Running from the war, their parents, the cops, whatever. He was with a girl named Sandy. They lived in the church, just below the ridge there. He was only here a couple of months. I didn't mean to upset you."

"You didn't upset me. I'd just like to hear the story."

"It's not much of a story."

"I'm not fussy."

She raised a dubious eyebrow before continuing. "We had the bluegrass music on Sunday afternoon, even back then. I was managing the café. We would get people from all over, straight, hip, bikers, you name it. One Sunday there was a tableful of engineers from the Sandia Labs, wise guys, they'd been drinking

73

beer for a couple of hours and were joking about putting a permanent rainbow over Madrid with lasers and zapping stray dogs and hippies. David finally told them to shut up. I'd never seen him get angry before. Afterward he apologized to me. He said he just couldn't stand all that macho shit, that his grandfather was one of the people who'd invented the A-bomb. It seemed like an amazing thing to say, but he refused to talk any more about it."

"What happened to this boy?" Gage said. "This David?"

"I think they were looking to buy a piece of land. At least that's what she was always talking about. She was a real country girl."

A boy pedaled his bike up the highway, glancing down at them as he labored up the incline past Gage's parked truck. How odd we must look, Gage thought, conferring in the middle of a deserted ballfield, as if we were going over ground rules for some imaginary game.

"And what did he look like?"

"He was tall. Taller than you. Dark hair. A handsome boy."

"That could be anyone."

"It's hard to remember, it's been so long. He would help me at the store sometimes, unpacking crates."

Gage rubbed the back of his neck. The clouds rolling in were darker now, heavy blue-black billows with tears in them, here and there, where it had already started to rain.

"I really need to go," she said. "I told Fiona I'd be at her house fifteen minutes ago."

Gage kicked at the packed earth with the heel of his boot. "The ballpark's held up pretty good, hasn't it?"

"Oh, yeah. They still have rock concerts in here." She brightened at the prospect of small talk. "Allen Ginsberg was here two years ago with Baba Ram Dass. Rally for a nuclear freeze. They filled the place up."

"Ginsberg, huh? You got to meet him?"

"Yeah, I've got a picture of him at home." Gage could tell she was starting to feel sorry for him. "We used to play big softball games here every Fourth of July. Everybody played, there was music and beer, nobody kept score. This David I was telling you about, he played once. He was a wonderful hitter and he could run like the wind. A lot of people had never seen him before and they started calling him the Secret Weapon. The one odd thing was that he threw everything underhanded. I thought he was just showing off and I teased him about it. It turned out he really couldn't throw overhand. He undid the top button of his shirt to show me. There was a big knob on his collarbone, as big as an egg."

Birds flew low across the ballfield, lighting for a moment and then swirling upward again, refusing to settle in the face of the approaching storm.

"I wonder why he chose the name David?" Gage said.

"Chose it? I don't understand."

He looked toward the shadowed grandstand with its collapsing roof, keeping his exultation under wraps. "You know what somebody told me once? That Babe Ruth played here, back in the thirties." He was too stunned to calculate how what she was saying was true, but he knew it was, he had known all along, Peter could never have died back there, he could never have done what people claimed he had done. "The Sultan of Swat. Hard to believe, isn't it? It was on one of those barnstorming tours."

"I know Madrid had really good teams back then," she said. "They've got pictures of them down at the Mine Shaft."

"I'll bet it is true," he said. "Did they say where they were going to buy land? David and Sandy?"

Lightning flared under the approaching front of dark clouds and for the first time Gage could hear thunder. "Why did you come see Neal, anyway?"

"It doesn't matter now. Did they actually say they were going to farm or what? Was there a piece of land they had their eye on?"

"I don't know. A lot of people were looking around Taos then, but some were going all the way up into Colorado. . . . I really don't know."

"What about this Sandy? What was she like?"

"She was from Texas. A Baptist. And she couldn't get over the fact that she'd broken away from all that." She grimaced and ducked her head for a second, then wiped at her lips as if she'd gotten some of the blowing sand in her mouth. "Neal must have known your son, then."

"Did they have a car? A van?"

"This is ridiculous! You can forget it, mister."

Tumbleweeds bounded erratically as loose footballs across the diamond. She was catching on. She sensed how mad his hope was. He was trying to rouse the dead.

"There must be other people who knew them."

"Not necessarily."

"Why not?"

"People come and go around here, that's the kind of place it is." Her voice rose with alarm. She had made a mistake. He was sure to cause trouble.

"There must be at least one person."

She backed away, terrified of him. On the hillside two hundred yards away, banners and streamers snapped above Airships. "People around here like to be left alone."

She turned and fled through the juniper at the far edge of the field, looking back once as if afraid he might follow her.

Gage did not leave the field right away. He looked toward home and the phantom-ridden grandstands that had been filled for Ruth and Ginsberg, then turned and scanned the outfield. His son had been on this field. Start here. Yes, Gage could imagine it, his son running, yes, she was right, he did run faster than the wind.

Seven

W HEN GAGE WALKED into the house there was a sizzle of grease coming from the kitchen and the strong, unmistakable smell of greens boiling down. Jody lay exhausted, still in her soccer uniform and shin guards, in front of the TV, watching *Square One*. Amy called out. She had made them fried chicken and cornbread and as soon as Gage set the table they could eat.

At dinner the big topic was whether Jody should stop going to soccer because there were no other girls on the team. Amy's point was that she didn't want Jody to get into the habit of quitting things. Gage sniffed at his fingers; the odor of coal dust was still on him. Back and forth they went with the news of the day: an emaciated deer dog had wandered up and gotten into a fight with their dogs and the stump-removal man came by with his remarkable machine.

Gage listened to his wife and child, soothed by their voices, by the light and warmth of the table. He was not going to tell them. There was no place for it here. There was no Vietnam War, no past. He would no more bring it up than he would drive them all over a cliff.

Amy leaned back in her chair and looked toward the kitchen.

"What's wrong?" Gage said.

"I smell something burned," she said. "I thought maybe I'd left one of the burners on. Did everybody wash their hands?"

"I did!" Jody said. She fixed her father with her most accusatory look. "Dad-dy!"

Gage lowered his eyes to his plate. With his cornbread he wiped up the pot liquor from his greens. "If you want any dessert, darlin', you better finish up your milk."

The next morning he drove back to Madrid and spent the day there. He tromped up and down the coal streets, keeping the village dogs in a constant uproar, methodically went door to door, speaking to anyone who would speak to him. He hit the Guatemalan fabric shop, the grocery store, the Mine Shaft Café.

Madrid was a small place and word got around quickly; several times people simply refused to come to the door when Gage knew there was someone in there. Of those who would talk, some were amused, others hostile. "Folks don't take kindly to being hassled around here. You start asking a lot of questions, no telling how people are going to react. And watch your step. Rattlesnakes love to nest up in these old mine shafts." A man who claimed he raised wolves for a living was incredulous. "You're looking for someone who passed through here fifteen years ago? You can't be for real, man."

Gage wasn't sure he was for real, that was part of the problem. Peter was dead. There was more than sufficient evidence. If one chose to doubt the charred, incinerated body, there was the burned clothing, the testimony of Benny Meinhardt, the old socialist farmer Peter had lived with during the years he was underground. Benny's son, Richard, had died in the explosion with Peter. During the investigation that followed the deaths, Benny had broken, poured out every damning, irrefutable detail.

Yet Frances had seen Peter play on that ballfield in Madrid four years later. There was only one way to solve it. Gage kept going, moving warily among the abandoned, snake-infested mine shafts that riddled the hillsides; all he needed was the one that would lead him back into the underground.

The woman in the antique dress shop said that Bradley Black-welder had lived in Madrid longer than anyone. She didn't know if he was in town or not, he'd been down in Central America doing a documentary on power spots, but she thought someone had said they'd seen him at the bakery in the last couple of days.

The ancient tipple jutted from the side of the mountain like a giant charred centipede. Two hundred yards beyond it, on the other side of the road, was the hand-painted sign: GILGAMESH PRODUCTIONS. The miner's shack would have been an embarrassment at a deer camp. Gage got out of his pickup and followed the mournful sound of whales around to the back.

Bradley Blackwelder didn't seem surprised at being interrupted. He was a small, tightly muscled man in his late thirties with a red ponytail. He wore Birkenstock sandals, and a pen-and-ink flowering peyote plant was stenciled on his purple T-shirt. He snapped off his mammoth tape deck. The sound track was for a slide show on Antarctica. A picture of glistening mountains of ice glowed from the back wall of the shadowy miner's shack.

Bradley sat with his legs crossed, nodding sagely and sipping cold coffee as Gage talked. "The kid's name was David," Gage said. "Frances remembers him. He lived in the church with a woman, I think her name was Sandy." As Gage's eyes adjusted to the darkness he could make out the posters of avant-garde film-makers on the wall, the silver cannisters of film. "I wondered if you remembered them, if any of this rang a bell."

"Oh, yeah. I helped them pack."

"You did?"

"Yeah." Bradley toyed with one of the spools of the tape deck. "David was far-out. I dug the guy a lot." Bradley seemed a little high-strung, like a cocker spaniel. There was New England somewhere in there, Gage thought, and overbreeding.

"But you don't know where he is?"

"No."

"You have any idea where they might have ended up?"

"They had their eye on this goat farm up around Gallina. He used to drive the ambulance for the county up there."

Suddenly it was all feeling a little too easy. "You're sure?"

"Absolutely. David. I'm a very visually oriented kind of guy, I never forget a face. His old lady had this red, red hair, came down to about here." He sucked coffee from his mustache meditatively. "Their daughter was just named rodeo queen up there."

"Daughter?"

"Yeah. Her picture was in the paper last week." As Bradley slid around on his stool, a red setter asleep under the desk awoke with a start.

Bradley rummaged through a two-foot-high stack of newspapers and film magazines on a twig couch. Gage sat utterly silent. The still-befuddled red setter sniffed his pants leg.

"This David," Gage said finally. "Did he ever talk about himself?"

"Oh, yeah. We used to have a beer now and then and the guy would really rap." For the first time Gage heard Boston in Bradley's accent.

"Really."

"He was from out East somewhere." As Bradley bent over the stacks of paper his T-shirt rode up in the back. "The Pine Barrens, I think he said. He'd wanted to go into Intelligence, but he couldn't get top clearance because he was an orphan."

"That's what he told you?"

The shack rattled as motorcycles roared past on the highway. Discarded newspapers slithered to the floor. "He was making artificial limbs for Vietnam vets for a while."

"Maybe you're getting him confused with someone else."

"Here it is." Bradley yanked a newspaper from the middle of the pile and handed it to Gage.

Gage stared at the picture on the front page of *The Rio Grande Sun*. A fresh-faced teenage girl on horseback, a dime-store tiara in her hair, waved into the camera. A stocky man with a black mustache held the horse's bridle. The photo stabbed at his heart. For a second Gage bought it. Anything was possible. Gage could have a granddaughter, and a rodeo queen to boot.

Then he read the caption:

> Chelsea Pinella, seventeen, daughter of Derek and Ruth Ann Pinella of Embudo, begins her reign at the County Fairgrounds.

The man steadying the horse was her father.

"Shit."

"What?"

"The guy's name is Derek."

"Let me see." Bradley grabbed the paper back. Gage, furious, turned away. On the back of the door was a color photo of a South American tribesman with his blowgun, peeping through banana leaves.

"David, Derek, so what?" Bradley said. "That's the guy. Maybe he changed his name."

"You said his name was David. He had a knot on his collarbone, right here," Gage said.

"Oh, yeah?" Bradley shuffled a handful of slides as if they were a disappointing batch of poker cards.

"Let's just think about this for a second," Gage said. Bradley leaned over the carousel and dropped the slides in one by one. His feelings were hurt. "It was a long time ago. I'm not doubting your word. But the guy I'm talking about worked with Frances at the store."

"This is the same guy." Bradley snapped on the projector. Two men stared together into a gleaming abyss of ice. "And I

81

met his brother once. Dwayne. He was into pit bulls down in Placitas."

"This is not the guy."

Bradley snapped off three or four pictures of penguins diving into the sea, ships churning through polar ice. Gage stared at the photos. This was Dead End City. He'd gotten to Bradley twenty peyote buttons too late. The man's mind had no more chance of holding focus than a kaleidoscope.

"What are you, some kind of detective or what?" Bradley said. "I'll tell you right now, you ain't gonna find him, not with an attitude like that. It's a big country, mister. Somebody wants to get lost, no one's going to find him. You're probably CIA, aren't you, man? If it's documents you want, forget it. What happened out here in the last twenty years, it's just written on water." Bradley hit the button to the tape recorder, the wheels began to move, and the echoing songs of humpback whales filled the desert room.

Two nights after his confrontation with Bradley Blackwelder, Gage sat at his desk paying bills while Amy put Jody to bed. He shoved the freshly stamped envelopes to one side and listened to his daughter's protests from the bedroom down the hall. He still had one more piece of unfinished business. He had been putting it off, but he saw now that he couldn't proceed until it was taken care of. He needed to talk to the man Peter had lived with the year he was underground. He pulled out the phone book, found the area code for southwestern Wisconsin, then dialed information.

"Reedsburg, please. The last name is Meinhardt, M-e-i-n-h-a-r-d-t, first name Ben or Benjamin."

He wrote the number down on the back of the customer's copy of the gas bill. He sat for a moment with the receiver in his hand, listening to Amy singing a verse from "Mockingbird" down the hall. He got up and gently shut the door.

He stood over the desk as he dialed, the reflection of the lamp shining off the dark windows. He misdialed once and had to start over.

"Hello?" The familiar, faintly Germanic voice was foggy. Gage must have woken him. Even socialist dairy farmers had to get up with their cows. "Hello?" Gage couldn't hear Amy singing anymore. If she came in now, how would he explain? "Who is this?" Benny demanded.

"Benny?" Gage said.

"Ya, sure it's Benny. Who is this?"

"This is Jeremiah Gage."

For a second the only sound between them was the static of a faulty long-distance connection. "Is this a joke or what?"

"No, Benny, it's not a joke." In the wastebasket under the desk was a crumpled piece of paper, scrawled with crayon, one of Jody's drawings. "I need to ask you something." Gage retrieved the drawing and smoothed out the wrinkles.

In the picture blue smoke curled out of an orange chimney, a little girl with a green dog stood in front of the yellow house. Jody always got furious when she discovered he'd thrown out one of her drawings. They were gifts, more of them every day.

"Is there any chance we could have been wrong, Benny?"

"What do you mean, wrong?" He could just about see Benny, bull-necked; the thick hand wrapped around the phone; the myopic, troubled gaze; the muddy boots by the door.

"Did you ever think that either of them . . . Peter or Richard . . . could possibly have come through that?" Again there was a long silence. The static came in flurries, as if they were on transatlantic cable.

"What the hell are you talking about?"

"I think Peter may be alive, Benny."

"Are you crazy, Gage? You've been drinking. I don't need to listen to this."

"I want to know, Benny, was there anything you didn't tell the police? Maybe you were trying to protect somebody. Maybe there was someone else with them. But I need to know."

"You've got no right to talk to me like this, Gage. I know where my boy is. He's buried in a cemetery six miles from here and he'd be alive if he hadn't met your kid. Just leave me alone."

Benny hung up and Gage was left with the squalling dial tone. When he set down the phone his hands were trembling. He could hear, faintly, through the closed door, Amy singing the final verse from "Mockingbird." He stared at Jody's drawing. There was no bringing the two worlds together. He picked up his pen and scratched out Benny's phone number with the thoroughness of an unfaithful husband.

The rasping of the door opening behind him made him jump. Amy stood in the doorway.

"Hey," he said.

"Did you call someone" she said.

Stupidly he lied. "No." She glanced at the open phone book. "Oh. I talked to the guy at the garage in Española. I want him to take a look at the Jeep. I'm going to run up there tomorrow." His glibness saved him. "She go to sleep okay?" He took Amy's hands in his own.

"She did fine," Amy said. "You seem upset."

"No, I'm fine."

"But I can feel your hands. They're trembling."

"I think I got a little chill from working outside today." Gage pressed his wife's hands to his guilty cheek. "You don't think I'm crazy, do you? When you met me, you must have."

"Well, you had a definite edge."

"And now."

"I hate to disappoint you. I think you're normal. Perfectly normal." The swivel chair creaked as she bent over him. Her auburn hair fell across his face like a soft net, pulling him back. "Is that okay?"

He began with the tax rolls and title transfers for Santa Fe, Taos and Rio Arriba counties for 1972 to 1976. There wasn't a single Anglo David among them, but he made a list of the more promising names and set off to work through them, one by one.

In the next five days he drove eight hundred miles. He drove into the mountains, through remote Hispanic villages, passing the graveyards with their simple wooden crosses and plastic flowers bright after a sudden rain. He drove west of the Rio Grande, through open rangeland, some of it barren as the Golan Heights, and alkali flats where shallow rivers wound through gravel banks. He tried to find owners, but in many cases the land had changed hands a dozen times, sometimes traded for a truck or a pair of horses, or simply abandoned. He bounced his pickup through a mile of dry arroyo to explore the remains of an old commune where a painted bus, cannibalized for parts, propped up the corner of a collapsing barn.

He met a renegade anthropologist who raised llamas on the ruins of an old hotel, talked to a Lebanese feed-store owner with a wiry black beard and rubberized hunting boots. He listened to the woes of a divorced fireman who raised ornamental corn. He followed the gutting sounds of chainsaws back into the forest to split a six-pack with a logger who looked like a muscular version of Sonny Bono, sleek shoulder-length hair and a gold star in one of his front teeth. Dope surveillance planes droned among the mountain peaks.

He knocked on the door of Spanish woodcarvers, a tiny old man and woman who knew no English but ushered him in with nods and smiles, thinking they had their first customer in months.

They lifted the white sheet off the coffee table to show him their prize creation, a cottonwood crèche of the Garden of Eden. The carved wood was as soft and smooth as soap. A mild serpent coiled among the biscuit-thick leaves. Gage tried to explain that this was not quite what he was looking for, the Tree of the Knowledge of Good and Evil, he was looking for a young man, or a not-so-young man anymore. They did their best to understand

85

his questions; in the end he bought a four-dollar pig for his daughter so he wouldn't totally disappoint them.

Gage, afraid of attracting too much attention, had a different story for everyone. Sometimes he posed as a man interested in buying land, other times he was a farmer looking for the young guy who'd sold him hay two summers before, a tall, dark-haired fellow named David. Or he was a businessman on his way to Denver who'd just decided on the spur of the moment to look up the nephew he hadn't seen for years, he just happened to have an old high school graduation picture in his wallet, maybe they'd recognize him from that. Or he was a rancher delivering a fine Missouri trotter and he'd driven all the way from Farmington and the buyer hadn't shown up, it was David something, he had the name written down on a slip of paper, but he couldn't seem to find it.

They weren't the most brilliant lies, but Gage milked them for all they were worth. "You must know the guy," he would say. "He told me he comes in here *all* the time." Gage would scratch his head and stare some. "Well, I don't know, then. You're sure, you're sure? Nice-looking boy. Moved up here, oh, it must have been the early seventies, you remember what it was like then."

Some people stared at him as if they had no clue what he was talking about, twice people laughed in his face. Once a heart-breakingly gentle guy, an ex–Hog Farmer who'd just returned from drilling tar sands in northern Alberta, got so concerned he brought Gage home and got on the phone trying to help. The ex–Hog Farmer and his family lived in a trailer at the base of a pumice cliff. In the front yard was a beehive oven and a satellite dish; in the backyard were raspberry bushes, cherry and plum trees. While the young driller made a half-dozen phone calls, his wife served Gage tea and talked of their worries. They had lived on the outside so long, they didn't know if they could get back in, and she was getting tired of living on bolita beans and bee pollen. She was hoping she could find work as a dental assistant. The young driller's calls yielded nothing.

There was one chance in a million someone was going to lead him right to Peter. Peter, if he was alive, could just as easily be in Colorado, Utah, British Columbia. The odds didn't concern Gage much. What he had trouble admitting to himself was what he really thought: he was going to find Peter in the simplest possible way. He would walk into a store and Peter would be there buying barbed wire and work gloves, or Gage would pass a pickup full of split firewood on one of those steep mountain roads and he would glance across and there Peter would be at the wheel.

There was one lie that was serious, that he was not going to be able to walk away from. He told Amy that he was working at a garage in Española putting a new engine in the Jeep. She never questioned why it would take five long days and never seemed to notice that Gage came back each night without a trace of oil or grease on his hands.

For about a day it seemed like a forgivable enough lie, but it grew. A half-dozen times Gage was on the verge of telling her, but backed off each time. Normal life continued: Amy found Jody a new soccer team that three other girls from her class were on; they spent one evening getting the winter quilts down from the old garage; one morning there was a pair of wild turkeys down at the fence line.

It seemed impossible that the truth didn't show somehow, that she couldn't read it on his face. Lying next to her in bed at night, his hand resting on her hip, he would close his eyes and see it all again, the curving mountain roads, the green river bottoms far below, a man on a tractor plowing his fields. The man would get off the tractor to open a gate, struggle with the loop of wire, then glance up as Gage passed. There would be the look of astonishment.

What had been put to rest was no longer at rest. If at first he had felt soaring hope, it was followed by old anger. If Peter had been alive all this time and hadn't chosen to contact Gage, he probably had sound reasons. If Peter was alive, then someone had died in his place. If Peter was found, there would be that to deal with.

Somewhere near the center of it was a hoax. The story people always loved to tell in the tiny New Mexico town where Gage grew up was of the financially strapped banker who had faked his own death. He went fishing one day and never came back. All the searchers found was the overturned boat and the hat floating on the water. Ten years later the man was discovered living in Texas with a new wife and a hefty bank account.

If Peter was alive, odds were it would be better for everyone if Gage didn't find him. Did he want to explain to his six-year-old daughter about her dead brother, about Vietnam? All the same, he kept on.

The land-sale records had come to nothing. He called Father Ortiz's brother, who refused to speak to him. He tried to trace Joan, the woman Peter had lived with just before he disappeared, through her parents' name in Winnipeg, but found no listings.

He checked the archives of the Española newspaper and talked to the editor there, who knew northern New Mexico like the back of his hand, who knew, better than anyone, who had come and gone in the past twenty years. Gage knew he was running the risk of being recognized, but the editor came up with a half-dozen fresh names, and Gage thought he had gotten away with it. He hadn't, quite.

While they were talking, Gage had noticed a big ponytailed reporter pass by the open office door three or four times and stare in. Just as Gage got up to leave, the reporter came in and lay a sheaf of fresh copy on the editor's desk, then turned to Gage.

"I'm sorry to bother you," the reporter said. "But I've just got to ask. Aren't you Jeremiah Gage? The movie director?"

"Me? No, sorry."

"You sure? You look just like him."

The editor was taking a closer look all of a sudden. Gage tried desperately to remember the name he'd given the editor, was it Vincent Fleming or Victor? His mind had gone into vapor lock.

"Absolutely," Gage said.

"You know, he lives right around here. This Gage."

"Oh, no wonder. See, I'm from Denver," Gage said as if that explained everything. He tried to remain offhand, but his heart was racing. He could see the doubt in the editor's eyes, see the older man trying to figure out if Gage really looked like a Colorado businessman trying to find a long-lost nephew. Gage knew if he was recognized it would blow the whole thing. Once the editor got hold of it, it would be only a matter of time before Captain Trevino got wind of it, before everybody knew.

"Well, that sort of clarifies it," Gage said. "I come through here on business every few months, but this is the third time somebody's asked me that. The other guy I get mistaken for is Lloyd Bridges. I can't see that one at all." He clapped the editor on the back of the arm. "Listen, thanks a lot." He glanced at the towering, ponytailed reporter, who still didn't look utterly convinced. "Jeremiah Gage," Gage said. "Isn't he the one who made *Stagecoach?*"

"No. That was John Ford."

"Oh, yeah. Same guy who made *The Searchers.*"

Every time Gage thought that he'd come to the end of the road, there was always someplace further. He drove across mesa tops littered with abandoned windmills and dead mufflers. He found a jive-talking, shifty-eyed Anglo shaman who'd spent twelve years of apprenticeship with an Indian healer in Guatemala before fleeing during the military violence. He lived now by a stream in a tepee with spotted horses painted on it. Magical leather pouches hung like Christmas tree ornaments in the cottonwoods along the river.

Gage met with a village *patrón* in Ojo Caliente who held court in an old Ford Maverick in the parking lot of the local package liquor store. The *patrón* suggested that Gage go around to the priests of the village churches. Gage objected: the man he was looking for wasn't Catholic.

"What does it matter?" The *patrón* shrugged. "If someone's been born, if someone dies, the priest's the one who knows." He gave Gage a wink and a confidential pat on the hand. "And the other good thing, you ask a priest, you know they're going to keep these things to themselves."

North of Abiquiu, Gage found a band of burned-out hippies planting trees for the Forest Service. They shuffled across an open field in a ragged row, bent and brown as peasants in a Brueghel painting, bags of wet seedlings on their shoulders, hoes in their hands.

Gage kept tiny, pocket-sized Woolworth notebooks that slowly filled with names and phone numbers and quickly scrawled maps, but more and more he felt as if he was losing touch with what he was looking for, as if he couldn't remember Peter's face.

There were so many people lost, too far gone to ever make it back. Gage felt as if he was unearthing the refuse of a generation. "Aquarian trash," one bitter Hispanic county patrolman called them, users, takers and losers, mountain junkies and juicers. The cop warned Gage to watch his step. It was marijuana-harvesting season and anyone wandering off the main road was taking their life in their hands. The year before, a deer hunter had walked into a trip wire and got skewered by a crossbow.

It wasn't the strangeness that really got to Gage. If anything it was all too familiar—the stacks of tin and scrap wood, the mangy animals and marginal land, the antiquated farm machinery, the hand-painted signs advertising chainsaw repair, the rusted automobiles and collapsed outhouses shoved over the embankments of the high passes. It was the same New Mexican poverty that Gage had spent a lifetime trying to get away from.

Gage began to feel as if he were skimming the surface, gliding through. Driving through the mountains he kept fiddling with the radio dial. He whizzed past something that looked like a witch's house, with a steeply pitched shingled roof and solar panels and tobacco drying on the porch. On his radio livestock-market reports faded and merged with mariachi music from Albuquerque. Gage had the eerie sense of the past and the present all garbled, sliding past one another, sending their distant signals.

Nina had been a staff photographer for *Life* magazine, assigned to do an article on the filming of Gage's second feature. She was tall, with tons of jet-black hair, a large, noble face and long, sensitive hands. She wore leather boots and long, dashing black capes and Gage's first impression of her was that she was haughty. Her father was Leon Friedman, a German-Jewish émigré physicist who had been one of the inventors of the A-bomb at Los Alamos. Gage figured that if you'd had Einstein to your house to play quartets with your father when you were twelve, you had a right to be haughty.

It turned out that haughty wasn't the right word. When Nina invited Gage over to her trailer for tea during a break in the shooting, she came up with a tin of English cookies and the whole thing was positively cozy. Later, a friend would say of her, Nina sets a rich table, and it was true, in a dozen ways. The talk was funny and quick, it got intense in a hurry, and then Gage must have said something he shouldn't have, though he never was sure what it was, and suddenly she grew distant and hurt.

Gage made a special project out of her. His first film had been a controversy-ridden success—acclaimed as brilliant by some, denounced as a new all-time low in blood-and-gore nihilism by others—and Gage suspected that *Life* might be setting him up for a hatchet job.

Even in the middle of a tight shooting schedule, Gage found time to pay court. In the evenings Gage would take her for walks past the corrals and the tents and the rented trucks and they would climb the mesa.

Being charming was just one of the tools of the trade. Gage played the country boy for her, pointing out owls and hawks and

91

jackrabbits with his flashlight. He told her stories about growing up in New Mexico, about rattlesnakes and tarantulas and the time his father went out to check the still and ran into Pancho Villa's men.

She wasn't that impressed. She had grown up in New Mexico too and she knew nearly as many good rattlesnake stories as he did. She was sixteen when she arrived in Los Alamos and, after the nightmare of wartime Europe, the high-mountain country seemed like paradise.

She learned to ride and fish, she learned the names of every flower and tree with good Germanic thoroughness, she explored the canyons and mountains and Indian ruins.

Her father never spoke of his work. It was made very clear to Nina that she wasn't to ask. All she knew was that it was very important to many, many people and probably much too complex for any seventeen-year-old to understand.

Everyone on the hill was a genius, of one sort or another. She remembered being wakened in the middle of the night by Edward Teller's piano playing, being given a volume of John Donne's poetry by Oppenheimer for her birthday. The aura of secrecy only added to the sense of being special, being one of the elect.

The aura of secrecy did not last forever. The first reports of the bombing of Hiroshima and Nagasaki were sketchy, but then the photos began to come in of the leveled cities, the half-melted, peeling bodies.

One of the reasons Nina had become a photographer was because anyone could understand pictures. Nina saw, finally, the fruits of her father's labor. They had a horrible row and for three years they didn't speak. She had not trusted polite surfaces ever since. It wasn't the showing of violence that scared her, it was the hiding of it.

"I grew up with people who really *knew* how to keep secrets. So if you think I can't tell—"

"Tell what?" Gage had said.

92

"That one of the reasons we go for these walks every night is that you're worried about being trashed in *Life* magazine and that you're trying to cut me off at the pass, so to speak. Well, just don't think that. I do know. And I've enjoyed the walks. All the same."

From his pickup Gage watched the comings and goings at the ancient church: the Hispanic family in their Sunday best, piling out of a Bronco with Arizona plates, the old man in a wheelchair, head lolling on his chest, being pushed by his sixty-year-old daughter, the spindly hunchbacked girl in a white dress carried by her stout, Pueblo-looking father. Grackles strutted and fussed on the gravel, and somewhere nearby someone was running a mower. At the far end of the parking lot a trio of Hispanic men sat in a rusted-out Impala with the doors open, laughing and telling stories.

The scene suggested peace—the slightly askew bell towers, the massive golden cottonwoods, the murmuring water running in the ditch, the cattle and horses grazing in the pool-table-green pastures below the two-hundred-year-old adobe church—but Gage felt no peace.

Five days and he had come up with nothing. He was going in circles now. He had come to the Santuario because of the *patrón*'s advice about priests being the ones who knew everything, but now that he was here he saw there was no point. What were they going to do, go through old baptismal records?

He had sat in his truck for twenty minutes without moving. It would be better not to find Peter. He saw that clearly now.

A loud thump made Gage turn. On the hood of a beat-up blue Chevy, parked ten yards away, sat a boot. It was no ordinary boot. It was of heavy black leather; it looked as if it must have weighed five pounds and was decorated with dirty red ribbons and chains.

Gage recognized it in a second. There was someone in the car, but Gage couldn't tell for sure who: the car door on the far side was open and it looked as if the driver was bent over, tending to something, maybe dusting off a sock.

The driver finally hopped up on one foot, supporting himself with a hand on the car door, and retrieved the boot. Gage saw just enough of the pitted cheek, the large jaw to be certain. It was the young thief who had stolen the cassette of Gage's film the day of Father Ortiz's funeral.

He still sported the silver-studded leather wristband, was still dressed in black. He leaned against the car while pulling on his boot.

Gage had not moved. He watched the punk kid go around to open the trunk and lift out a heavy red gas can. The grackles flapped off as the young thief slammed the trunk shut. The boy clomped off, gas can swinging heavily at his side. He moved through the courtyard and disappeared into the church.

Gage got out of his pickup. If he couldn't get satisfaction for one grievance, maybe he could get satisfaction for another. Gage walked through the courtyard with its gravestones and plastic flowers and entered the church. He scanned the windowless sanctuary, baffled; he saw no sign of the young thief.

Gage had been here just a couple of times before. A toy-church, he thought, that was part of its power. Ancient as it was, it looked as if a child could have built it.

Massive reredos hung on either side of the nave, the blues and golds fading on the three-hundred-year-old paintings. Carved wooden saints peered from their niches in the wall. The front of the church trembled with the light from a hundred flickering candles. Above the altar hung Our Lord of Esquipulas, the Guatemalan crucifix around which the church was built, the dark green body scarred by long red wounds.

Gage came up the aisle, running his hand over the pews. The young thief could not just have vanished into thin air. Gage squinted at the painted wooden panel of Our Lady of Sorrows with a dagger in her heart, the panel of the saint with the flowering staff. Each saint was frozen in its gesture, each represented a

94

story, a letter for the illiterate. Gage was surrounded by signs he could not read.

He stumbled over buckled linoleum where it looked as if the floor had started to give way, then walked past the altar and ducked his head to slip into the side room. There was still no one.

Gage stared at the crutches and braces, the corsets and baby shoes hanging from the flaking adobe walls. Family snapshots and graduation pictures and handwritten testimonials were stapled to beaverboard, slipped under the glass of portraits of eye-rolling saints. Dog tags hung from a crucifix like so many snapped fishing lures. On a scrap of lined paper someone had written in large block letters: PLEASE HELF ME FIND A JOB.

A soft scraping noise startled Gage. He swiveled quickly and stared through the next narrow doorway. Two figures, backs turned, knelt inside the tiny room.

He hesitated for a second and then moved quietly toward them. They never looked up. It was a man and his young son. They were Hispanic and poor. The man seemed almost diminutive, with wide Indian cheekbones, and he wore a thick blue suit, his knobby dark hands protruding out of starched white cuffs. The boy couldn't have been more than thirteen and wore a neatly pressed white shirt.

The father scooped the red dirt out of the hole. There was no indication that either of them knew Gage was there. The boy leaned his head back, his eyes closed, and opened his mouth. When his father put a pinch of dirt on his tongue, some of the fine red dust fell on the boy's clean shirt.

Gage braced himself in the narrow doorframe, both appalled and moved. He knew he was in the presence of something potent. So many miracles had come out of this place, this pozito, this sacred hole. Gage knew the stories, the mysterious appearances and disappearances of saints and relics and lights on hillsides in the middle of the night—the usual paraphernalia of legend.

Yet he would never mock this place. He had seen the pilgrims on Easter, walking on their knees for miles to reach the Santuario. The one part of it that he did believe was that if one believed powerfully enough, almost anything could happen. The trick for Gage was how to believe; he was not a man who could easily surrender his skeptical eye.

He took the snapshot of Peter from his shirt pocket and stuck it into the corner of the frame of a velvet painting of a saint, then ducked back into the sanctuary.

Gage lifted his head at the long, liquid boinging of a full gas can hitting against something. At the other end of the church the young thief stood, the red metal container in his left hand, while an older man fiddled with the lock of what must have been a janitor's room.

Gage moved down the aisle toward them. The older man looked up. He was small and wiry, dour-faced and wary as an ex-bantamweight boxer. Gage guessed he was in his late sixties. The young thief looked up too, but didn't recognize Gage at first.

"Can I help you?" the caretaker said.

"Yeah, you can," Gage said. The young thief's eyes widened. Maybe it was Gage's voice that did it, but the kid suddenly had Gage placed.

Gage kicked at the cracked linoleum. He had the choice of being a real bastard or not. The scene was easy enough to read. The old man must be the kid's grandfather, the boy had been running errands, gone to get gas for the lawn mower. What was Gage going to do? Turn the kid in? For stealing a twenty-dollar cassette? Gage had it in him to be vengeful, but not here, not in this place. Gage had no right to turn anyone's son in.

"You should do something about the floor," Gage said.

The caretaker gazed down at the buckled linoleum. "Oh, I know. Seems like every couple of years now, we've got to tear it up and put down a new one."

The young thief set down the gas can warily, as if to free his hands.

96

"Now, why would that be?" Gage said.

"The priests," the caretaker said.

The punk kid fiddled with his studded wristband. "Listen, Grampa, I got to go now."

"All right. But your grandmother, she's expecting you for dinner. Six o'clock."

The young thief backed off, giving Gage the faintest of nods, then drifted out the door into the sunlight.

"The priests," Gage said. "You mean they make you put in the new floors?"

"No. Not those priests. The dead ones. Buried under the church." Grackles shrieked and whistled out in the churchyard.

"Come on," Gage said.

The caretaker shrugged, not taking offense. "That's what they say. Supposed to be in big stone caskets. I haven't actually seen them, but my uncle has. He says that when he was a boy, they opened them up and he saw the bones."

"You believe that?"

The two men moved toward the door of the church, the caretaker dragging a gimpy leg. "I believed it then. We were children. He told us there was a tunnel under the church. Went all the way back to the stone wall down in the pasture. The priests built it a couple hundred years ago so they could escape during Indian attacks. They would crawl out, go hide out in the mountains."

"And are there still people hiding out?" Gage asked. The caretaker stared, missing the jump. "In these mountain villages."

"Oh, sure," he said.

The two men stepped out of the church into the late-afternoon sun. The beat-up blue Chevy gutted its way out of the parking lot, sounding like an outboard motor, with blue smoke billowing from the tailpipe.

"But usually all that means is that they've killed somebody and they're staying at their mother's house and the state police are afraid to knock on the door."

"And who could tell me about this?" Gage asked. The caretaker frowned. "No, I'm serious. This is something I need to know about."

"I'm not the one to talk to."

"Then who is?"

"There's a man named Knapp. He's a little crazy. But he knows. And he'll talk. You got no problem there."

Eight

GAGE'S FIRST IMPRESSION of Nina's father had been that he was a man ready to give correction. They had gone to seek his blessing. He was at an institute in New Jersey, a summer camp for geniuses, Gage called it, an impressive colonial mansion flanked by angular glass offices tucked under earthen bunkers as if the builders had been worried about mortar attack.

On a long walk through the Institute woods, among magnolia and flowering dogwood, they told him they wanted to get married. He was polite enough on the spot, in a superior sort of way. Only later, after Gage had been sent off to a Wine and Game Shop in search of bourbon, did Leon Friedman lay it on the line. The match was preposterous, Gage was beneath her, a professional vulgarian, a maker of horse operas. The zinger that Gage always remembered was, "A man like that is too hungry to love anyone."

Leon Friedman didn't back down easily. He didn't attend the wedding, and at Peter's birth the best he could manage was an ambiguous telegram. Gage found the whole act unbelievable. Nina's father was the kind of guy you wanted to get even with, sooner or later.

Gage wasn't the only one who felt that way. Leon Friedman had been an American hero. He'd worked with Teller on the theory of implosion hydrodynamics, which led to the bomb that defeated the Fascists, but he'd been an increasingly irritating presence since. He'd opposed the development of the H-bomb, had spoken against the intensification of the Cold War and the arms race. He had not minced words. His one miscalculation was thinking he couldn't be touched.

He was called up in front of the McCarthy hearings and grilled. There was a matter of an eighty-three-dollar check he'd written to some two-bit lefty organization in the early forties. The committee wanted to know about his relationship with his various émigré friends, many of whom were socialists or acknowledged Marxists. Witnesses were called who testified that Friedman might have been giving information to the Russians for as long as ten years.

Nina's father didn't have the sense to keep his head down. When asked by a reporter what he thought of McCarthy, Friedman reverted to German. *"Der Mann ist ein Narr."* The translation made every morning newspaper in the country: PHYSICIST CALLS MCCARTHY FOOL.

Nina's father's security clearance was withdrawn. It was never clear whether he was forced out of the Institute or resigned voluntarily. He was a shattered man. His lifetime of work had been predicated on the deep, underlying lawfulness of the universe; the world he lived in now had no laws. He moved from one teaching position to the next; the focus of his research had shifted to particle-antiparticle annihilation.

Nina was the one to catch the full weight of his fall. Her father had never been able to give her a word of praise, but now she was his lifeline. At first there were just the weekly phone calls, but later came the emergency visits. Nina flew to Massachusetts after his apartment was burglarized. She ended up staying the week, cooking his meals, paying his overdue bills, sewing the leather patches on the elbows of his jackets. Later came the trip to northern California to help him pack after his mid-semester resignation. She went to Houston to be with him after a CAT scan picked up what they thought was a brain tumor, but after a harrowing two weeks of tests, the team of doctors agreed there was no physical basis to the slurring of speech and dimming of vision Leon Friedman had been suffering.

Nina was a massively competent person, but she was being whipsawed between a father on the way down and a husband on the way up. There was a child to be raised and Gage was gone, five months at a shot, making films in Canada, Mexico, Arizona. Each film was the big one, the breakthrough movie for which nothing could be spared, no personal sacrifice withheld. When Gage was home, most of his time was spent in the exhausted trance where ambitious men pass their private lives.

Something had to give and it did give, periodically. Nina would grow tense and remote. When she finally broke, there would be a great outpouring: she was being pulled apart by everyone's needs, she couldn't do everything herself, once in a while she needed someone to take care of her.

Gage would try harder and things would improve for a time. She was a wife to be proud of. She was striking and smart and she had a kind of class Gage would never have, no matter how hard he worked at it. Fatally unsure of herself in private, she was impeccable in public. Gage sometimes accused her of being a classic Hollywood liberal; he wasn't crazy about her picketing Woolworth's or raising money for the farm workers' union, but he respected the fact that she was a woman of conscience. It seemed to Gage that they had achieved a fragile but workable equilibrium, until the night that Nina's father hanged himself in a New York hotel room.

101

The next year was a long, downward spiral. She blamed herself for her father's death. He had called her a week before his suicide. He had gotten an eviction notice and begged her to come, but he had cried wolf once too often, and she refused.

Nina would not be consoled. She was alternately furious at Gage, her father, herself. Gage was less than perfectly sympathetic. He had never liked her father and couldn't really swallow the line that Leon Friedman had been a great martyr to Principle. Gage didn't believe in principles. He really didn't believe in anything he couldn't see. He was the ultimate show-me guy.

Her behavior became increasingly erratic. She fired the Japanese gardener, claiming that he'd stolen money from her purse. She ran a traffic light on Sunset Drive and totaled her car. It got to the point where the simplest tasks seemed to confound her. Some nights she would break down and weep like a child.

Gage backed out of a picture a month before shooting in order to spend time at home with her. He found one doctor for her and when that didn't take, he found a second. Nothing he could do helped and he found himself growing more and more angry.

"Do you think I'm crazy?" she would ask him.

"No," he would answer, not seeing how it would help to say yes. "It's just a hard time."

In his heart he knew they could not go on like this. They were both worn out. Gage knew how to get what he wanted out of actors and he knew how to get what he wanted out of a crew. He could flatter and bully and cajole and he had been known to slug people when it was called for. This is different. She was like a closed watch to him now; he could hear the ticking, he could see the hands move, but he could only make conjectures about the mechanisms that truly drove her. He was out of his depth and, though he would have never admitted it to anyone, he was intimidated.

They tried to hide what was going on from Peter, as if their pain was unexposed film to be kept from the light, but Peter knew there was trouble. He wouldn't talk about it, but he drifted more and more into his own private worlds, setting box traps for rabbits in Topanga Canyon and becoming a baseball statistics nut.

Gage got the invitation to go to Africa a full year after Nina's father's death. Uwe Krohn, a wealthy young German heir to a publishing empire, wanted to get into the movie business. He had been trying desperately to sign Gage to direct an overly meaningful adventure film set in Kenya. Gage protested that he just made cowboy movies, but Uwe wouldn't take no for an answer.

"I want to make a gift to you, my friend. I want to fly you to Africa, you, your wife, your son. For a week. No strings attached. I will take you to these places, so beautiful, you will have to make this movie, I have no doubt."

When Gage got off the phone he was almost laughing out loud. If Uwe wanted to pay, let him pay. This trip was going to be just what the doctor ordered. He wouldn't listen to any of Peter or Nina's objections. It would be a lark, a chance to wipe the slate clean. If Peter was worried about missing summer baseball, he could just pack his bat and glove and they would shag flies on the Serengeti.

Uwe turned out to be good company and a great tour guide. He drove them into the highlands to see Isak Dinesen's farm, rented a plane and flew them to Victoria Falls. It was the most spectacular country Gage had ever seen. It should have sent anyone's spirit soaring, but it only made Nina seem more disoriented, more out of place.

By the end of a week, Nina had given up. She felt they were there under false pretenses. Gage had no intention of making Uwe's film, Gage was ripping him off. She did not approve of any of it. She stayed in the hotel while Gage and Uwe toured game parks. Peter, caught between his mother and father, chose to stay behind with his mother. Gage, returning from a day of chasing lions through thorn trees in a Landrover, found his son sitting in the lobby, reading the baseball scores in the *International Herald Tribune* and refusing to look up.

The climax came one night in Nairobi. Gage and Uwe had gone off to a club, just the two of them. Uwe had arranged for an anthropologist friend of his to take Nina and Peter to a lecture at the university.

At the club a Congolese rock band played tinny French rock and roll for its Kenyan audience. Uwe had invited some British television people, a Czech cinematographer, a white hunter who had once boxed middleweight in Madison Square Garden. Gage held court. The liquor flowed. Uwe abandoned the soft sell. Hawks and Huston had made their best pictures in Africa and Gage's film would be twice as good as theirs. What was he afraid of? All Gage had to do was say yes and they would have themselves a masterpiece, they would get very rich, and on the side there would be the greatest big-game hunting in the world.

One of the African prostitutes tousled his hair and tried to pull him toward the dance floor, while the Czech cinematographer was trying to get him to tell the story of how he had sewn the jaws of a rattlesnake together and dropped the snake down an actor's shirt in the middle of a take.

Gage was a little drunk, more than a little drunk, and he was having a good time. He had a right to a good time. They hung on his every word. He had the power to make things happen or not happen. It was all coming back to him now, that power.

The Congolese band took a break and Kikuyu dancers took their place, great hemplike manes around their necks, imitating lions or monkeys, Gage wasn't sure which. The drumming became urgent. Three or four people in the audience hollered encouragement.

Gage tried to remember the story about the snake, but he was fuzzy about details. The one thing he did remember was the cold, crazed look in the snake's eyes when he realized he couldn't strike, the writhing frustration as he tried to break the stitches in his jaw. A snake not able to strike was like a filmmaker not able to make films, you just had to swallow all that venom yourself. Masterpieces, why not. All he had to do was say yes. The Czech cinematographer, playing with a candle, spilled a load of hot wax on his hand. He leaped up with a shriek and plunged his burned hand into a pitcher of beer, the spray exploding the length of the table.

It was after midnight by the time he got back to the hotel. He assumed that Nina would be asleep so he didn't turn on the light.

He had one shoe off and was working on the second when she called his name, startling him. He had to put a hand against the wall to steady himself. She snapped on the bedside lamp. She pulled herself up in bed, wide awake and luminous as a bride.

The lecture had ended two hours before, but she hadn't been able to go to sleep. It had been the most extraordinary talk, she said. The speaker was an African graduate student who had spent two years in a highland village studying spirit possession. He had shown the audience slides of the exorcism of a nineteen-year-old girl and played them tapes of the voices that had taken control of her.

After the exorcism the girl had to go back to relearn everything, like a child. One of the slides was of her mother's hands over her hands on the hoe, another of her mother teaching her how to balance a water jug on her head.

Gage brushed his teeth, bent low to spit in the sink. He glanced up at the mirror. Nina sat on the edge of the bed, resetting the alarm clock. She seemed as fragile and pale as a Victorian doll with her long black hair and white cotton nightgown.

"But one of the points he was making," Nina said, "was that there was some payoff for going through all that suffering. They believe that there is a certain wisdom you acquire. The person is treated with great respect in the village."

His clothes still reeked of beer. Gage wriggled out of his shirt and leaned back against the sink to undo his trousers. "Did Peter enjoy it?"

"I think so, yes."

Gage wadded his clothes up in a ball. Nina was wired, ready to go on, but Gage was too tired and drunk to focus. "He's asleep, then?"

"Yes." Gage snapped off the bathroom light. He padded across the zebra-skin rug toward the second of the single beds. The door to Peter's adjoining room was closed. The lion's head mounted above the bed was half in shadow, the soft plastic eyes glistened. Gage pulled back the covers.

"You know what it made me think of?" Nina said. "English poetry. Wordsworth. Or Blake. Or maybe Blake showing up on Ginsberg's windowsill in Harlem."

Gage crawled into the cool sheets. "Maybe we should be getting to sleep. Uwe's going to be flying us down to Mombasa tomorrow."

For several seconds Nina didn't say anything. The only light in the room glowed through a lampshade of cured animal skin. Gage was prepared for her to say that she was refusing to go.

"Somehow it felt like confirmation," she said.

"Confirmation of what?"

"I don't know," she said.

Sometime in the middle of the night Gage was awakened by Nina's crying out and thrashing wildly in her bed. He got up and stood silently above her. At first he couldn't make out what she was saying, just a word here and there. Her long hands groped feebly in the air, as if she were trying to fend something off.

Gage thought he heard a sound behind him. He turned and looked toward the window. Charcoal fires burned in the alleyways far below, the dark silhouettes of beggars and lepers gathered around for warmth.

Nina moaned again and cried out more sharply. Gage knelt beside her, put a comforting hand on her shoulder. Her voice was low and exhausted. "Tell me the names of the gods," she cried, "tell me the names of the gods."

He shook her gently. She shuddered and rolled away from

him, threw an arm over her face. He snapped on the bedside lamp. When she opened her eyes she stared as if she didn't recognize him.

"You were having nightmares," he said. "You were talking in your sleep." Gage sat down on the bed and wiped a strand of damp hair away from her face. She put a hand on his chest; her fingers were trembling.

"I was having a terrible dream."

"Can you remember what it was?"

"No. Just that something had been taken from me and I didn't know what it was. I was running and I had to keep saying over and over again, 'My name is Nina, my name is Nina.' The thief was sitting in a car and I had a knife in my hand. His window was rolled down just a few inches and I stabbed at him, over and over again."

"Yes."

"What was I saying? What did you hear me say?"

"Nothing," Gage said. "Just gibberish. Don't worry. Everything's going to be all right."

"All right?" Suddenly there was mockery in her voice. She lay back against the pillow and Gage could see the streaks of silver in her dark hair. "No, it's not going to be all right. You know it's not. We can't go on like this. You and I."

"No."

"So what are we going to do?" she said.

He took both of her long, slender hands, icy cold, and pulled her to him, held her. He had not slept with her for a year, yet he still knew her body as well as his own. They both knew they were not going to back down from what they had just said. They clung to one another for a long time, Gage's face buried in her thick hair.

Finally she lay back and was asleep, almost at once. Gage stood and pulled up her covers. He heard footsteps in the other room and then the creak of bedsprings. Gage did not move for a long time, overcome by dread.

No one had the heart to say anything at breakfast, so events carried them. They flew to Mombasa with Uwe, even went through the elaborate charade of checking into a rambling hotel on the beach. But when Gage returned to the room after a brief tour of the grounds with the manager, Nina was on the phone, making plane reservations for London and L.A. She looked up as he came in, but her voice never wavered. Gage didn't interrupt her.

When she hung up the phone she stood up and brushed off her khaki shirt. "I called Louise in L.A. She said I could use their guest house until I find something else. I've got a flight out in the morning."

"Tomorrow morning?"

"Yes. Is there anything wrong with that?"

He could stop her. The scent of bougainvillaea drifted in through the open window. The first thing Nina always did when she came into a room was open the windows. Directly below, white-jacketed waiters swept up broken glass in the palm-thatched bar and far off was the sound of the sea.

"I'm letting you off the hook, Gage. Isn't that what you want? Just take it."

"Have you said anything to Peter?"

"I thought I'd let you do that," she said.

"Where is he now?"

"I think he went down to look at the water."

"Do you want him to fly back with you?"

"He can do what he wants," Nina said.

There seemed to be hundreds of crabs, nearly invisible against the white sand, scuttling for cover at Gage's approach. There was no sign of Peter. Far out, tankers crawled on the horizon of the sea. A hundred yards down the beach a band of monkeys leaped down from a viney grotto, galloped along the sand until Gage picked up a stick to wave them off. As he moved around the rock outcropping, he heard a knocking sound.

Peter stood at the water's edge, tossing up small rocks and hitting them with his baseball bat. The wood-struck stones sailed and darted, plunged into the softly rolling surf.

"Peter." The boy turned, startled, stone in his right hand, bat in his left. "I was just talking to your mother. You know she hasn't been feeling that well." Gage avoided his son's stare. A crab appeared at the mouth of its hole, one periscopelike eye raised, scanning for trouble. "She's decided to fly back tomorrow. You can go back with her or go on with me. Uwe said he'd drive us into Tsavo for a few days. He's friends with the warden there."

"You're not going back with her?" Peter said. Gage didn't answer. He took the bat from his son, ran his hand along the barrel. The wood was badly pitted from hitting stones; it was a great way to destroy a bat. "But she's sick, Dad, she's not well."

"I know that, Peter. But it will be better this way."

"Better? How will it be better? Better if you don't help her?"

What Gage wanted to say was that he couldn't help her, but that wasn't something you say to your son. Instead he handed him the bat. "This wasn't just my decision, Peter."

"I'm going back with her."

"Fine. Whatever you want."

Far down the beach two women in saris walked at the water's edge. A tanker steamed toward Malindi. We are halfway around the world, Gage thought. We could not be farther from home than this.

Peter turned and ran. Crabs fled across the sand in pale waves. When Peter reached the tree line he whirled and hurled the bat high into the blue African sky.

Nine

THE SIGN on the wall announced: KNAPP'S GALLERY. The stone building, painted in bright colors, looked like a badly funded day-care center. Gage slid out of his pickup.

The yard was full of weeds and old wagon wheels; carved wooden saints guarded the door. The place had the air of a colonial outpost years after the collapse of the empire.

He trudged toward the house. Heavy-headed sunflowers drooped over a woodpile. Sun gleamed off tin roofs five miles away. There were traces of new snow on the high peaks surrounding the town and soaring birds played on the currents above the canyon that plunged five hundred feet below.

A bell tinkled when Gage pushed open the door. He quickly scanned the room. On the walls hung a couple dozen oil paintings, mostly mountain scenes, well-done imitation Cézannes.

Religious objects were piled in the corners: crucifixes, rosaries, retables, a miniature oxcart with the grinning figure of Death riding inside, his bow drawn. The building smelled of animals.

Gage peered down a narrow, dark hallway that led to the back.

"Hello." The light, birdlike voice, so close, startled Gage. He turned quickly. A wreck of a man sat behind a typewriter in the corner. He had a plastic tube up one nostril and his ankles were heavily taped. His chest was so caved that his massive turquoise belt buckle seemed to balance on his stomach like a glowing blue domino. His long white hair and beard were uncombed and electric, wizardlike. He must have been watching Gage the whole time, silent as an owl. He stared at Gage with baby-blue eyes. He might have been amused; it was a hard face to read.

The old man gestured with an open palm. "Feel free to look around." Gage nodded. He turned back to the paintings for a moment, as if trying to decide on his favorite.

"And you're Knapp, right?" Gage asked.

"That's right."

"Well, I've heard a lot about you," Gage said. "I've seen your stuff for years and I always meant to stop by, but you know how these things go." Gage stared at the bumps on the back of his left hand. "I'll tell you the truth. A man sent me to you."

"Oh, yes?"

"He said you knew a lot of stories."

"That depends. Stories about what?"

"About the people who got lost up here."

"You're talking about a lot of people."

It didn't take much prodding to get Knapp going. He had come to the mountain village twenty-five years ago, intending to become the Georgia O'Keeffe of the Sangre de Cristos. He was about the only Anglo up here then. He had been a painter, a newspaperman, he'd run a small grocery store. In the late sixties he had been the justice of the peace when the wars started between the hippies and the Spanish villages. He had tried to help, to be a reconciler, and he got caught in the cross fire. He had been burned out twice, his animals killed, his store ripped off dozens of times.

Knapp spoke in a mild, matter-of-fact voice, stopping every so often to blink, owllike, regain his breath, be sure that Gage was still with him.

Gage did nothing to discourage him. The stories got wilder. Knapp claimed he had fed fugitives from the Manson gang in his kitchen. The two boys who had blown up the tower in San Francisco had lived in the goat shed out back. Janis Joplin had come looking for a mountain man and Knapp had found her one. There were people with mythological names buried in the hillsides, One-eyed Dave and Badger, Puck and Captain America. Knapp told of tough East Village kids who came out to play cowboy, riding through Spanish villages sky-high on acid, shooting out windows, making ends meet as rustlers and poachers. A man was pulled out of his house next door to Knapp and shot in front of his family, and police were too terrified to investigate.

Knapp's pale blue eyes grew moist. "I don't tell these stories to just anybody. No one believes me. They just wave their friends over. 'Come on, listen to crazy old Knapp, he's got some good ones.' But what I'm telling you is true. There is no law up here, there never was. My neighbor came to me, he said, 'Are we dogs? When a man dies, they write it down on a piece of paper. When a dog dies, no one writes it down. When we die, no one writes it down.' " Knapp threw up his hands, making his point.

"So why do you stay here?"

"Where would I go? Santa Fe? Let them put me in a hospital so I can rot to death?"

"There are not many left, are there? From the old days."

"A few."

"And where are those few?"

Knapp teetered forward on his cane. "There was a place people used to go. It's about the last stop on earth. I haven't been up there for a long time, but somebody told me there were still a

couple people living up there. You can't get there by car. You'd
have to walk in."

"Could you draw me a map?"

"Sure. But why would you want to go there?"

"I'm looking for someone."

"Oh, I knew that as soon as you walked in. But who?"

"My son."

"I see. But you're not going to find him up there."

"How do you know?"

"Boys always come home, sooner or later. You just have to
give them a little time."

"I've given him plenty of time."

"Well, then, he's probably on his way home now."

"Why don't you draw me the map all the same?"

Knapp took his map drawing seriously. What he ended up with
could have come off the inside cover of *Swiss Family Robinson:*
artful little pine trees and crosshatched ridges, a series of dashes
for trails and a squiggly line for the stream Gage would have to
cross. Knapp beamed like a child as he handed it over for Gage's
approval.

Gage followed the old painter's map, leaving the pavement
after three or four miles. The pickup bounced and scraped along
a dirt road, passed a half-dozen tin-roofed houses and a trashed-
out church with a gold cross gleaming in the sun. Gage crawled
along behind a Hispanic farmer and his horse-drawn hay-rake
for almost five minutes until the farmer finally turned his team of
clopping bays into one of the narrow lanes between the fences.
Red-tailed hawks floated in a brilliantly blue sky.

The road got rougher, Gage's wheels spinning and throwing
up stones as he bucked up through red rock cliffs into a long
valley. The road finally petered out altogether.

Gage got out of his truck. Cattle raised their heads to stare at
him, calves trotted to their mothers for protection. Above the
pasture was a heavily wooded ridge. Gage stared at his home-

113

made map. It was impossible to figure. Maybe Gage had misread the map or maybe Knapp had just sent him on a wild-goose chase.

There was a gap in the trees at the top of the ridge. It wasn't marked on the map, but Gage had come this far, it wouldn't hurt to take a look. Gage locked the truck and started walking. The huddled cattle trailed him at a distance until Gage climbed a fence and left them behind. It took Gage twenty minutes to get to the top of the ridge. He stared down through a dense, silent grove of ponderosa. There was no sign of a settlement. A ravine lay thirty yards below. Gage sidestepped down the slope, digging his heels into the slick brown mat of needles.

He stared up and down the boulder-strewn ravine. The lower branches of the trees were matted with the debris of spring floods. A squirrel clattered up an aspen. As soon as it was safely out of reach it stopped to scold him, its tail pulsing like a striking snake.

There was nothing here. Gage kicked at a small rock, sent it rolling down into the ravine. Watching it bound, Gage's eye was caught by a bit of color, bright blue wedged between massive boulders.

Gage half stumbled, half slid down to the bottom of the ravine, then yanked a child's Big Wheels out of the rocks. It was caked with mud and leaves; there was no way of knowing how long it had been there. It didn't matter. Gage's hands trembled. He could hear the sound of water.

He climbed out of the ravine and followed it downhill. After a hundred yards he came out of the trees into a meadow. There were three or four plots, fenced in by rusting mattress springs and old tires. He could see some buildings on the next rise and the top of a tall pole. On a winding footpath Gage stepped over a rotting rug that looked as if it had been left out in the rain for a decade.

A yellow dog bounded down through the weeds, barking, then pulled up short and wagged its tail. Gage put his hand out, scanning the horizon for any movement. The dog sniffed Gage's pants.

Gage called out, waited, then called out again. A gust of wind came up the long meadow, swaying the long green boughs of the ponderosa. There was the booming sound of loose tin on a roof.

Gage began moving again. He passed two slightly domed ovals of packed and sunbaked earth. His first thought was that they were root cellars, but they both had wooden doors and smoke holes and he realized that someone must haved lived in them once. There were raised tepee poles and a couple of abandoned cabins, one with owl wings mounted over a busted window, another with an ancient Forest Service sign tacked to the wall. He stuck his head in. There was nothing but torn feed bags, mice droppings and spiderwebs. A half-dozen other eccentric structures dotted the meadow. Wind rippled the torn yellow plastic of an empty greenhouse, brought the faint smell of something rotting.

He stared up at the twenty-foot pole at the center of the settlement, decorated with elk antlers and a dozen skulls of different sizes, cow and horse, coyote and deer.

Gage spun around. At least half the buildings were marked by animal skulls or horns. The chalky white pelvis of a cow stood on end in the weeds like a Halloween mask. Rusting car parts swung softly on a rope from one of the trees like chimes.

Gage circled the greenhouse. An orange twenty-year-old Volkswagen van with a mural of blue lagoons and palm trees painted on its side panels sat in the shade. Gage stared in the window. In the back were gold and white cigar boxes full of geodes and agates, cut and polished stones. On the dash was a dog-eared copy of *No Exit*.

The yellow dog had run on ahead, but stopped now and looked back, tail still pumping, waiting for Gage.

Gage moved more slowly now. From where he stood he could look all the way down the meadow, look all the way down to the tawny orange canyons of the Rio Grande, thirty miles off. Sixty

yards away were the ruins of a corral, built to resemble a geo-
desic dome. There were racks of some kind. Then he saw movement, the switching tail of a tethered horse. The smell of rotting
meat had grown stronger.

"Hello!" he called out again. Again there was the booming of
tin loose on a roof. The sound came from the woods still ahead
of him. The yellow dog still waited for him. Gage decided to
follow.

The grass was littered with more and more bones. The dog
darted and sniffed under a juniper, tail wagging furiously. Gage
stared in through the gnarled branches and saw the severed
deer's head, the flies buzzing in the eye sockets, the hardened
black collar of dried blood. The dog scampered ahead, blithely
leaped a downed tree. On the far side of the tree was a shed, one
corner of its tin roof bent back and waving in the air like a
pennant.

Gage shimmied over the dead tree, spied the snowmobile
parked behind the shed. Hanging from a limb along the riverbank was a quarter of deer or elk in cheesecloth.

Gage pushed open the door of the shed. As he stepped inside
something soft brushed his face. Instinctively he swatted it away,
felt it tumble silently to the floor. He stared at the crumpled bear
pelt at his feet. There were furs, mostly coyote and bobcat, piled
on the long shelves. Traps with heavy chains hung from the wall.
A shotgun rested on wooden pegs. On a crudely carved stool was
a box of shells and a bottle of yellow liquid, bait of some kind.
The smell turned Gage's stomach; it must have been bear or
skunk urine.

He backed out of the shed and pushed the door shut. He
stared at the racks next to the corral, realized they were for
drying pelts. It was a whole operation. His head pounded with
the sound of the rushing water.

He glanced back toward the settlement, but still saw no sign of
anyone. He walked toward the racks, the dog happily at his side.
They passed a massive woodpile, some of the logs freshly split.

Gage bent down to pick a metal wedge out of the grass when he heard an explosion, muffled by water. The bullet whined overhead and ticked into the stack of split logs.

He threw himself down quickly behind the woodpile and didn't move for several seconds. Alarmed ravens sliced into the dark woods for protection. The dog trotted over to Gage, figuring that a man on all fours was an invitation to play. The dog buried its muzzle in Gage's armpit and Gage shoved the animal away. He peered through a chink in the woodpile.

A figure in a shapeless brown hat bounded through the woods like a blind bear, arms and rifle held up in front of his face as a shield against low branches and brush.

Gage watched the maniacal figure leap and stumble and weave, a brown stain flickering through the trunks of the ponderosa. Gage rose, forgetting the danger for a moment. He needed to see a face. He was ready to believe, then that it was Peter, ready to believe that Peter would be willing to kill him if he needed to, but in the next second he was thinking, no, that cannot be my son, my son always ran like a deer, my son would never be so clumsy. This is just some lunatic, trying to outflank me, angling for a clear shot.

The wind banged the loose tin on the roof of the shed. Gage remembered the shotgun he had seen in the corner. He made a run for it, zigzagging through the long grass, nearly tripping over some bones half buried in the matted weeds. The dog cavorted at his side.

Gage hurtled into the shed and slammed the door behind him. He scissored the shotgun open on his knee. The chamber was empty. He grabbed the box of shells, but he didn't even need to open it, it was light as air, empty.

He peered through a gap in the wooden slats. Maybe it was over. Maybe the guy was as terrified as Gage was, maybe he'd taken off. The yellow dog whined outside the door. After two or three seconds Gage saw the brown hat emerge behind a rise, then the stooped shoulders. The stench of bait inside the shed

117

was intense. The man poked at the woodpile with the barrel of his rifle, then trudged toward the shed.

Gage scanned the shed for another weapon. As he ran his fingers across the heavy traps hanging on the wall, he accidentally knocked loose a bundle of furs. It tumbled from the shelf and bounced noiselessly across the dirt floor. A knife fell free of the bundle.

Gage picked it up. The knife was hand-flaked stone, the handle wrapped with a leather thong. The dog barked, but at some distance now. Gage looked out through the gap in the beams. The man lumbered steadily toward the shed, his face still hidden by his floppy hat.

The sudden banging of tin, right above his head, made Gage start. He glanced up and saw the loose corner of corrugated metal still shaking, and a bright triangle of sky.

Gage stuck the stone knife in his belt and climbed onto the low wooden stool. He grabbed hold of the beams over his head, found a toehold on one of the heavy rusted nails on the wall. He let go with one hand and lunged for the roof. Tin cut into his open palm. He got one elbow up and then the other, shinnying onto the corrugated surface. The slant of the building still protected him from view.

He lifted his head slowly. The man swung his rifle carelessly through the grass, thirty yards away now and still coming. That cannot be my son, Gage thought, my son would never carry a rifle like that. In the valley, thirty miles below, the bright canyons welled with shadow. In one long, careful motion Gage pulled the stone knife from his belt, lowered his head again and flattened out on the roof. The hot tin burned his bare forearms, prickled through his trousers.

Gage held the stone knife just inches from his face, careful not to let it scrape against the corrugated metal. The stone was milky white with blood-red flecks. Gage had never seen a stone like it. He ran his thumb along the jagged, keen edge. It must have taken fifty hours to make a knife like this.

118

The man's boots rustled in the grass below. Again Gage lifted his head. He looked down at a grease-stained oval of hat, sloping shoulders. Gage wrapped his fingers tight around the handle of the knife. The man poked at the door of the shed with the rifle barrel, still a couple of steps too far away for Gage to jump him. Gage brought one knee up, crouching, one hand down for balance.

Gage never knew what it was the dog picked up—a sound, a smell, a sudden shift—but before he had a chance to do anything the dog was leaping in the air, barking triumphantly up at the roof.

The man hissed something at the dog, then grabbed it by the scruff of the neck. In another second he understood. He let go of the dog and backed away slowly, yanked the rifle up where he could use it. Gage had nowhere to go. The two men stared at one another.

Gage gazed at the long, slack-jawed sharecropper's face with orphanage eyes and strands of dirty hair sticking out from under the floppy hat. The man gave a short sniff of surprise. He couldn't have been more than forty, but his face was deeply lined and the left side of his mouth was drawn by some kind of paralysis.

He backed off a couple more steps, lowering the rifle. He wore a faded COUNTRY JOE AND THE FISH T-shirt, bib overalls and a rawhide pouch strung over his shoulder. He swatted away the barking dog with his free hand. Gage had not moved.

Gage could see him begin to smile, could see a broken front tooth. Maybe there was something to smile about: a stranger coiled up on a roof with a knife in his hand and nowhere to go, like a diver poised on the board looking down to discover there was no water in the pool.

"So get off my damned roof," the man said.

Gage tossed the stone knife out on the grass and nodded compliance. He backed around on all floors, lowered himself over the edge of the tin roof, dropped the last two or three feet.

119

He straightened up and brushed off his hands, trying to appear friendly. His shirtsleeve was in tatters, torn on the tin. The fingers of his cut hand felt a little numb: he had to be thirty miles from the nearest tetanus shot. The rifle pointed at his chest, dead center. Even ten yards away the man reeked of bait, bear urine or something worse.

"I told you," the man said. "Didn't I tell you?"

"Mister, you never told me anything. You've never laid eyes on me in your life."

"Oh, man!" For the first time the man seemed outraged. He snatched the shapeless hat off his head and crumpled it in his fist. He was balding. Above the sprigs of unwashed hair was a bird's-egg-pale dome. "Oh, man! You can stand there and tell me I never told you?" He dropped his hat and raised the rifle. "Take off your boots."

"You're kidding."

"Take off the boots, man!"

Gage considered a smart reply, then decided against it. Hopping on one foot to keep his balance, he pulled off his left boot. The mountain man came forward a couple of steps, knelt quickly and retrieved the stone knife from the grass.

"Never saw a knife like that," Gage said. He pulled off his other boot. "You flake it yourself?"

"Socks too," the man said. A breeze came up the meadow, the heads of the sunflowers swung in circles.

Gage pulled off his socks and stuffed them in his boots. "Don't think I ever saw stone like that. Where'd you find it?"

"Only one place you can find it. A place over on Pedernal Peak. Even if I told you, you wouldn't be able to find it. I'd have to show you." The mountain man ran his tongue over his broken tooth. The brittle grass jabbed at Gage's tender feet. "So empty your pockets."

"Now, hold on. The least you can do is tell me just who you think I am. Let me guess. Forest Service, right? Or game warden, that's more like it. Mister, I don't work for anybody and I don't

120

give a damn what you got going back here. I came looking for somebody who used to live here."

"Who was that?"

"Somebody named David."

"I never knew anybody named David that lived here."

"Okay. So I was wrong. Sorry to bother you."

"Empty your pockets." The rifle draped over his arm, as if it were as harmless as an old raincoat. "Everything. Wallet, car keys too. Just leave 'em there in the grass."

Gage tossed his wallet out first, then slowly turned his pockets inside out, releasing a spray of coins and keys and old ticket stubs.

"So now what?"

"You can go."

"Let me ask you one thing. Do you know why you're doing this or is it something you just saw somewhere?"

The mountain man stared at him with the big blank eyes of someone who'd been outsmarted more than would have been good for anyone.

"Just get the hell out."

Gage put his hands up, conceding. "Whatever you say." Gage glanced back toward the pole with the skulls. It was probably ten miles back to the main road. A good four-hour walk, if Gage's feet held out. The guy, if he thought about it, had to know he was just inviting more trouble. But maybe he hadn't thought about it.

Gage moved gingerly, watching for yucca and hidden cactus. The sharp grass and stubble cut his feet with every step. He'd gone maybe twenty yards when he glanced back over his shoulder and saw the mountain man move toward the shed, then kneel and set aside his rifle. Gage kept walking. The trees were still sixty yards off. He stepped down on a small bone hidden in the grass, bruising his foot. He looked back again.

The mountain man shook the cards out of Gage's wallet and raised his head. "Hey." he called.

"Yeah?" Gage said. The mountain man held up a handful of credit cards. When he spoke his voice was like a little kid's.

"Is this you?"

"Who else you think it could be?"

"Jeremiah Gage."

"Yeah."

"You the one who made *Renegade?*"

"Yeah."

"Well, dog." His voice welled up with awe. "That movie changed my life, man."

Gage drove down from the mountains. Dark clouds built quickly over the high peaks, and sunshine and shadow slid in alternate bands across the canyons below.

He had had enough. He needed to get home. It had taken him nearly another hour to get away from the conversation-starved mountain man and his disjointed stories of harassing game wardens, stolen horse trailers and friends in distant V.A. hospitals. Maui was the name the mountain man had given himself and he made a living trapping, poaching and selling his polished geodes to rock hounds. He took Gage to the grave of the last woman to have lived there and they sprinkled bourbon over a mound of dirt decorated with cheap blue bottles, pieces of broken glass and plastic dime-store daisies. Staring down at the red dirt, all Gage could think of was: if you have any power in the world, don't give it up.

He felt like a man crashing after a binge. He had overdosed on too many lies and too much loose talk. Something in him had finally recoiled. No one's memory could be trusted, not tuned-in flag makers, church caretakers or recluse trappers. He had had enough of the hypothetical to choke a horse. He just wanted his life back.

It was nearly six by the time he passed the roadside fruit stands and the weaving shops of Chimayo. He was late; Amy would be angry. He sped past the sign for the Santuario; there wasn't any more time for talk of underground tunnels and ancient caskets.

His tires squealed on the sharp curves as he climbed out of the valley, sped through the arid reservation land. On both sides rock formations jutted up like eroded altars. Dark clouds and lightning filled the horizon. Ravens skimmed low, anticipating the storm. Gage braked for a white stallion that stood in the road, dreamlike, framed by the black sky.

The wind came and then the rain and, seconds later, the hail. Gage crept along for a couple of miles until it was coming down too hard for him to even see. He pulled off the road to wait it out.

He sat for twenty minutes, covering his face with his hands. Hail pounded on the roof, water streamed down the windshield. The only sound inside the car was the blinking of the hazard light.

He had seen Nina for the last time in New York, in 1968. They had made a date for lunch on the West Side. He sat for an hour in the window of a sidewalk café, growing more and more certain that she wasn't coming. Then he saw her, weaving her way through the Columbus Avenue crowds.

She wore dark glasses and a hat. She never wore hats. She was drinking a cup of coffee. She stuffed the empty paper cup in her purse, still a half block off.

When she sat down she was scattered and frantic, launching into a long description of her work on a documentary film about the excavations of newly discovered Hohokam ruins in Arizona. *Hohokam,* she explained, was an Indian word for "vanished ones." The director was an absolute genius, only thirty years old with a Ph.D. in anthropology from Chicago, but they'd run out of money. Couldn't Gage introduce her to producers? She did not touch her food. They were the only ones in the restaurant and the place smelled faintly of ammonia, as if it had recently been mopped.

Gage stared at her long, delicate hands, a pianist's hands.

123

There were one or two places she had picked raw and not allowed scabs to heal. "Are you going to see Peter?" he said.

She stared out the window and pushed up her dark glasses. "No," she said. "I wouldn't want him to see me like this. I've failed everybody, haven't I?"

"You haven't failed me," Gage said. "I was such a crazy son of a bitch, I was amazed you stood it as long as you did. And you didn't fail Peter."

"I'm so ashamed, Gage. This isn't me. I'm an attractive, intelligent woman." She was in tears.

"I know you are. Let me help you, Nina."

"You mean doctors? No, I don't need more doctors."

The waitress arrived to clear the table. Nina asked her if she would mind wrapping the untouched sandwich in a doggie bag. She hated letting anything go to waste.

They walked through the park; it was a beautiful October afternoon. Steel drums echoed across the Sheep Meadow and nurses pushed carriages on the curving walks. Nina slipped her hand under his arm.

"You know," he said, "one thing I never did understand. When your father talked about antiparticles . . . what the hell was he talking about?"

"Oh," she said, "it's simple. An antiparticle is just a particle. Except it's moving back in time."

He walked her to the elevator of the apartment building, where she was staying with friends. He said he would call her that night. There were several other people jostling to get on the elevator; Nina accommodated them, moving to the back, holding her doggie bag high so it wouldn't be crushed. She cocked her head and gave him a brave smile as the doors rolled shut.

That night he called her friends, but they didn't know where she was. Several days later he tracked down a number in Arizona. He left four different messages on her answering machine, but she never called back.

Two days after Thanksgiving Nina was dead. She had been on

124

location and wandered off one night. They searched for a day and a half before they found her body. A twenty-three-year-old cameraman who had been her drinking buddy offered the closest thing to an explanation, as appalling as it was. She had confided in him that she was in communication with her dead father and had been going off on nightly walks in search of him.

Every couple of minutes there would be a hiss of water and a glare of lights in the side mirror as a foolhardy pickup passed. Gage sat immobile. He realized how exhausted he was, how utterly depleted. He began to shiver, his teeth chattering. He folded his arms tight around his chest, but it didn't help.

The rain finally stopped and Gage started the engine. The ground was covered with hail. It looked like a March snowstorm, but it was melting quickly. The ditches swirled with muddy water.

Gage passed a half-dozen abandoned cars. Torn tree branches were everywhere and wet matted leaves covered the pavement.

By the time he turned into the dirt road to home, the setting sun was out again, but there were still incredible lightning displays over the mountains to the south.

Gage braked when he saw someone standing in the road in from of his house. Amy, in a yellow slicker, held Jody in her arms. A section of the stone wall next to the gate had collapsed and boulders were strewn halfway across the road. Gage knew this would happen, sooner or later, the way the wall had been constructed. The sudden deluge and the pressure of the heavy wet earth behind the wall had been too much for it.

Gage pulled to the side of the road and got out. He felt the spitting rain in his face. Jody wriggled from her mother's arms and ran toward him, calling his name, her frog boots splashing through puddles. Gage scooped her up. Her arms tightened around his neck.

"Hey, darlin', hey, darlin'," he murmured.

Amy had not moved. Her eyes were down as she wiped some mud from her hands.

"Amy?" Gage said.

Amy looked away, toward the jagged gap in the wall, then glanced back at him. He could see the distress in her face, a distress too deep to have anything to do with collapsing walls. Gage set Jody down, whacked her on the behind as she hopscotched across the puddles. He moved slowly toward Amy, trying to understand. The faintest of rainbows glowed above the dark mountains.

"Hey, Amy."

She ran her fingers through her wet hair. She kept her voice low in front of the child. "You lied to me," she said.

Ten

"BUT YOU buried him."

"Buried someone."

Gage sat on the edge of the tub and Amy sat in a chair facing him. His swollen left foot rested in her lap and his trousers were rolled up to the knee. They kept their voices down; Jody had been asleep less than half an hour.

She leaned forward for better light, brushed the tip of the tweezers across the ball of his foot. Gage felt a prick of pain, but tried hard not to wince.

"And what am I supposed to do with that?" Amy said. The mirror was misted over, the bathroom steamy from the hot water in the tub. "That really helps a lot. You've been looking for your dead son. You lie to me, every day for a week, and when I ask for an explanation, I get this totally incredible story."

127

She had found something. She squeezed his foot tighter, closed in with the tweezers and gave a quick yank. Gage flinched. "Hold still," she said. She wiped an almost invisible cactus hair from her tweezers.

"You want me to take you down to the police station? I'll show you the newspaper."

"You don't have to do that." She moved his foot over a few inches, leaving a damp spot on her skirt. "I believe there's a newspaper with Peter's picture in it. And I believe there's a woman in a flag shop who knew a kid ten years ago with an egg on his collarbone."

"Don't make fun of me. It doesn't help."

Amy had found another barb. She pushed it gently to the left and then to the right, trying to get hold of it. Gage gripped the sides of the tub with both hands.

"I'm sorry," Amy said. "Let me see your other foot," Gage switched feet. "I'm not making fun of you. I think you saw that picture in the paper and it set off all sorts of alarms in you and you began to talk to people and eventually you found someone who fit the description."

"No one fit any description." He pulled his foot off her lap and set it down on the wet floor. His voice became harder, overriding. "It was Peter. The woman knew Peter. It couldn't have been anyone else."

"Here." She handed the tweezers to him. "Most of them are too small to see. I'm sure you can do a better job than I can."

He soaked his feet for another half hour and then hobbled into the kitchen to call Simon Huerta about repairing his collapsed wall.

Huerta was his usual maybe-I-can, maybe-I-can't self. He had done a half-dozen jobs for Gage, everything from digging trenches to reroofing to landscaping and his prices were the best around. The word around town was that he was the godfather of wetbacks. He'd started out draining old batteries and selling the lead for scrap. He'd come a long way and he liked playing the small-time *patrón*. It took fifteen minutes of courtly flattery and bargaining to get Huerta to promise he'd have a crew out in the morning.

Gage hung up the phone and hiked his bare left foot up on his right knee. He ran his fingertips over the swollen sole of his foot, exploring for more thorns and prickers.

He heard the low, gutting sound of scissors cutting through something thick, coming from the direction of the living room. Gage knew enough to keep his distance. Amy needed time to cool out; they both did.

Amy's finding him out had been a fluke. Someone from *The New York Times* had called, interested in doing an article now that all his films were being re-released. They were desperate to get in touch with him. Amy, trying to be helpful, called the garage in Española and discovered that Gage had not been there in months.

He went to the refrigerator and opened it, but found nothing to his liking. He shut the door and scanned the counter, then spied the crinkly yellow plastic bag on the folding stool. He picked it up; the feel alone told him it wasn't food.

He lifted out the cassette. It was *The Outriders*. Amy must have gotten it in town, earlier in the day. He was sure that she had done it to please him. He still heard the laboring scissors from the far side of the house.

He walked into the living room. Amy stood with a pair of shears and a narrow cardboard box, maybe five feet long, cutting one end into a wedding-cake-like top. On the couch was a roll of silver duct tape and Jody's stuffed orangutang with a Barbie Doll clutched to his rust-colored chest.

"What are you doing?" Gage said.

Amy consulted a book laid open on the side table. The left-hand page had a full-color photo of the Empire State Building.

"This is for Jody's carnival at school. She told me yesterday that she wanted to go as King Kong climbing up the Empire State Building."

"She came up with that herself?"

"Apparently. So I thought I'd see if I could make it work."

Gage fingered the two cardboard flaps Amy had cut out half-way down the box to serve as windows and eyeholes. "You think she'll actually wear this?"

"We'll see."

Amy finished cutting the top and tossed the scrap pieces in the wastebasket. Her voice still had its edge; she had not forgiven him.

He picked up the orangutang and propped him against the cardboard building. The whole thing was very clever. Amy cut two long strips of duct tape and ran them along the freshly cut edges of cardboard.

He tossed the orangutang back on the couch. "I want you to know that I'm sorry," he said. "I shouldn't have lied to you."

She didn't answer at first, pressing the silver tape flat with her thumb and forefinger. "Here," she said. "Why don't you get into this? I'm not sure if I'm going to cut armholes or just make some kind of handles."

Gage cocked his head, considering for a second, but decided not to pursue it. He lifted the cardboard box above his head as Amy lent a guiding hand and then slid into it. The tip of the building fit just under his chin.

"Now just lift it up a bit," she said. "So you can see through the eyeholes."

Gage did as he was told, peering out through the two tiny windows at his tight-lipped wife like a man condemned to solitary.

"Now, where are your elbows?" she said.

"Her arms are going to be a lot shorter than mine."

"I was counting on that," Amy said. She slashed two dark lines on the sides of the box with a Magic Marker. Gage let his cardboard prison slide down and lifted his arms free.

130

"Amy, we've got to talk this out," he said.

She snapped the top back on the Magic Marker. "Maybe you couldn't tell anyone," she said, "because you knew that no one would believe you. In your heart you knew it was ludicrous. Isn't that right? You never believed it yourself."

"I did believe it," he said. What was ludicrous was having a conversation standing in a cardboard box; he felt like a character in some old Fatty Arbuckle routine. "I still do believe it."

She picked at the silver duct tape with her fingernail, trying to get it started. "I knew there was something wrong all week, but I thought it was me, something I might have said. If you really believe that your son is alive, then I think you need to go see someone. I think you need real help."

"You're not hearing what I'm saying."

"Just stop it! Stop! Don't I live with all your ghosts the way it is? I've got Nina's photographs on the wall and Peter's college textbooks in the back of the closet as if we were just waiting for him to come back from vacation. Sometimes I feel like I'm just renting a room here. I don't need this." She slammed the silver tape down on the side table, turned her back on him, moved to the fireplace.

He couldn't go to her because he couldn't walk. She was treating him as if he were nothing more than a clown. He wasn't going to let her mock him. He lifted the slick cardboard around him, wriggled and thumped his way out of it, leaned it against the couch.

Amy turned to face him. "Even if he is alive, living up in these mountains somewhere, he's never contacted you in seventeen years. What sort of son is that?"

"Amy, we should go to bed," he said. "It's been a hell of a day for everyone."

She brushed her hand across the mantel. "You go ahead. I want to finish this. I promised Jody I'd have it ready by tomorrow."

He reached out and felt the starched coolness of a pillow and realized he was alone. He looked across at the clock on the bookcase. It was a little before three in the morning. His first thought, his only thought, was that Amy had left him. He rolled out of bed and lurched down the hallway on sore feet, his heart pounding. He stopped at the doorway of his daughter's room. Amy's long silhouette lay in Jody's bed, one arm around their daughter. Gage moved to the bed and stood over the two of them, watching the soft rise and fall of Amy's shoulder. She was still in her clothes from the night before. She was not going to get over this one in a hurry. A quilt had slipped to the floor. Gage picked it up and spread it lightly over both of them.

He prowled through the house, checking the locks, closing a window in the spare room that had been left ajar. He was too churned up to go back to sleep for a while. He went into the kitchen and poured himself a glass of juice.

The cassette of *The Outriders* still lay on the counter. Gage drank his juice, eyeing the tape warily. Did Amy think he'd be pleased? She knew he'd refused to watch any of his films for more than ten years, why should she think anything was different now?

He rinsed out his glass and picked up the cassette. He remembered the other copy, crushed beneath the wheel at Father Ortiz's funeral. Maybe everything was different now; plus he had time to kill.

In the living room the cardboard Empire State Building leaned precariously against the mantel, its strips of silver tape ghostly in the darkness. He snapped on the television and fed the cassette into the VCR. He turned the sound down as low as it would go so he wouldn't wake Amy and Jody. Something thumped against the glass doors and he looked up. The two dogs stood outside, wagging their tails, hoping to be let in.

The film's opening shot slid across a mountain meadow, angled toward the river as the credits rolled. Gage smiled, watching

132

the baptisms in the stream, the grizzled faces of the born-again miners emerging from the water, sputtering and snorting.

Deacon Wiggs looked so young in the picture. He'd done all right for himself, with a long run as a second banana on some TV detective series. Buster Graham had ended up as a bail bondsman in Reseda, and the snaggle-toothed kid, Christ, Gage couldn't remember his name now, but that kid had cleaned up in the poker games each night even though he claimed he'd never played before.

Scene by scene Gage fell deeper into the world of the film. There were things he hadn't thought about for years: the miserably miscast actress whose lines they'd had to cut by half, the chickens loose in the whorehouse scene, how many times had they had to reshoot that one?

The dogs outside the glass fell asleep again. The only light in the room came from the screen, reflected off the panels of glass and white walls. It was as if Gage were alone in a cave staring at a fire, but the fire he was staring at was his old dreams.

Interviewers had loved to ask him about his vision, but he hadn't started out with any vision. He had wanted to make movies for the usual reasons, he had wanted to be rich and famous. He had been a kid desperate to be extraordinary and willful enough to achieve it. He had learned from every director that was around and had stolen from any that weren't.

Gage was no philosopher, he just wanted people's attention. He figured out early that the trick of keeping their attention was to take his most violent dreams, his most disturbing nightmares, and work them into pictures, shadows, images. A poet of violence, one critic had called him. Maybe he was a poet and maybe he wasn't; but he made them look. He made them admit there was a kind of liberation in violence, he made them take pleasure in it. It always amazed Gage that what really got to audiences was violence to animals, not people: a calf hung from a tree, children torching a nest of snakes. They objected, too, to the way the camera lingered.

Maybe a trick you repeated often enough became a vision. But Gage was sure one thing it did become, after eight, ten movies, was a kind of devil's bargain, a feeding on his own entrails. After so many years of making movies, he felt like one of those mad hatters who'd spent too much time sniffing arsenic. He sometimes imagined that all the images he'd created were out there in the atmosphere, like radiation, harmless enough for the vast majority of the population. Except that Peter had had a hundred times the normal dosage, it was in his bone and marrow.

Gage slouched in his chair, heavy-lidded, letting the images flow silently over him. Eloi and Crow were trying to evade the bounty hunters. Horses splashed through streams, labored up canyon walls. Every time Crow looked back the trackers were still out there, sometimes dots on a plain, sometimes nothing more than haze on the horizon. He knew every cut by heart: close-ups of horses' legs and frothy bellies, long shots of ghostly riders distorted through shimmering waves of heat.

It had been a hundred and five degrees for three days running, riders and horses and camera cars all breaking down in the heat. They had called Gage in to save the picture. He had saved it all right. He had been like a god, a decision-making machine, shooting all day and writing the next day's scenes at night. He had never been better, a damn superman.

Crow and Eloi picked their way across a maze of deadfall timber and the bounty hunters climbed below them. The Indian tracker found the abandoned horses and waved to the others.

Crow crouched quickly behind a downed ponderosa and raised his rifle, balancing it in the crook of a dead limb. Eloi screamed, but with the sound off, his protest was mute, grotesquely comic. The rifle jerked, the scout fell backward, tiny figures scurried for cover. Guns blazed soundlessly. Eloi grabbed at his shoulder. One of the bounty hunters grabbed the reins of an abandoned horse and tried to mount it, clutching the horn, but the horse was shot out from under him. Blood spurted from the animal's neck. Suddenly the shot went to slow motion,

134

horse and rider floating as they fell, light as feathers, graceful as dancers.

In the dead silence of the living room the distant report of a rifle sounded like a muffled thud. Gage pushed up in his chair. His first thought was that his mind was playing tricks on him, or that he had dreamed it, but then he saw that the dogs, who had been lying asleep just outside the sliding glass doors, had raised their heads, ears perked.

Gage leaned forward to push the sound lever down, but it was already as far down as it could go. Silver light flickered in the room, but he was staring now out at the darkness. After almost a full minute, there were two more shots, sharper and closer than the first.

He pushed away from his chair, unchained the sliding glass doors and yanked them open. The dogs jumped up on him, whining to be petted. He pushed them away. He stared down toward the barn and the road. He saw nothing at first, feeling the bite of night air, but then two pale fans of light appeared, maybe a quarter of a mile past the barn. It looked like the headlights of a Jeep or a three-wheeler, bouncing over rough ground and then coming to a stop.

Gage heard a soft rustling behind him. He turned quickly to see Amy, still half asleep, running her fingers through her tousled hair.

"What is it?" she said.

"Hunters, I think," Gage said. He pulled the glass doors shut, reached down and snapped off the flickering movie. He put a hand on Amy's shoulder and gave her a quick pat. "Why don't you go back to sleep?" He moved toward the bedroom.

"Where are you going?" she asked.

"I'm going to put an end to this. I'm really sick of this crap."

"Don't," Amy said. Gage snapped on their bedside lamp. "You don't know what they'll do."

Gage grabbed his trousers from the back of the chair and

pulled into them, then sat down on the bed to put on his socks and boots.

"We've been through this many times," Gage said. "These guys are going to have to learn."

"Let me go with you, then."

"No. You stay here." He found his jacket in the closet and wrestled into it, then pulled his rifle off the top shelf. He rummaged around on the floor of the closet to find the old tackle box. He unlatched it, took out the box of shells and stuffed it in his jacket pocket.

Amy chewed on her lower lip, sitting on the edge of the bed. "Don't go. Please. Don't do anything crazy."

He looked back at her angrily. "I'm not going to. I'm through doing crazy things."

It took a couple of tries to start his truck. The dogs leaped around the pickup, bit at the tires, ready for a run. The hole in the stone wall gaped like a missing tooth, filled with an etherlike night mist.

He did not turn on his lights. When he came to the gate that led down to the barn he had to get down to undo the chain. The Jeep headlights, a half mile away, had not moved. He could hear horses galloping in the dark pasture; it sounded as if they were racing from one fence line to the other.

As Gage pulled himself back into his truck he saw the distant Jeep headlights flare, grow dim, then flare again. Gage cursed. The Jeep had turned around and was bouncing back toward the mesa.

He rolled the truck down the slope. His rifle bounced on the seat next to him and he reached across to keep it from falling to the floor. Sheep bunched up in the corral next to the barn. Gage wheeled the pickup past the corral, into the lane beyond, saw the knot of the dark shapes standing against the pale hillside. He pulled on his lights.

Three horses stood shoulder to shoulder and they shied at the sudden light. As they wheeled away, Gage saw that there was a

136

fourth horse, down, that tried to rise but couldn't and collapsed heavily on its side.

Gage pulled the pickup within ten feet of the injured animal. He got out, but left his headlights on. The two-year-old mare had been shot twice, once high in the right front leg and once in the neck. The leg was shattered, the splinters of bone breaking through the skin. Blood pulsed slowly from the tiny neck wound.

As Gage moved closer the horse thrashed, lifting its head. "Hey, girl, hey, girl. It's going to be all right," he murmured. The other spooked horses regathered, watching from just beyond the circle of light. The dogs sniffed their way around the wounded mare, their tails wagging. The mare quivered and then was still again, following Gage's every move with one huge brown eye.

Gage stared up toward the mesa. You had to be a real son of a bitch to do something like this. There was no sign of the Jeep. There were only two or three passable roads off the mesa and if Gage stepped on it and got around to the Trillo drainage and waited he would have at least a fifty-fifty chance of catching them.

The sound of a motor made Gage look back toward the house. He saw the headlights of Amy's car. He moved quickly to his truck and got his rifle, yanked the box of shells from his jacket pocket. The metal shells were cold to the touch. He slipped one in the chamber. He wanted to finish this before Amy got here; he didn't want there to be any argument.

He moved slowly toward the horse, talking to her, soothing her. The dogs backed off, intimidated by the sight of the rifle. The mare's labored, growling breath hung ragged white umbrellas in the chill air. Gage knelt in the cone of the truck's headlights and lay the rifle on the ground. The mare shuddered at the touch of his hand. Gage ran his fingers lightly over the warm belly, scratched the horse behind the ears. The pulsing of blood from the neck wound seemed to be slowing. Gage could see the other horses watching him just beyond the pool of light, silent as a jury, their eyes shining.

137

When Gage stood and backed off a couple of steps, the mare tried to rise too, lurching forward, but the shattered leg buckled and she whomped heavily on her side. Amy's car was nearly down the slope; headlights flared along the wall of the barn. Gage raised the rifle to his shoulder and aimed just behind the ear.

The mare's body jerked at the shot, there was a rattling in her throat as she pawed the air weakily and then was still. The other horses wheeled and thundered off. Gage heard one of them hit a fence in the darkness and then whinny in pain. As Gage moved around the body the huge soft brown eye of the mare did not follow him; blood had begun to seep from the mouth.

Gage threw his rifle back in the truck. Amy's Datsun bounced up the slope toward him. It's crazy for her to bring a car out here, he thought, she's going to tear the bottom out of it.

She slammed the car door behind her and stared at the dead horse, her knuckles pressed to her lips. "Who did this?"

"I've got my ideas," Gage said. "It could be one of fifty people."

"Maybe it was a mistake."

"Maybe. Maybe they were drunk. Maybe they saw the eyes in the darkness and thought it was a deer. And maybe not." Gage tossed the box of shells across the seat of his truck. The dogs sniffed daintly at the dead horse.

"What are you doing to do?" she asked.

"The first thing I'm going to do is get this animal out of here." He gathered a long chain from the bed of the truck, metal growling on metal, and then moved toward the mare.

"You can do this in the morning," Amy said. "Come back to bed. It can wait."

Gage didn't bother to answer. He wrapped the chain around the two back legs of the horse and jerked it tight. The body was still warm. Amy did not move, her hands tucked up in the sleeves of her shapeless Irish sweater, as Gage backed the truck up and attached the chain to the trailer hitch.

138

"Amy, just go back to the house. Just let me take care of this."
He sidestepped down the slope toward the barn and she followed him.

"I want to know what you're going to do," she said. The sheep
bolted out of the corral at their approach.

"I'll tell you what I'm not going to do. I'm not going to sit
around for two weeks watching buzzards picking over the body,
I'll tell you that."

He opened the door to the dilapidated toolshed behind the
barn and found the can of kerosene behind the door. He shook
it; it felt three-quarters full.

"You're not going to try and burn it?" Amy said. Gage didn't
answer, slamming the door shut and securing the sagging latch.
"This is crazy."

"Is it?" he said.

They moved back toward the two vehicles. The can of kerosene banged hollowly against Gage's leg.

"What happened last night . . . we were both upset," Amy
said. "Things get blown out of proportion. We can talk this out.
We're two adults, after all."

"I just want to take care of this, Amy, all right?"

He swung the can of kerosene into the truck, then turned and
put his hand on the back of her neck. "We will talk it out, we will.
Just not right now, okay?" She didn't say anything. He stepped
across the slack chain, went around to the other side of the truck
and pulled himself in behind the steering wheel. He checked the
glove compartment to be sure he had a box of matches. When he
looked up, Amy was on her way back to her car.

He started the engine and edged forward. He looked back,
watched the chain slither and tighten. The truck shuddered and
he gave it more gas. The wheels spun, dug in, and the mare
began to slide.

Gage followed the rutted switchbacks that worked their way to
the top of the mesa. The mare bounced along behind, head
flopping like a rag doll, raising dust in the red glare of the

taillights. The dogs raced gleefully alongside, tongues wagging, going all out. Halfway up the trail Gage glanced back and saw Amy's headlights. It looked as if she was nearly back at the house.

As the trail steepened, the truck began to whine and strain from the weight. A couple of jackrabbits jumped out, bounding in the headlights for twenty yards before one of the dogs spied them and gave pursuit, dog and rabbits plunging into darkness.

Gage had brought it all on himself. He had always refused to lease his land to the local hunting clubs and that had created resentment. It was a matter of local custom, a matter of neighborliness. The argument ran that hunting clubs at least gave you some protection; they policed themselves and ran off poachers and trespassers. Gage never bought it. He'd never played by other people's rules. So he'd paid the price. Over the past several years there had been a half-dozen incidents—cut fences, gates left open, people shining deer on the mesa at night—but there'd never been anything like this.

At the mesa rim there was a shallow draw, protected from the wind. He parked as close to it as he could. He wrestled a posthole digger out from under the clutter of tools in the truck bed and used it as a lever to nudge the heavy body of the mare over the edge. The horse rolled over and then slid down another five feet through brush and loose gravel.

Gage splashed kerosene up and down the length of the mare, washing away gravel and blood, anointing the body as the exhausted dogs watched, panting. He gathered armfuls of dead piñon and juniper and heaped them on the body, creating a pyre. When he saw that wouldn't be enough he got a pair of oil-stained two-by-fours and split them with the ax and wedged them under the mare's neck and legs.

He poured the remaining kerosene over the tangled pile of brush and went back to retrieve the matches. A cold wind off the dark mountains caught him full in the face. The night was clear; stars were everywhere. He saw a light moving slowly on the road four or five miles to the south.

140

The first match he lit blew out. He cupped the second in his palm, nursing it for a second, then tossed it into the tangled pyre and stepped quickly back. The match lay there, rose for a moment, and then died.

Gage moved closer for his third try. There was a whoosh and flames exploded upward. Gage flinched, felt the searing heat against his face. The dogs backed off, cowering as the fire rose, brush crackling.

Gage retreated too. He stuffed the box of matches into his back pocket. He brushed the back of his hands, not sure if he'd been burned or not. The flames licked ten, twelve, fourteen feet in the air.

This was the only way to go. He wasn't going to have coyotes and neighbors' dogs trotting across his pasture for days; he didn't want them to develop a taste for it. He wasn't going to have flocks of buzzards perched in the trees like dark candles, waddling in the grass, wheeling lazily in the sky. Gage had always hated stench. He wanted things disposed of. He wanted things behind him.

It was a huge fire. Embers floated on the night air, drifted down into the surrounding brush. Gage beat them out with his shovel or stomped them out with his boot. For a moment there were three or four tiny blazes spreading at once, reflecting off the Spanish bayonet, and Gage thought he'd blown it, he was about to set the whole mesa on fire. It took ten minutes of furious work to get it back under control.

The fire roared fifteen feet in the air. The blaze could be seen for miles; the hunters who had shot the mare were probably watching it now, wondering what was up.

Gage gathered the chain and threw it in the truck. The pickup glowed in the glare of the fire. He got out the tarp and spread it twenty feet from the roaring pyre and lay down. The dogs crept back and lay down next to him. As the fire shifted, some of the burning piñon branches collapsed in on themselves. Gage stared at the shovel resting across his knees. Looking through the waves

141

of heat was like looking through faulty glass. Gage could see the horsehair curling into filaments of ash, see the hide charring.

This was how his son had died, in a fire ten times more searing than this. The reports had said that people had seen the flames from the exploding powder tank fifteen miles away. The firefighters had to work for eight hours to put out the conflagration.

A new popping sound in the fire roused him. The flames had burned through the skin, and the fat just beneath had begun to sizzle. For the first time there was the smell of roasting meat.

This was how his son had died. He'd better get used to the idea. He'd better sit here and watch until he finally got it through his thick skull. Because if he didn't get it, life was going to be torture. Things had to be disposed of. People shot horses for spite, children died, that's the way the world was, get used to it. When Abraham offered up his son Isaac, God had put a ram in the thicket just in the nick of time, or so the story went. The problem here was that the animal had been sacrificed seventeen years too late.

As the fire began to die down, Gage got up to gather more wood. This time he took the ax with him, ranging further out into the darkness. He could hear small animals rustling in the brush. A hawk or an owl exploded out of a clump of piñon. He hacked away at a couple of good-sized scrub juniper and dragged them back, rolling them onto the fire. He used the shovel to flip some of the smoldering wood back into the heart of the blaze.

Gage lay on the tarp, staring dully into the flames. The fire hissed as the scorched stomach wall gave way and the wet intestines slid into the flames.

Tending the fire, Gage began to drift in and out of sleep. He lost any sense of how much time had passed. He finally curled up with his hand under his cheek, staring at the flames licking up and down the mare's body. Get used to it. This was the way it had been.

The dogs' barking woke him. Instinctively he grabbed for the shovel, thinking the fire had gotten out of control, but the half-burned carcass lay smoldering tamely below him. It wasn't sunrise yet, but the edge was off the darkness. What the dogs were barking at was the figure in a hooded slicker sitting on the far side of the draw, knees pulled up to the chest.

Gage lurched up on one elbow. His body was stiff from sleeping on the ground. "Peter?" he whispered. He staggered to his feet, he didn't have his balance yet and his heart was leaping wildly. The figure on the far side of the draw rose at the same time he did, mirroring him, but with the ease of someone a generation younger.

The hood of the slicker fell back. Amy shook out her hair. She came sideways down the draw with careful steps so she wouldn't slide and then leaped across. Gage came to meet her, offered his hand and pulled her up.

She put her arms around him, her head to his chest, without even looking him in the face. Gage lay his cheek on her hair, ashamed and moved all at the same time. He finally took her face in both his hands, forced her to look at him.

"How long have you been sitting there?"

"Not so very long," she said. She reached up and pulled a twig from his matted hair. "We should get back," she said. "Jody will be waking up any time now."

Eleven

ON THE LAST DAY of May in 1970, Gage had buried Peter's remains in a grove of redwoods halfway up the California coast. It was land he had bought ten years before; he had promised Peter that sooner or later they were going to build a cabin there. The only people at the ceremony were the redheaded wife of a producer, whose son had been Peter's best friend and was now in England on a Marshall Fellowship, and Unita Phelps, the black woman who had been Gage's cook and housekeeper when Peter was young. The minister read from Dylan Thomas and the Psalms; the prayers were silent.

Gage tried to tough it out. People told him to take time off. "Anybody who's gone through what you've gone through needs time, Gage."

"But I'm not anybody," he told them.

He went into the studio and functioned, seven days a week. He made a point not to read any newspapers or watch any television. He never really broke, but the mind played funny tricks on him. When Pete Rose started the rally in the twelfth inning of the All-Star Game, Gage's first thought was, "I've got to call Peter to tell him, he must be lovin' this. . . ."

The one part of his life he couldn't control was his dreams, and there grief raged and mocked. He had one dream in which Nina had been taken off to the hospital for what the doctor called acute sexual therapy. Peter had been taken to an institution. In the dream, Peter's fourth-grade teacher explained to Gage that the court had decided he was not capable of caring for a child by himself and Gage kept shouting at her, "It's not fair, it's not fair."

It became very clear very quickly that he was not going to be able to stay in California. People were getting weird around him. Guys he'd known for twenty years walked past him in the halls of Paramount without speaking. One night at Scandia a group at the next table kept glancing over and finally the host got up and asked the waiter to move them. Gage couldn't handle it: the fearful rolls of the eyes, the too-sympathetic catch in the voice.

He cut a deal with the studio. He got a nice chunk of money for a screenplay and went off to write it in New York, where he figured he wasn't going to be running into people he knew every five minutes.

He took an apartment on Central Park West and holed up. The writing did not go well and he started drinking, seriously. One night he got into a brawl in a Village bar and nearly got his nose bitten off by a Greek muralist.

His agent, a tall, languid and kind woman, flew into town. She read without comment the first draft of the screenplay it had taken him five months to write.

"I'm concerned," she said. "You're too isolated. It wouldn't be good for anyone."

"But I'm not anyone, remember?"

There was a young woman his agent wanted him to meet, a recent NYU film school graduate who was working at the Museum of Broadcasting.

Gage and his agent went to dinner at Amy's apartment, a tiny sixth-floor walk-up in SoHo. It was the most eclectic-looking place Gage had ever seen. A Gogodala sculpture, huge, wooden, beaded, feathered and phallic—a gift from her sister who'd lived in New Guinea for five years—was poised above a marble-top antique sideboard, given to her by her ninety-nine-year-old grandmother. Rusting bits of farm machinery hung on the walls as decoration.

She was attractive, with the long, defined lines of someone who'd taken dance lessons for years. She was not afraid to speak her mind and at the same time seemed a bit scattered. She had made a southern meal of fried chicken, greens, black-eyed peas and blackberry pie. They ate crowded around an old gate-leg table. Gage's agent asked her where she'd got it.

"I found it on the street," Amy said.

"You *found* it?" The agent seemed astonished. "But weren't you worried that it would be gone by the time you got back?"

"Oh, no," Amy said. "I just carried it up."

Gage looked up from chasing black-eyed peas around his plate. Any New York woman who was going to carry a table up six flights with nonchalance deserved his attention.

They began to see one another. She took him to avant-garde performances where they sat in folding chairs watching tiny tin-foil boats being pulled across a stage for twenty minutes. He took her to Yankee Stadium and helped her build a darkroom in her cramped apartment. She insisted on their getting up at 5 A.M. to take the train out to Jones Beach, when he could have gotten them the use of a house in Sag Harbor with ease. They were both so tired they slept through their Jones Beach stop and had to take a cab back. More than once Gage thought he was too old for this kind of stuff.

It seemed like a classic mismatch. She hated his drinking. The

146

third time they went out she told him she wanted two children and a house and he hadn't even kissed her yet. One night they got together with her friends from her therapy group. It was a disaster. First of all, they seemed like children, and second, they sat on the couch staring at him with knowing looks as if they had spent many a good hour discussing his hang-ups. Gage finally launched into a tirade about what a rip-off therapy was, which brought the evening to a quick close.

Somehow Gage and Amy continued. They each had their chances to end it and couldn't. Gage worried about her riding her bike to work through midtown traffic. He did not talk to her about Peter and she did not ask.

The afternoon that Gage heard his script had been put into turnaround, he was supposed to meet Amy uptown to see *La Strada.* He was stunned. He didn't believe it. The only explanation his agent had was that the studio's new president was bringing in a lot of his own projects. "You don't put Jeremiah Gage into turnaround with a bullshit excuse like that! Do they know who they're dealing with? Do they?"

He walked the thirty blocks uptown in a fury. They had cold noodles with sesame paste at Empire Szechuan and Gage had a couple of bottles of Chinese beer. He said nothing about what had happened. Amy was filled with stories about "the funeral boy," the middle-aged man who came into the museum faithfully once a week to watch tapes of whatever funerals he could get his hands on: Kennedy, Churchill, the Queen Mother.

Afterward they walked up to the theater. A half-dozen pickets paraded outside, chanting. One or two of them clapped gloved hands, trying to stay warm in the cold December night. A stout man in a navy blue car coat waved people on. "Pass 'em by, pass 'em by."

Gage felt Amy's hand tighten on his arm. "What's the matter?" he said.

"Nothing's the matter," she said. "We can go somewhere else." A gust of wind blew a sheet of newspaper down the street,

147

pinned it momentarily against the shin of one of the pickets; he kicked it free.

"Hey, we said we were going to a movie, we're going to a movie."

"Gage, don't."

"No, you leave this to me. I'll get the tickets."

Gage left her and moved toward the ticket window. He wasn't really even thinking about what he was doing; when he finally had enough it was like a burner kicking in somewhere in the back of his head.

The stocky man in the car coat had already picked him out as trouble. "Projectionists on strike here, pal, let's just pass 'em by."

Gage careened into the picket line, as if to somehow make it look accidental, but nobody was fooled. He caught one guy with his shoulder and stumbled back against another.

"Hey, man, what the hell you doin'?"

"I'm trying to buy a ticket, that's what the hell I'm doing," Gage said. "I'm trying to walk down the goddamned street, that's what the hell I'm doing."

The pickets surrounded him, most of them looking more stunned than angry, but the man who'd been hit shoved Gage and Gage shoved him back.

"You don't touch me, cowboy, you don't want any of this, I'm telling you, man!"

"Aww, he's nuts, just leave him alone."

Gage was suddenly dizzy; he could still feel the effect of the beers from dinner. Beyond the circle of angry men he could see the *La Strada* poster in its display case, Anthony Quinn busting chains across his bare chest, the doe-eyed Giulietta Masina in the background.

"This is a free country and you guys were taking up the whole sidewalk."

The crowd was growing; a couple of older Puerto Rican men had come out of the Chinese-Cuban restaurant next door, seen

148

the excitement, and were waving through the window for their friends to come watch.

The man in the navy blue car coat put a hand on Gage's back, trying to be a peacemaker, but Gage swatted the hand away. He glanced through the gathering crowd and saw Amy's horrified face. Her hand was at her mouth. He tried to form a sentence, but before he could shout anything, she turned and ran.

Gage made a move to go after her, but a cop car had just pulled up and someone was blocking his path. Accusing fingers jabbed at him. Gage turned slowly as if he were going to take them all on, one by one. In the crowd a trio of black teenagers laughed and exchanged handslaps.

It took twenty minutes of fast talking for Gage to extricate himself. As soon as he was free he called Amy's, but there was no answer. He took a cab downtown, hit her buzzer a dozen times, but she wasn't at her apartment. He wandered around the Village for an hour, calling every fifteen minutes, and finally got her.

"Amy, I'm sorry about what happened. I need to see you."

"Not tonight, Gage. I don't want to see you tonight."

He stood on the corner of Eighth Street, late-night shoppers milling at the fruit stand behind him. "Amy, I can explain. The studio called this afternoon. They put me into turnaround. I was pissed, I had a couple of beers."

Yellow cabs jockeyed for position on Sixth Avenue. "A bunch of poor men are striking for five dollars an hour and you're going to knock them down . . ."

"They were blocking the sidewalk."

"You provoked the whole thing, Gage. You ran into them."

The metal sides of the outdoor booth were cold to the touch. "What is this, I can't go to the movies until everybody's got justice in the world?"

"I can't believe you're saying these things, Gage. What's happening to you?"

"I don't know. But I had a son, he would have agreed with

149

everything you're saying. He felt for everybody. And look where it got him."

Suddenly Gage couldn't speak anymore. He leaned into the booth, hiding his face, the rectangular metal sides of the booth shielding him like the blinders on a horse.

"Gage? Gage, are you all right?"

He was weeping. No one noticed. The shoppers still picked over the fruit at the stand ten feet away, the prisoners in the Women's House of Detention screamed obscenities to the pedestrians passing below. Suddenly Gage was just anyone; weeping, like anyone who had ever lost a child.

"I think you'd better come up," she said.

The war had started to fade and cool. The pictures sent back were of South Vietnamese troops clinging to the skids of departing American helicopters. The protests were subsiding.

Once, in the dentist's office, Gage picked up a *Harper's* magazine. The lead editorial was about the waning peace movement.

> When the Vietnam conflict finally ends, all a lot of people are going to remember about the antiwar movement are the explosion in the townhouse in the Village, Bernardine Dohrn's gleeful remark about the Manson murders and Peter Gage's bombing of the powder plant. What they need to remember are the millions of law-abiding Americans of conscience who opposed the war, not the pathological aberrations. . . .

Gage gave up his screenplay. It should have worked, but it didn't. He had no more stories in him. The projects his agent showed him were all second-rate; the fingerprints showed.

One night over cappuccino at Dante's, Gage told Amy, "I'm getting out. It's no good. No more movies."

"But you're a director."

"What's a director? A guy who goes around making little pictures with his fingers? No, I'm not a director. Not any more."

150

"But why, Gage? I don't understand. You've spent your whole life making movies."

"I don't expect you to understand. I know what movies cost and you don't, all right? Let's just leave it at that."

"Then what are you going to do?"

"I'm going to go back to New Mexico. Buy some land, maybe." She was silent for a moment. "Hell, you don't like the city anyway. You've got this frog record you play every night to remind you of the country."

"What are you saying?"

"I'm saying I want you to come with me."

They flew to Atlanta to tell her parents, who were furious. Her father, a former All-Georgia basketball player who still sported his crew cut, threatened to punch him out. Gage, a model of restraint, heard them out. He didn't quite win them over, but in the end achieved at least a grudging truce.

They were married six months later and moved to New Mexico. Gage gave up drinking altogether. When, in their eighth year on the ranch, they discovered Amy was pregnant, the *L.A. Times* movie critic sent him a pair of bronzed golf balls in tribute.

Amy and Jody had saved him. He had lucked out. He knew he was not an easy person to live with. He grumped and bellowed and demanded more attention than was anyone's due. There were nights when he felt he was too old to be raising a small child, but he was a playful father; he would get down on the rug and rub his head into Jody's belly until she was helpless with laughter.

He was a protective father too. Amy teased him about it, Gage, the great master of violence, who didn't like the idea of his six-year-old dancing around to the sexually explicit lyrics of Tina Turner. When some of Jody's first-grade classmates were off to see *The Terminator,* Gage refused to let her go.

He knew that one day she would see his films and ask questions. If he'd had his way, he would have destroyed all his films, every last print. He didn't want that record of pain and cruelty around, however veiled.

Amy said that sometimes it felt as if they were living on a desert island—doing their buying through mail-order catalogs, marooned behind thick stone walls—and in the past year she had begun to make changes. She was on the road to Santa Fe a lot more, joining a book group, working at Jody's school, no longer willing just to play Girl Friday to Gage's Robinson Crusoe. It irritated Gage from time to time, but if anyone had asked him if he was happy, he would have said yes, happier than he had any right to be.

Amy had started to wear more straw hats and long-sleeved shirts. Gage had warned her for years about the dangers of the New Mexico sun, particularly for someone with her fair skin, particularly when you grew older. It took a scare or two, but she was finally taking protective measures.

Twelve

GAGE WOKE to the soft, steady clicks of rocks being wedged into place and the Spanish voices of Huerta's crew. He rolled over and stared at the clock. It was ten-thirty in the morning. He got out of bed and pushed the curtains aside. Huerta's men—Mexicans, Indians, God knew what else, but brown-skinned and aliens all, dismantled the damaged sections of the wall.

He padded into the kitchen. Amy had left a note for him on the refrigerator; she had taken Jody with her to the grocery store and they'd be back by eleven. Sun streamed in the windows, but the house was cold. He felt as if someone had been pounding his body with mallets for hours; he needed to warm up.

He went into the living room and saw the logs laid in the fireplace. He rubbed the back of his hands, felt the fine, singed

153

hairs. He still smelled of smoke from the night before. He should have had enough of fire to last him a lifetime, but he was chilled. He folded the fire screen and set it to one side.

Gage knelt and shook out a half-dozen sheets of newspaper from the stack in the brass bucket next to the hearth. He balled them up, one by one, and wedged them in under the logs. One of the balls of paper fell through the grating and Gage retrieved it. His eye caught on a picture on the wadded-up paper.

He smoothed it out on the stone hearth. The photo that had gotten his attention was of a sourpuss janitor holding a box of votive candles; the picture was one of eight color photos on the front of the "Living" section, a special article on the cathedral.

Gage remembered the face. He remembered the day too, the day he'd run into Tina Lancet. He remembered how surprised he'd been to find her in a church and he remembered how she'd explained that she was shooting photos for a newspaper article. The only problem was that now, as Gage checked the credits, her name wasn't to be found. All the pictures had been taken by a man named Rob Singer.

All of a sudden he didn't feel cold anymore. He went back into the kitchen, taking the newspaper page with him, and dialed in a series of quick strokes. He let the phone ring, staring out the window. Huerta leaned against his truck, cowboy hat tipped forward, playing the *patrón*.

"Hello?"

"Hey, Rudy?" Gage said.

"Hey."

"It's Jeremiah Gage. I've got a question for you. You know Tina Lancet?"

"Of course. Who doesn't?"

Gage turned, the telephone cord coiling tight around him. "You know the full page of pictures you ran on the cathedral . . . what was it"—he checked the date on the newspaper—"a week ago? Was she ever assigned to that?"

"Are you kidding? She hasn't worked for the paper in over a

year. We had a massive blowup when she claimed we lost some pictures of hers."

Gage stood frozen at the sink. Outside, the workers pitched boulders from one set of hands to the next, dumped them on a growing pile. The size of the hole was appalling. But that was the problem with stone walls, they were like jigsaw puzzles. One piece faulty or weak or out of place and you had to take the whole thing apart and start over from scratch.

"Uh-huh. Have you talked to her at all?" Gage asked.

"Not for months."

"Thanks, Rudy. That's all I need to know."

Gage hung up. He moved to the counter, opened the cupboard door and shut it again. So Tina had lied. Such a dumb lie too. It wasn't like her at all. He picked up the wrinkled paper again and stared at the pictures of the cathedral. He tried to go over all the details of the afternoon: Tina in her wide straw hat, waiting in the pew for someone, the grim-faced young priest on the other side of the church. He remembered how tense and skittish she had been, how quickly she had gotten rid of Gage. It almost made him laugh—to think that he had spent all that time looking in the wrong direction, when it had been right there, in front of his nose.

It took just a second to look up her number. Someone picked up on the second ring; a child's voice answered.

"Hello, this is the Lancet residence."

"Hello. Is your mommy there?"

"No."

"Do you know when she'll be home?"

"No." The child didn't sound older than ten.

Gage kept his patient tone. "Will she be home this afternoon?" He paced the floor restlessly, the telephone cord pulling him back like a tether.

"I don't know."

"Do you have any way to get in touch with her?" Gage kept his voice soft as a feather, trying not to scare the kid off. He heard a

155

second voice in the background. Two children quarreled for possession of the phone.

"Excuse me," Gage said. "My name's Jeremiah Gage. I'm a friend of your mother's. What's your name?"

"Gaia."

"Listen, Gaia. Your mother used to work for me. She was in a movie I made a long time ago." An engine sputtered and then roared outside. Gage peered out the window, his heart pounding like a man about to be caught at something illicit, but it wasn't Amy's car, just Huerta backing his truck up to one of the rock piles. "Did she ever tell you about that?"

"I think so," the girl answered.

"It's very important that I speak to her, Gaia. As soon as possible."

"Well . . . she had to drive to Texas."

"Texas."

"She left yesterday." Again the two children argued.

"Excuse me," Gage said, "but where in Texas? I can call her there if you have the number."

"I have to hang up now," Gaia said. Gage heard the phone being wrestled away, heard the disconnecting click.

Autumn light swelled within the room. Gage balled up the wrinkled newspaper, tossed it in the air, caught it with one swipe. Everything now was suddenly fuel for the fire. Part of him was saying, don't even think about it, don't even start, you owe it to your wife and kid not to, and part of him was already out there, back in the chase.

By the time Amy and Jody returned, Gage had it all planned. What they needed was an outing. The storm the day before had dumped a couple of inches of snow high in the mountains; they would bundle up, take the dogs and Jody's plastic saucer and go have an adventure.

It took them forty minutes to drive up to the Ski Basin. Jody was the first to spot snow, white patches deep in the ponderosa pine just beyond the Black Canyon campground. The winding road became wet and then icy; on the curves they could see the valley miles below and the endless unfolding of tawny mesas. A big van passed them, chains clanking on its massive tires, skis strapped to the roof. As they eased around the bend at Big Tesuque they were suddenly surrounded by solid banks of snow.

Twenty other vehicles were scattered across the Ski Basin parking lot. Skiers waxed down their cross-country skis, dogs romped, voices rang like crystal in the crisp air. None of the lifts were operating and the lodge would be closed for at least another month; days like this came gratis. People slid down the lower slopes on sleds, toboggans, sheets of plastic. The driver of the county snowplow had his feet up, the flaps of his hat down; he sipped at a thermos of hot coffee and watched the madness.

Gage and Jody and Amy crossed the bridge and headed up the trail; the narrow stream seemed black as tamarack against the white snow. The dogs plunged ahead of them, chasing fresh scents, playing tag with one another like puppies. The sun was warm; Gage had to narrow his eyes against all the dazzling whiteness. Snow was already dropping silently from the branches. It wasn't going to last long. It would probably all be melted in three or four days.

Jody was sky-high, racing after the dogs, then plopping down to make a snow angel, then dashing off again. Amy stayed up with her, but after a couple of hundred yards Gage fell behind, short of breath on the steep slope.

He stepped off the trail to let a pair of dispirited backpackers clomp past—it looked as if they'd gotten caught by the storm. Gage sat down on a log to get his wind back. He stared down through the barren aspens at the black rushing stream. He had said nothing to Amy about the photos in the paper or his phone call to Tina's. As long as he didn't pursue it, there was no point. The question was whether or not he was pursuing it.

He heard them shout his name. He looked up and saw Jody and Amy on the switchback above him. Jody threw a snowball that disintegrated midair. Gage rose and hurried to catch up.

157

They labored up through the hushed trees. Jody started to weary and wanted to swing on their hands; in the end Gage and Amy pulled her on her plastic saucer.

At the top of the ridge there was a meadow. The view was incredible; they could see a good thirty miles, across desert and Indian land to the blue shapes of the Jemez Mountains. Gage glanced at Amy. Cold had brought red to her cheeks and her gray-green eyes were luminous with delight. Whatever he did, Gage thought, he'd better not blow this. Amy sensed him looking at her and smiled back. Amy was not the kind of person who always needed to have things named for her; she sensed why he had brought them up here.

Jody's snowball hit Gage on the boot. He knelt quickly and tossed his gloves aside, dug deep in the snow with his bare hands, packing one snowball after the other. Snow was a blessing; it blotted out everything, it buried the past. What Gage needed was to cleanse himself, wash off every old scent, every last odor of death.

He threw three snowballs at Jody, rapid-fire. His hands were stinging. Jody tried to run and fell back in the snow. Gage tromped back to retrieve his gloves.

"Isn't that cold?" Amy said.

"A little." He touched his red, cold hands to her cheek. She flinched, but took his hands in both of hers, rubbing them warm. Gage leaned across and kissed her on the cheek. A snowball hit him solidly between the shoulder blades.

They played in the snow for almost an hour, all three of them taking turns sliding down on the plastic saucer, fending off the dogs that leaped all over them every time they took a spill. They tried to teach Jody the rules of Fox and Goose and even made the start of a snowman, when Jody's hands got too cold and she got snow down her boot.

It was dark by the time they got home. Amy was running Jody a bath and Gage was making them all cocoa when the phone rang. It was one of the parents from Jody's school. They were setting up for the carnival and they'd found a wagon for the hayride, but they had no hay. Gage held the receiver in place with his chin while he sprinkled the tiny marshmallows in the hot cocoa.

"How late will you be there?" Gage asked.

"Oh, all night. Eleven at least, we've got so much to do."

Amy came into the kitchen with Jody's wet snowsuit balled up in her hands and a hint of alarm in her eyes.

"Well, let me put Jody to bed," Gage said, "and I'll bring you in all you need."

It was a quarter to ten by the time he got into Santa Fe; it had taken him nearly an hour to first sing Jody to sleep and then load the hay bales into the back of the truck. On a Sunday night the town was shut down tight, the dark streets empty except for a few prowling dogs.

He tried to tell himself that he wasn't pursuing anything, that taking a quick swing by Tina's house did not constitute any violation of trust, but when he made the turn onto Alameda, heading west instead of east, he knew he was just kidding himself. He took the corner carefully. The tarp was strapped down tight over the twenty bales of hay in the back; even so, he could feel the weight.

Tina lived on the west side of town, in a lower-middle-class neighborhood just beyond the projects, a neighborhood of small yards, decorative stone rabbits or deer every block or so, vegetable gardens out back. He drove slowly, leaning forward on the steering wheel, trying to make out the house numbers. It turned out he didn't need numbers; Tina's old hippie van with the rainbow stickers, parked in the driveway, was landmark enough.

A child's bike lay on its side in the front yard. The house was dark. Gage turned off the ignition and sat watching for five minutes. He chewed two sticks of spearmint, a dog barked, a paint truck with the ladders up top rattled past. He could see the silver flicker of a television through a front window on down the block, but at Tina's there was no sign of life. A garage door opened and a man came out lugging his garbage can. He deposited it at the curb and then stared hard at Gage's pickup, his hands on his hips. Gage never moved and the man finally went back in, the garage door rattling shut behind him. The whole thing suddenly seemed stupid. He had to deliver hay to a hayride. He tossed his gum out the window and started the truck.

When he arrived, eight or nine people were still at work in the school auditorium, sorting out prizes, putting up decorations, piecing together a tape for the spook house. Gage got a hero's welcome. He and two of the other fathers unloaded the hay bales onto the long rickety wagon and then Gage, getting into the spirit of things, stayed another half hour to help hammer together the booth for the second-graders' football toss. It was past eleven by the time he left.

He cruised through the silent town, feeling oddly exhausted, not all there. He didn't see them until it was almost too late; three or four drifters had come up from under the bridge and were squatting in the middle of the street with their bedrolls. They seemed to writhe in the headlights. Gage swerved. There was a quick flash of an angry, drunken face at the side window, a thump as the man banged against the glass. Gage looked back, instinctively searching for Peter's face among the homeless, wraithlike figures.

Everything came back, like the ache of an old fracture. He wheeled the car into a U-turn under the blinking yellow caution light by Albertson's and headed back into town. Damn it, he just had to know.

The second effort paid off. Parked behind the hippie van in Tina's driveway was a gleaming silver and maroon monster of a truck. The house was no longer dark; a lamp glowed softly behind the curtains in the front window.

He drove slowly past and parked around the corner. As he walked back a dog barked from a fenced-in yard. He ran his hand over the massive silver haunches of the truck, kicked at the freshly caked mudflaps. He peered in the dust-streaked windows, saw the police scanner under the dash, the blankets and pillows and Chicken McNuggets cartons strewn across the back. If there ever was a doper's truck, this was it.

He walked to the front door. He listened to the voices inside; one of them was Tina's. It was impossible to make out what they were saying. Gage paused for a couple more seconds and then knocked.

The voices stopped. He stepped back from the door. The dog barked again, several houses down. He saw the ripple in the curtains on the front window. He knocked again, harder.

"Hey, Tina," he called out, not loud enough to wake the neighbors, but loud enough.

"Who is it?"

"Jeremiah Gage."

He heard the click and slide of locks and the door opened a crack.

"What do you want?"

"I want to talk to you."

"Great. But not now."

Gage's hand was on the door. He felt steady pressure from the other side.

"I think now, Tina. You lied to me."

He hit the door with his shoulder and caught her off guard. She cried out.

For a second the scene in front of him was perfectly still, like some murky, underexposed photograph: an olive-skinned woman crouching on the floor, holding a blanket to her throat, child curled up on the couch above her and, above the couch, the skinniest, most Lutheran-looking man Gage had ever seen.

Tina banged the door off Gage's shoulder, trying to shut him out, but it was too late. "You've got no right!" she hissed. The man behind the couch still hadn't moved, standing as ramrod erect as the farmer in the Grant Wood painting. "Just get the hell out!"

The olive-skinned woman scooped up her sleeping child and

161

her blanket slipped to the floor. She wore a cheap, high-waisted, baby-blue dress, something out of Woolworth's. The buttons on the back were undone. Her pencil-thin legs were scarred. The Lutheran-looking man moved finally, came forward to put a sheltering arm around her.

"I'd leave if I were you," the skinny man said. His shoes were thick-soled and black, night-watchman's shoes. "Before we call the police." He was trying to sound tough, but he had no more potential for violence than a giraffe.

"I don't think you want to do that," Gage said. The woman backed toward the kitchen with her baby, "You can tell her it's okay," he said. "Don't be afraid. We're all friends. Amigos."

The woman stopped. She had the dazed look of someone who'd just stepped off a roller coaster. The sleeping child clung to her, froglike, slender brown legs wrapped around his mother's waist.

Everyone waited on Gage. He took his time scanning the dim room. The floor was strewn with toys and books and stray socks. A couple of days on their own had been enough for Tina's kids to turn the place into a real mess. One wall served as a gallery for Tina's photographs. A lot of them Gage remembered: the picture of Dylan in bib overalls milking a cow, the shot of Janis Joplin asleep backstage at the Fillmore East, the toothless, grinning Peruvian shepherd in his brightly knit beanie.

"So," Tina said, "you satisfied?"

"No. Not yet," Gage said. He gazed at the tall, gentle man. "You look like a preacher. What denomination? Let me guess."

"Stop trying to show off," Tina said. *"Maritza. Puedes poner el niño en mi cuarto de dormir."* She gestured to the minister. "Why don't you go with her? This will take me just a couple of minutes."

Gage smiled; he recognized the bossy tone. It was what Gage used to call her Emma Goldman voice. This was the kind of woman you'd want in charge of feeding two hundred thousand

162

people at a rock concert. The tall man and Maritza and the sleeping child dissolved into the dark hallway.

"So where's she from?" Gage asked. The woman's shoes lay beside the couch, scuffed, black plastic pumps. "Salvador? Guatemala?"

"None of your damn business, Gage. Everyone's exhausted. Whatever it is you're here for, it can wait till morning."

He ruminated, still sizing up the house. Piled up on the kitchen counter were jackets, a canteen, a hefty black plastic flashlight the size of a salami.

"I don't think so. You lied to me, Tina."

"Now when was that?"

"That day in the cathedral. You said you were doing photos for *The New Mexican.* It wasn't true."

She flopped down in a frayed easy chair. Her hair was in pigtails, the way she'd worn it years before. Her laughter was high and incredulous. "So I like people to think I'm working, what's wrong with that?"

He picked up the pile of cassettes stacked on the VCR: *Mask, The Neverending Story, The Breakfast Club.* "When I saw the truck outside I thought you were running dope." He could see the gaunt minister standing in the dark end of the hallway, his arms wide, touching the walls on either side. He had the wingspan of a condor. "But this is even better."

Tina pulled at the wispy strands on the arm of the worn chair. The only light in the room was from the single low lamp; shadows of their smallest gestures fled upward, as if they were in a cave. "Better?" she said.

"This is a real cause, real Robin Hood stuff." Gage circled behind her and picked the canteen off the kitchen counter.

"Don't try and bait me, Gage. No one in this is playing."

"No one?"

Tina said nothing, her head bowed. The minister's voice caught Gage by surprise. "There was a man who came through here last month. The police had taken his son and beaten him."

163

The thin man drifted to the center of the room, reached out and touched Tina's shoulder. "They took the boy to the square and poked his eyes out with a machete. Anyone who tried to help they shot on the spot." He gazed steadily at Gage, his voice gently threading the darkness. "They killed the boy and hung him upside down from a tree, cut off his testicles and stuffed them in his mouth. For three days the army guarded the body. Anyone who tried to retrieve it for burial they shot. The father finally had to leave his son unburied. A priest found him on the road, drove him to one of the refugee camps."

Gage took a swig from the canteen. The water was still warm from its trip through the desert and tasted like metal.

"Do you know how many people have been killed, Gage?" Tina said. "Do you have any idea?"

He screwed the top back on the canteen. "People die everywhere," he said. "That priest who died in the desert two weeks ago, what was that? Thirty miles from here?" He came back into the living room and leaned forward to examine the Dylan photo up close, squinting like an art critic. "You ever meet him, Tina?"

"Don't play cop with me, you bastard. You don't know shit about this." The minister stiffened at Tina's language.

"More than you think," Gage said.

"Like what?"

"Like what the cops found in the trunk of Father Ortiz's car."

"What was that?"

"An old newspaper."

"How old?"

"Real old. The lead story was about Peter's death. What wasn't old was that someone had taken a ballpoint pen and scratched out Peter's face."

The minister stood behind Tina, closing ranks, both hands resting gently on her shoulders. Now that he was closer to the light, Gage could see how sunburned his face was. He had the hollow, haunted look a couple days in the desert will give anyone.

"But why?" Tina said.

"I don't know."

She pushed out of her chair, out of the minister's comforting grasp. "I knew Father Ortiz. We both did."

"Tina, good God . . ." the minister said.

"He has a right," she said. She walked to the curtains, parted them and looked out on the dark lawn. "Father Ortiz helped us. From the beginning. As much as he could. His bishop didn't know. No one ever really knew . . ."

"And would someone kill Ortiz for that?"

"I don't know." She let the curtains close again, ran her tongue across parched lips. "The reason I was at the cathedral that day was that we were afraid."

"Afraid of what?"

"If the police figured out that Father Ortiz was part of the sanctuary movement and started coming after people . . . well, you can imagine the nightmare that would turn into."

"And had they? figured it out?"

"Not that I know."

"All they found was an old newspaper. With Peter's picture scratched out," Gage said. The minister's long face furrowed with concern. "This probably doesn't make any sense to you, does it, preacher? I'll let Tina tell you. It's quite a story." He roamed the room. "You would have liked my kid. He believed in causes too. A big sweet kid, not a mean bone in his body. He was in Guatemala in '68, teaching Indian kids to read before anybody gave a damn."

"And then . . ." The minister was tentative. "He died."

"No. He didn't die. He's alive." No one moved, no one said anything. "I know. Everyone thought . . . I did too. Sounds nuts, doesn't it? But I've got proof. And if you don't think that's crazy enough, listen to this. Father Ortiz knew him, I'm sure of it. If Ortiz was helping refugees, he would have helped Peter. If I'm right, if Peter's alive, he's been running and hiding for seventeen years."

"And what do you want from us?" Tina's voice was flat with resistance.

"I want you to help me find him. Help me bring him back."

"We don't know anything."

"What about you, preach?" The minister said nothing, his big brown eyes soft and sad as a horse's. "Okay, maybe it doesn't sound like much. I mean it's not thousands of people fleeing death squads, it's just one white boy . . ." He pointed back toward the bedrooms. "You believed her story, why won't you believe mine? I'm telling you the truth, dammit!"

There was the unmistakable sound of a chair scraping the floor in the dark kitchen. For a second they all froze at the ghostly sound. Tina recovered first, snapping on the wall switch, flooding both rooms with light.

A blond child, maybe eight years old, lay under the kitchen table, perfectly still, eyes wide open, peering out through the welter of wooden legs like a small caged animal.

"What are you doing up?" Tina demanded.

"I was thirsty, Mommy."

All three adults were on their feet. There was no way of knowing how long she'd been hidden under there or how much she'd heard.

Tina crouched and offered a hand. "Come on, let's get out of there." The girl did not move at first, still half asleep, staring out at them from some other world. "You can't stay under there all night. Let's go." Tina's voice got sharper.

She gently extricated her daughter from the stockade of table legs, moving chairs out of the way, and pulled her to her feet. The girl grimaced in the light, bewildered and soft as a sleep-walker, clinging to her mother.

"I missed you, Mommy," she said. The minister stared down at his night watchman's shoes.

"I missed you too, pumpkin." Tina rubbed the girl's back through her pajamas. The girl was a beauty, with slightly punked-out hair and the kind of clean all-American features

166

found only in soap commercials. "But it's the middle of the night. And you have school tomorrow. Go back to bed. You can get a glass of water in the bathroom." Tina gave her a push, but she didn't go. She stared at Gage.

"You shouldn't shout at my mother."

"No, I shouldn't," he said. "Your mother's terrific. That's just the way grown-ups talk sometimes. It doesn't mean anything." He slapped the minister lightly on the back and moved toward the door. "Don't mind me. Go on, get some sleep. You all deserve it."

Thirteen

GAGE COULD ALWAYS COUNT on Huerta having a new story. The two men strolled side by side, beers in hand, inspecting the wall. The workers behind them wedged and chinked rock into rock. A couple of the younger guys, skinny as bantamweights, shuffled up the plank ramp with forty-pound boulders.

"Last week this woman she came to me," Huerta said. "You probably know her. Her husband used to be a big-time stockbroker back East. He loves to canoe, right? Goes out to Lake Cochiti every week. But his canoe takes on a little water. So this Sunday he's wearing a new pair of socks and he doesn't want to get them wet. So he takes off his shoes and socks and he leaves them by his car."

Gage took a sip of his beer and glanced back. A big-bellied

168

Mexican in a Pittsburgh Pirate hat dressed out a slab of rock with a sledge. The air rang with the blows. The sun was low in the sky, filtering through the cottonwoods on the far side of the road, sending long shadows across the fields.

"He goes for his canoe ride and when he comes back, his shoes are there, but he can't find his socks. So he looks over and he sees this group of Mexicans standing by some old Chevy. And one of the guys has on sandals and a pair of socks that look real familiar. He goes over and asks, 'Excuse me, are those your socks?' Of course they don't speak no English and they go into a little conference. The stockbroker starts to get a little hot, he points to his own bare feet and then to the guy's socks, he starts to get a little loud. 'Those are *my* socks!' The Mexicans go into conference again. Finally the guy takes off the socks and hands them over. Stockbroker goes home, gets out of his car, looks in the backseat, what does he see? A pair of black socks." Huerta hooted and took a swig of beer. "Good one, huh?"

Gage laughed, running his hand along the rough surface of the stone wall. "And why does the wife call you?"

"She was embarrassed. She wants me to find the guy whose socks they were and give them back. Can you believe that?"

"So did you do it?"

"You kidding? What am I, a miracle worker? I like that one, though. This Mexican comes to America and the first thing that happens is he gets mugged by a stockbroker!"

Huerta finished off his beer, crushed the can and looked back toward the workers. "Yo! Severino!" The hefty man stopped his hammering. "Enough for one day. Go pass out the beer, man."

The big-bellied worker pushed the sledge aside, took off his hat and wiped his forehead with his elbow. Gage had brought beer for everyone: a pair of six-packs sat on the hood of one of Huerta's two trucks. Severino retrieved one six-pack and raised it for his fellow workers to see, as if it were a prize stringer of fish.

"I want to ask you a question," Gage said.

"Shoot."

"You ever heard about this sanctuary movement?"

"You mean those church people who play cops and robbers with the border patrol?" Huerta said. "No, I don't get involved with politics. A man wants to work, I'll find him work. You got a job, I'll find somebody to do it. No reason to cut God in on the deal."

Severino distributed the beers to the other workers. Some glanced at Gage and Huerta to make sure it was all right, but one after the other they all took off their stiff, crusted working gloves and jammed them into back pockets.

"But what about you? You still bring people across?" Gage asked.

Huerta sucked on his teeth. "Who told you that I brought people across?"

"Nobody *told* me, Simon."

"Well, you got it wrong. I never did that."

"Never?"

"Why would I want to get myself mixed up with that? Run all the way down there. You can get yourself into big trouble, man." Sunlight glared off the cracked windshield of Huerta's truck. The second truck, its bed bristling with tools, straddled the ditch. "Why you want to know about that stuff, anyway? You making a movie?"

"Maybe. Yeah."

"Bad idea, man. Who's gonna look at that stuff?"

The workers sat against the wall drinking beer. In the low light the brown faces and the dusty clothes seemed to fuse with the rusts and burned orange of the rock. All his life Gage had witnessed scenes like this, crews of wetbacks, barely visible men, squatting by the side of the road with their hoes or riding in the back of trucks with their picking baskets. Now he scrutinized the faces as he would have studied the faces in a police lineup.

"I take care of my people," Huerta said. "I give 'em houses. I feed 'em."

170

Gage said nothing. He had seen the houses, the four adobe huts, not fit for chickens, lined up behind Huerta's house.

"I might have another job for you," Gage said finally.

"What's that?" Huerta was giving him the cold shoulder, offended. He waved in the direction of the workers. "Hey, Matín!"

The smallest of the five workers stood up, pointing to himself to make sure. He was scarcely five feet tall with prominent Indian features. Gage thought he seemed familiar.

"*Sí,*" Huerta shouted. *"Tráeme mis cigarros, por favor. Están en el piso de mi troca."*

Matín smiled easily and ran off toward the pickup with the cracked windshield. Huerta watched him, stony-faced for a second, before speaking again.

"What job is that?"

"I need you to find somebody for me."

"Oh, yeah? You need a good yard man, there's this kid I've been working with on the other crew, he's real good, a Navajo boy, right off the rez, he won't cost you much."

"No. I need you to find me a gringo."

"A gringo?" Huerta's face fell in disbelief. "You crazy?"

"Not just any gringo," Gage said. "I think some of your people might know him. Or if they don't, their friends might."

"I don't think so," Huerta said. "They don't know many gringos, these boys."

The door to Huerta's pickup was open and Gage could see the worker crouched on the seat, searching for the pack of cigarettes. He seemed to be having trouble, flipping the visors, looking in the glove compartment.

"This one they might," Gage said. "He spent some time in Guatemala, he speaks whatever it is they speak."

Huerta seemed to relax a little for the first time. "And he's mixed up with these church people."

"It could be."

"And you want me to be your private eye?" Now Huerta was amused. He looked back and saw Matín still kneeling on the

171

front seat of the truck. *"Matín! Están en el asiento. Usa los ojos! Están abajo de tu nariz!"*

Gage bent low and retrieved a bull-point from the brittle grass. "Just see what you can scare up," he said. "The guy I'm looking for, he's got a big knot on his collarbone, right here."

"That's all you're going to tell me?"

Sunlight glanced off the cracked windshield of Huerta's truck, bathed the faces of the workers who rested against the wall of fissured rock. The light at this hour made everything seem so close at hand. A juniper on the hillside a mile away looked near enough to reach out and touch.

"He's thirty-six, thirty-seven. Big guy. Dark, wavy hair."

Huerta picked at a discolored nail. "And what's his name?"

"I don't know."

"You don't know?" One of the workers pushed to his feet and began shoveling the spoil against the base of the wall.

"He uses different names. I've got an old picture." He took Peter's high school graduation photo out of his shirt pocket and handed it to Huerta. "Add twenty years to that."

Gage turned away as Huerta scrutinized the picture. Matín had found something. He still knelt on the seat of Huerta's truck, but he was motionless now, his head slightly bowed, like a man at prayer. Or hiding something. It was very hard to see. The sun was directly in Gage's eyes and it flashed off the cracked windshield of Huerta's pickup, flared around the hunched, dark figure. Gage smiled. The little bastard was stealing something.

Huerta turned the picture over as if expecting an inscription. "And I thought the woman with the socks was crazy."

"If you can find this guy, I'll double what I'm paying you for the wall." Gage glanced back over his shoulder. Whatever it was that Matín had been inspecting he shoved under the seat of the pickup.

"What's this guy to you?" Huerta said.

"You can guess."

"I already have. But it's pretty hard to believe."

172

"You don't tell anybody about this."

"No. I've learned my lesson. I don't tell anybody anything, not anymore." Huerta looked across at Gage, his face softer, more filled with sadness than Gage had ever seen it. "Things can get pretty screwed up, can't they?"

Matín walked toward them, the package of cigarettes in his left hand. Huerta raised his eyes.

"What are you looking at?" he said. "Can't you see we're talking business?" Matín stood his ground, offering the crushed pack of Camels. His face was masklike and grave. *"Gracias. Cambié de mente, no los necesito. Te los regalo, vete."* He waved Matín off, then turned to Gage. "I shouldn't be smoking anyway. The doctor, he told me, no more, those damn things will kill you."

Gage hadn't taken his eyes off the retreating Matín. It came to Gage suddenly where he had seen the diminutive man before. It had been at the Santuario. Matín had been kneeling at the *pozito*, putting sacred dirt on his son's tongue.

Huerta smiled, cupping Peter's picture in his hand.

"What are you smiling at?" Gage said.

"I don't know. It just reminded me of a story, something. There was an old guy, he lived in Ojo Caliente, Coyote, I forget which, but he went up to Utah to pick potatoes. He was making good money, so he stayed a couple of years. Finally he comes back. He walks into the village, it's the dead of night. He knocks on the door." Huerta slipped Peter's picture into his shirt pocket. He was telling the story with relish, as if a great weight had been lifted.

"His wife, she's scared, she gets a candle and a shovel. She opens the door just a crack. Her husband, he's standing there holding a cheap little brooch with a mirror in it that he's brought her as a present, but it's so dark, with just the one candle. She peers out and sees her reflection in the mirror. 'Ahh-h-h,' she says, 'so that's the whore you've been living with in Salt Lake City!'"

173

Fourteen

HUERTA'S WIFE called at six in the morning to say that her husband had been killed, stabbed to death along the Santa Fe River sometime during the night. Her voice sounded miles away, a spider thread tugging him steadily out of his world of dreams. She was fine, she insisted, she didn't need help, her family was all there with her. She just wanted to call and explain why the work crew wouldn't be there at eight. She would have someone take care of it as soon as possible, she knew Simon would have wanted it that way.

Amy propped herself up in bed, trying to figure out who he was talking to. After he'd hung up he gazed at Amy's questioning face for a moment before speaking. "Simon Huerta's been killed," he said. "I'm going in to see if I can help."

It was too early for there to be traffic. He drove seventy-five

174

miles an hour all the way, passing an empty school bus and a couple of semis on the long hill up to the Santa Fe Opera. He snapped on the radio, hoping for news, but all he could find was farm reports and a bouncy Rosemary Clooney singing, "When the Red, Red Robin Comes Bob, Bob, Bobbin' Along." The first rays of morning sun lit the peaks of the Jemez Mountains twenty miles to the west.

He had no plan. All he had was the one dumb thought that his son was poison, one look at a picture and you were dead, this was the second time it had happened.

Huerta's wife had said that he'd been killed on the river, but the river ran the length of the town. Gage drove west along Alameda for a mile and when he found nothing he doubled back. He was a half block from Palace Street before he found what he was looking for: the police cars, the people out in bathrobes and shiny exercise outfits standing on the curb, talking and pointing.

Gage pulled over. The action was all on the far side of the river. Three more police cars angled in among the cottonwoods, a cop with a metal detector combed the ground, a couple of others stood guard at either end of a dirt path, waving off dog walkers and early-morning joggers.

Gage ambled across the wooden bridge like a man for whom the rules did not apply. He zipped up his jacket; it was still cold.

A beer can tumbled slowly in the rushing stream. A pair of detectives sat in one of the police cars drinking coffee while a bearded reporter in tennis shoes waited patiently for an interview. Gage remembered the snapshot of Peter he'd given Huerta. If Huerta had still had it on him when he'd been killed, it didn't seem like the kind of thing a cop was going to miss.

Gage smiled at the big-bellied policeman standing at the north end of the footpath. "Hey, LeRoy," he said.

The cop turned, surprise prying his lips open like a big-mouthed bass. "Hey, Gage, what you doing here?"

"I was just driving by." LeRoy was in Gage's gun club, a deer

175

hunter, geniality run amok, the kind of policeman you'd send out to talk at elementary schools. "What the hell happened?"

"A guy got stabbed." The cop with the metal detector circled one of the big cottonwoods with the care of a man edging his lawn.

"That's what I heard." Gage glanced up the hillside. A couple of cops he hadn't noticed before were knocking on doors, exploring the maze of driveways. This was the backside of Canyon Road, the side no one bothered to look at, a tangle of garages, half-constructed additions, adobe huts without plumbing or electricity where gallery owners' gardeners and maids lived.

"Huerta," Gage said. Again he saw the surprise in LeRoy's eyes. "He was building a wall for me."

"I guess you're going to have to find somebody else to finish it for you." LeRoy hitched up his trousers. "I've been meaning to ask you, Gage. You know we've got this little hunting club, great bunch of guys. We're looking to lease and I know when we talked about it a year ago . . ."

"I'll tell you, LeRoy, I think that would be fine. I think I'd like to do that."

LeRoy was astonished. "Really?"

"Long as you don't cut up my pastures with those three-wheelers."

"Gage, we'll take real good care of the place, I promise you. I can't tell you how much I appreciate this. . . ."

One of the detectives opened the police car door and stood up, saying something to the bearded reporter. It was Captain Trevino—Gage had not seen him since that morning at the police station.

"They have any idea who did this?"

"Not yet. We got a call at three in the morning. Neighbors heard a scream, saw somebody running. Huerta and whoever it was had been drinking and arguing for a couple of hours. Same old story."

Trevino had seen Gage, but he seemed more interested in

176

answering the reporter's questions. The reporter bent over the hood of the police car, scribbling madly on a pad.

A woman in gray sweatpants and a horned-toad T-shirt jogged out of the woods. LeRoy raised both hands in warning. "Sorry, lady, you're going to have to go around."

The woman stiffened, about to take offense, but then she saw the other cops and the cars. Gage watched the fear come into her eyes. LeRoy gave her a reassuring smile. She walked off, hands on her hips, trying to get her breath back.

Gage patted LeRoy on his ample shoulder. "Okay, LeRoy, I'll get out of your way."

"Now, Gage, how about if I bring a copy of the hunting lease by sometime, what do you say?"

"Anytime, LeRoy."

Gage wandered up the hillside, between two police cars, daring Trevino to say something. Trevino stared at him, but went on talking to the bearded, burly reporter. Gage glanced in the window of the second car. The Ziploc bags of evidence sat on the front seat, all clearly labeled. There was a bloody sock, a pair of broken sunglasses, and a long, hand-flaked stone knife, milky white with blood-red flecks.

He didn't bother to call Amy, just took off, following the highway north. He felt dizzy, as if he were being turned in tighter and tighter circles, carried inward like a needle on a warped record, skittering from groove to groove: Peter's picture, scratched out with a ballpoint pen; a stone knife on a bundle of bobcat pelts; Peter's picture, slipped into Huerta's pocket; a stone knife in a Ziploc bag; a Guatemalan kneeling on the seat of a pickup as light flared through a web of cracked glass. Gage knew he was almost to the center of it; he dreaded what he would find there.

He was so intent on where he was headed he'd already made the turn off the highway before he saw it, big as a barn door: the twenty-year-old orange Volkswagen van with the mural of blue lagoons and palm trees painted on the side—Maui's van. It was parked with three or four other cars in front of the Float Shack, a tiny, cedar-shingled restaurant perched above the river.

He squealed to a stop, made a big U-turn and came back. He parked next to the van and just sat for a moment, considering his options. He had a pistol under the seat. He decided against it.

He got out of the car. A hand-painted sign on the roof of the restaurant read: RIO GRANDE ZOO: FREE.

A bell tinkled as he opened the door. A gaunt waitress with a long hazel braid looked up, coffeepot in one hand. Maui's back was to Gage. He had cleaned up his act. He wore sandals, bib overalls, and his hair was pulled back in a short ponytail. He had laid out his cigar boxes of agates and geodes on several rickety tables and was explaining their origins to a pair of thick-thighed cyclists, and a gaunt, white-bearded cook with bad teeth.

The waitress gestured toward a possible table, but Gage paid her no mind. Maui was getting animated. He still had not looked up.

Gage came up from behind, smiling mildly at the blond woman cyclist and nodding to her curly-headed boyfriend. With one quick move he twisted Maui's arm behind his back. Maui let out a short cry before Gage slammed him forward into the wall. Tables overturned, polished rocks rolled across the floor, spun and wobbled like tops.

"What the fuck, man?" Maui shouted, face pressed to the wall, eyes rolling back, trying to see who it was. Gage yanked Maui's arm up another couple of notches, felt him rise up on his tiptoes.

"Hey, mister, leave the guy alone!" The curly-headed cyclist put a firm hand on Gage's shoulder. Gage swatted the hand away and the guy didn't try again.

Maui did a little dance like a boy trying not to pee, but Gage had him locked up tight, thumb and wrist bent as far as they would go.

"Don't even try to screw with me or you'll find yourself in a world of hurt," Gage said. He had his nose right in the middle of

178

Maui's back and the guy still smelled of bear urine. Out of the corner of his eye Gage saw the cook slip out the door.

"Just get the hell off me!" Maui bellowed. "You crazy, man?"

"What do you want to do? Call the cops? Call 'em. You're the one guy they'd really like to talk to right now."

Maui got very still all of a sudden; like an animal in a catch pen, only his eyes moved. "What do you want?"

"I want to talk."

"Well, I can't talk like this."

Gage stepped back, letting Maui go. Maui turned, gave Gage a quick dirty look, but there was no real fight in him. He checked the scrape along the side of his face for blood, then shook out his arm to get the feeling back.

Gage tried to hide how winded he was; he felt too old for this. He scanned the room with quick eyes, knowing the whole place was against him. The waitress huddled in a far corner dialing the phone. The curly-headed cyclist had pulled the fire extinguisher off the wall and looked as if he intended to throw it.

"Forget it, Sally, it's no big deal," Maui said, "I know the guy." The waitress hung up the phone reluctantly. "It's not a problem, okay? I'm going to take care of it."

Maui, still pouting, set one of the overturned tables back on its feet and knelt down to retrieve his scattered agates and geodes. The blond cyclist came over to help. Gage picked up a broken chair and propped it against the wall. The waitress still had one hand on the phone.

"Didn't you hear what I said, Sally? Don't worry, I'll take care of everything." Maui puffed up his cheeks and sighed, then went back to putting rocks in cigar boxes.

Gage stared out the window, waiting. Down below was a half acre of wire fences and cages, the only animals visible some sheep, an emu and a flea-bitten llama. It was a sorry excuse for a zoo.

Maui set two of the heavy-laden cigar boxes on the table. "Sally, listen, I'll get this all cleaned up when I come back." He ran a finger gingerly over the raw scrape above his cheekbone. "I just need to talk to this guy, okay? We're cool, right?"

Maui and Gage went outside. The cook rummaged through the trunk of his car and froze when he saw the two of them. The bastard was looking for his gun, Gage thought.

"We can walk down here," Maui said. "No one will bother us."

The two men shuffled down the steep bank, down into the hog-wire labyrinth of fenced-in lanes and enclosures. The caged animals rose up, expecting to be fed.

"Guess you know why I'm here," Gage said.

"No."

Gage glanced at the long, vacant face. Maui wasn't smart enough to even think of bluffing. "You ever heard of Simon Huerta?"

"Nope."

As they moved up one of the narrow lanes between pens, the imprisoned animals pressed to the wire, moving with them, the long-necked emu undulating on one side, the black-snouted llama skittering on the other.

"Well, you probably will," Gage said.

"Why is that?"

The llama banged impatiently against the wire. Most of the hutches and pens were empty. "Somebody stabbed him to death last night. Down in Santa Fe."

"So what does that have to do with me?" The archaic head of the emu floated above the wire.

"He was killed with this big stone knife. Handmade. Milky white. Little red flecks. Only one guy I know makes knives like that."

"Come on."

"It's true, Maui." The emu snaked its slender head through the wire, trying to get a peck at them. Gage raised a threatening hand and the bird backed off. "We're not talking about a two-hundred-dollar fine for poaching, Maui, this is really heavy duty. You make a lot of knives like that?"

180

Maui scrunched up his face. Panic was taking hold. "No, just a couple." The ram chased the two skittish ewes in mad circles in the outer lane. Beyond the dismal flats were thickets of salt cedar and willow, a few big cottonwoods.

"You sell 'em to somebody or you just give 'em away?"

Maui stepped around some rotting feed sacks and accidentally kicked over a stack of plastic insecticide buckets. "I don't remember."

"I think you'd remember, Maui, those knives took a lot of work."

"I sell things to all kinds of people, man." He yanked open the flimsy wooden door to the outer lane and ducked in. Gage followed.

"Well, I'd try to remember if I were you."

"Did you tell 'em, man? Did you tell those cops?" The ewes stood on alert as the ram approached the two men warily.

"I haven't told anybody anything. And if you can tell me where you got rid of that knife, maybe we can just leave your name out of it altogether."

"There's a guy, a farmer named Walter," Maui said. "I gave him the only other knife I made like that. About a year ago." The ram trailed behind them. "But he wouldn't do something like this. He's the nicest guy in the world."

"And where do I find him?"

Maui saw the ram lower his head just in time. He turned and caught the horns in both hands before the animal had a chance to butt. The ram bucked two or three times, trying to get free, but Maui held on and finally tossed the animal back. The ram scrambled to its feet, stared at them for a second, thought better of it and ran off to join the ewes. Maui watched the animals thunder off.

"Where do I find him?" Gage repeated.

Maui turned to Gage, pleading. "He couldn't have done this, man!"

"I don't care."

"You go down the highway about a mile and a half and just before you get to the Exxon station there's a dirt road going off to your right. You take that across the river, they've got a wooden bridge, and it's right there."

"And how will I know it's him?"

"He's the only guy who lives back there, him and his old lady and kids." Maui rubbed his hands together, trying to get rid of the slick feel of lanolin he'd picked up from the ram's wool. "Big, tall guy."

Fifteen

THE LOOSE PLANKS of the wooden bridge volleyed like pistol shots and then Gage's pickup bounced down into the dust of the dirt road. He wound through the big river cotton-woods into a small apple orchard. Beyond the orchard, set up against the mesa, was a series of adobe and stone buildings and corrals and a windmill. When he came to the rise in the road, he could see, just beyond the main house, a dark-haired woman loading apple crates into the back of a truck. Two blond children played in the road, riding plastic motorcycles. The woman stopped loading crates and looked up.

Gage turned off the ignition. A light film of dust coated the windshield. He stared down at the children coasting their motor-cycles through a shallow puddle, knees pressed to their chests.

He got out of the car and began walking toward the house.

Hollyhocks leaned against the adobe wall and there were rose-bushes.

The woman shielded her eyes. "Can I help you?"

Gage just kept walking toward the main house. A mare and a colt raised their heads in one of the corrals. Gage thought he saw a curtain move in one of the front windows.

"Can I help you?" The woman's voice became more strident. "What do you think you're doing?" She moved quickly toward him.

Just outside the front door was a cardboard box of mewling, blind kittens, tumbling over one another. Gage gazed down at them, considering.

"Don't go in there!" The woman began to run. The children stood stock-still, straddling their plastic motorcycles.

Gage threw open the door. A middle-aged farmer held a twelve-gauge shotgun leveled at Gage's chest. He was a big man who had to stoop a bit in the dark, low-ceilinged hallway. The muscles worked in his jaw like he meant business. He wore a faded jean jacket over a pea-green T-shirt, oil-stained khaki pants, and black irrigation boots. A leather thong around his forehead held back shoulder-length hair that was dark, but flecked with silver.

Neither of them had taken a breath. The only sound was the mewling of the cats. Gage stared at the callused hands holding the shotgun. The forefinger on the man's left hand was a stub.

One of the children cried out on the road. The farmer lifted the barrel of the shotgun, pursing his lips in irritation, bent slightly to gaze out one of the low windows. He ran a hand through his hair. His face softened at whatever it was he saw and became suddenly perplexed and gentle. For the first time Gage realized that it was Peter.

Gage was not prepared for this moment. The dark hallway was filled with long shelves of canned fruit, children's lunchboxes, some flashlights and pruning shears. Open sacks of animal food sat on the floor next to an array of muddy boots and an oversized

184

red plastic bat. The adobe walls kept everything tomblike and chill. Gage still had not moved, as if the slightest gesture might scare Peter off, spook him like some skittish animal.

Peter stared at the floor, then took a deep breath and lay the shotgun carefully on one of the high shelves. He had put on a good twenty pounds since Gage had seen him last, but he carried it easily; he was a formidable-looking man.

"Peter?" Gage's voice caught, came out so softly he wasn't sure his son had heard him. But he had. He looked up, his face frantic, the plea written all over it: why the hell did you have to do this?

They were rescued by the shadow in the doorway. "Walt? Are you all right?" Gage turned and saw the woman just outside, the two children clinging to her legs.

"Sandy. Come here. Come meet my father."

The woman stared at Peter, as if waiting for the punch line, then realized one wasn't coming. She stroked her children's hair and then looked up at Gage, smiling bravely. She wore Reminiscence overalls and scuffed leather boots and had a nosering in one nostril. She was small and quick, with sharp features and generous brown eyes. She made a nice recovery. She extended her hand. "Good to meet you." She turned to the children. "And this is Shelby and Jason. Come say hi. There's nothing to be afraid of." She put a hand on each of their backs, ushering them forward. "This is your grandfather."

The children didn't buy it for a minute. The boy kept a cool and skeptical distance. The little girl finally came forward a couple more steps. She wore double-strapped high-top tennis shoes.

"I like your shoes," Gage said. "I have a little girl with shoes just like that." She looked up at her mother and father to see what she should say.

Peter picked up his little boy whose green wool hat with earflaps was down around his eyebrows. "You know who this is, Jason?" Peter said. "Your daddy's daddy. What do you think about that?" Jason just looked bewildered. Peter reached under his son's chin and began to tickle him. "When I was your age, he used to play with me, just like this." The boy began to laugh, wonderful laughter, and it made his father smile. Gage hadn't seen a smile come that easily to Peter for years—not since Peter was, what, twelve, thirteen, before Gage and Nina started the real battling, before Peter knew what the real world was.

Gage stared sadly beyond them, into the living room with the big stone fireplace, kerosene lamps with smoky chimneys on the mantel, a magenta Indian print covering the wall. There was almost nothing in the room: one big chair and some overstuffed pillows, a couple of blue plastic milk cartons filled with Superheroes. How could they possibly live like this, Gage thought.

The little boy rocked back and forth in his father's arms, trying to duck out of the way of more tickling. "So say hello, then," Peter said.

"Hello." Jason kept his chin down, protecting his weak spots, green hat totally cockeyed.

"We have kittens."

Gage turned. The little girl held up a black and tan kitten for inspection. Gage took the animal carefully from her. It squirmed in his hand, warm and delicate, the tiny claws pinpricking Gage's fingers.

"We had four, but one died because it couldn't go pee-pee," she said.

"I'll take the kids out," Sandy said.

"No, we'll go for a walk," Peter said. He set his son down and straightened out the green hat. "It will be easier that way."

They walked side by side through the orchard, stepping across gurgling irrigation ditches, ducking gnarled apple tree branches. Neither spoke. Peter picked up a fallen limb and tossed it across a barbed wire fence.

"This is not an accident," Peter said. "Your finding me."

"No," Gage agreed. He felt as if he were holding a sword

186

above his son's head and Peter didn't even know. "You can make a living? With this?"

"You mean from the orchard? No. Sandy substitutes at the Dixon school. I do construction when I can get it."

Peter did not meet his father's gaze. They were still shy with one another. Gage scanned the horizon. On the mesa above the house were silver-tip poplars and a stand of aspen, golden in the autumn light.

"You been here a long time?"

"About ten years." Peter held back a low-hanging branch to let his father pass. Wind swirled yellow leaves through the aisle of trees. "So how did you find me?"

Gage pretended he hadn't heard the question. "All this time we were just thirty miles apart."

"Yeah. I guess it was four or five years ago that I saw your picture in some local paper. Until then I hadn't realized that you'd moved out here."

Gage stepped carefully across rotting apples. "It never occurred to you to—"

"Oh, it occurred to me," Peter said. They had come out of the orchard and moved down across a meadow that sloped gently toward the river. "You want to know the truth?"

"Yes," Gage said.

"I did come by once. Almost three years ago. Did it on my own, I never told Sandy what I was up to. I asked around and found out where your place was. I parked across from that big stone wall. Just sat in my truck. There was somebody working in the backyard. I thought at first it must be you. I could hear the snipping of shears, see the branches waving over the top of the wall. Then the gate opens and there's a Mexican worker with a trash can full of dead branches. He was as surprised to see me as I was to see him. I just took off."

"Why?" Gage said. He could see the swirling water through the trees. The river was still running high from the storm three days before.

187

"I'm supposed to be dead, remember?"

"Yeah. I remember all right. I buried you once." Gage hesitated, sidestepping the spears of a huge yucca, then went on. "On that little piece of land up the coast where we were going to build a cabin. It was a windy damn day, I'd never seen breakers like that. The minister read some Dylan Thomas poems. You'd been on this Dylan Thomas kick, remember? Unita cried her eyes out. I think it broke her heart."

Peter's glance was fierce; they both knew Gage had meant it to hurt, but Peter didn't yield. "And you? What did it do to you?"

Gage didn't answer. He snapped off a brittle milkweed pod, popped it open and let the fuzz drift away in the wind.

"You said you did construction?" Gage said.

"Sometimes."

"You ever heard of a guy named Simon Huerta?"

Peter looked as if he'd just been hit by the flu. "I'm not sure. Why?"

"No reason," Gage said. Peter was lying. It was written all over him. As they moved down into the mammoth cottonwoods a jay cried out in alarm. Gage stared at the brown water, swirling senselessly past; whatever hopes he'd had were disappearing beneath the brown water.

When they came to a fence Peter held the strands of barbed wire apart so his father could duck under.

"All the trees down at the far end we planted," Peter said. "We should be getting fruit from them next year. We built the main house ourselves. Nobody'd worked the place for years when we got here, it was a real mess."

"You must get floods."

"Yeah. The first year we woke up one morning and all the fences were three miles downstream. It was a joke. We made about every mistake you could make. One year we set the disk too deep and plowed under a whole field of alfalfa." He held up his left hand with its stump of a forefinger. "Lost this to a chainsaw."

188

"Do you know he's dead, then?"

"Who?"

"Huerta."

Peter's eyes were unreadable as stones. He pulled at his nose and said nothing.

"Don't lie to me, Peter. It took me a long time to get this far. Don't lie. You know a guy named Maui?"

Peter walked to the water's edge. "You mean the guy who lives back of Truchas? Sure. He helped me build this bridge a couple of years ago."

"And he gave you a stone knife."

Something slithered through the reeds and plopped into the water. Peter looked bitterly back at his father. "And what if he did?"

"Huerta was stabbed to death with that knife."

"So that's what you're here for? You think I killed somebody in a drunken knife fight?"

"Peter, I don't know what you did."

Peter laughed. A pair of wood ducks whirred up from the river, wings beating along the water, then rose and circled above the trees, crying out.

"This is perfect!" Peter said. "We pick up right where we left off. This just proves your point, doesn't it?"

"What point?"

"Twenty years ago. In Guatemala. Remember? We stayed up half the night arguing. You were trying to convince me that a man was a killer before he was anything else. And I refused to believe you. But I believe you now. I'm the living proof of it, right?"

"You didn't kill him, did you?"

"You believe what you want to believe."

"You know what I want to believe."

"No, I don't. Everyone's a killer, except your son, is that it?"

"Maybe."

"You want your son to be spared?"

"Yes."

"Well, he hasn't been." The current eddied around a rusted-out car buried nose-down in the river, sand up to its back windows.

"Did you ever miss me, Peter?"

"No." Peter stared across the water at the muskrat dens pocketing the far bank. "How could I miss you? I've been arguing with you every damn day. It's like a knot that I try to untie, but I can't. I try to run away, but I can't. Remember that old trick you used to do? Pretend that you could swallow a spoon? And I'd invite all of my friends over so they could see it and we never could figure it out. I do that trick for my kids now."

"You wanted to know if my finding you was accidental. No, it wasn't. A priest was killed. Three weeks ago. Father Ortiz. Did you hear about that?"

Peter's eyes widened. "Yes."

"Well, the cops found an old newspaper in the trunk of his car. With your picture in it."

The chalky white bones of a calf lay scattered in the grass. A few ribs had been carted off by coyotes and the rest had been gently floated apart on the matted reeds by the passage of time. Peter turned the skull over with his foot.

"Except someone had scratched it out," Peter said.

"Yes."

Peter bent over to examine the calf's skull. "I did that."

"You did?"

Peter turned the bleached-white skull over in his hands. The nose of the skull was badly fractured and he tossed it away. "He was a friend of mine."

"And you *gave* him the paper?" Gage asked. Peter was silent, his face red and flushed. Suddenly he was a boy again, being chastised by his father. "Now what person in their right mind . . ."

Peter stepped out onto one of the river boulders. He squatted down and let the water rush against his open palms, then wiped his hands on his jeans. "Maybe you made a big mistake coming here," he said. "Maybe you should go now."

Gage didn't answer at first. There were great clots of debris and driftwood matted halfway up some of the trees, left by the old spring floods. It seemed impossible to believe that the water could ever have been that high. It must have cut this place off entirely, he thought, turned it into an island.

"Do you know who killed Ortiz?"

"No," Peter said. He stepped back onto the bank. "So what did the cops think? When they saw the newspaper?"

"They didn't think anything. They didn't know what to make of it. I didn't either. At first."

"But it was enough to lead you here."

"No, not really."

They walked silently along the bank. Just ahead was a set of old concrete pilings and thirty yards beyond that was the bridge. An uprooted tree had floated down and snagged, held by a snarl of roots. It writhed from side to side in the roiling water like some living thing.

"I find myself telling the kids things you told me. Remember the story about the time you worked for the loggers?"

"No," Gage said.

"Really? When you were fourteen and you spent Christmas Eve in the ice wagon, chipping away at the walls with a pick to keep them from freezing. Jason always asks me, 'He didn't get any presents? He didn't have any family?' "

"You're protecting someone, aren't you?" Gage said. "Why can't you tell me the truth? You owe me that much. After what you put me through. . . ."

"Where would I start? When I came out here I would hear the sounds of tires crossing the bridge and I would think, this is it, it's all over. My palms would sweat, I'd actually go hide in one of the sheds until I was sure who it was. And then, after a couple of years, that feeling went away. I never thought I'd be able to lead a normal life. But somehow that happened. And now it's going to end. In a million years I would have never guessed that you'd be the one to end it." The cables beneath the bridge squealed and groaned.

"Peter, I want to help. Any way I can. Whatever happened twenty years ago, that's old history. You've read the papers." Peter gave no sign that he was listening, his eyes darting up and down the river as if he were a driven animal looking for a crossing. "All those old radicals, they're working on Wall Street, writing their memoirs, for God's sake. It's over."

"It's not over," Peter said. The half-submerged tree surged forward on the current and then slid back, creating its own rapids. "Everyone wishes it was over, but it's not over."

"You're going to need a lawyer, Peter."

"I'm not getting a lawyer. Wasn't this the last conversation we had? In the parking lot in Madison? About how I should listen to my lawyer?"

"So what's your alternative?" Gage said. "You want to go on playing Swiss Family Robinson? Wake up. The world has arrived and you're just lucky that I was the first one here."

The huge, dark corpse of a tree rolled in the muddy water, seeking release from the relentless pressure. There was a loud crack somewhere under the bridge.

"Come back with me now," Gage said. "You and Sandy and the kids. We'll have a chance to at least talk this out."

"Where was Huerta killed?"

"In Santa Fe. On the river. Last night about two, three."

"And they don't know who did it?"

"No. Neighbors saw somebody running, but that's all. Come back with me now," Gage said. "There could be cops pouring over that bridge any time."

"No, I can't do that yet." He walked off several paces and ran his hand through a stand of young willow, set it rattling. "We need to talk it over."

"Who needs to talk it over?"

"Sandy and I do."

192

"So I'll wait."

"No, you won't wait. You go back home. We'll call you." He turned away from his father, staring at the squealing metal cables under the bridge. "Listen, I gotta take care of that before it takes the whole bridge out."

At an impasse, neither of them spoke. They had come to another fence. The barbed wire gate was down, lying in the grass. Peter walked through, glanced back up toward the house. They could both hear the distant shouts of the children.

"You want me to close this?" Gage said.

"Sure."

He shook out the snarled wire gate, the slender cedar poles waving like batons, and pulled it toward the massive oak post. There were two loops of shiny smooth wire, top and bottom. Gage thrust the scrawny cedar pole in the lower loop, then tried to lever the top into place. He came two inches short of the upper loop, yanked again, but came no closer. He felt his son's eyes on him.

"Let me help you," Peter said.

"No, hey, I've got it," Gage said.

Peter strode toward him. Gage was not going to be weak in front of his son. He pressed forward with all his might, one hand on the wire loop, the other on the top of the pole. The whole thing was ridiculous, not being able to close a gate. He was getting the shakes in his upper arms. All he needed was another half inch. Lunging for it, Gage lost his hold. The gate sprang back, barbed wire cutting between his thumb and forefinger, raking his clothes.

"Goddamn!" Gage spun around, grabbing at his hand.

"You okay?"

"I'm fine."

"You cut yourself. Let me see."

"I told you, I'm fine. Go on, you close the gate."

"Forget the gate," Peter said.

193

"What do you mean, forget the gate? You said you were a farmer, didn't you? Close the gate!"

For a moment it wasn't clear whether Peter was going to obey or not, but then he did. Gage clutched his wounded hand and watched Peter flip the tangle of cedar fence poles and barbed wire and stretch it out. Peter jabbed the base of the pole in the lower loop and, in one strong move, slipped the upper loop in place. As he came back toward his father he swatted at the chamisa, not meeting his father's eyes, not wanting to make too much of it.

"The gate was a little twisted, that's all," Peter said.

"No, it wasn't twisted," Gage said.

"Come on up to the house, we'll put something on that."

"You forget, Peter. I'm an old man now. Twenty years is a long time. I can't do the things I used to do."

"The gate was twisted, I was trying to tell you. . . ." Peter's voice was shaky, strangely fissured. "Let me see your hand."

Gage held out his hand. It was a good-sized puncture, blood oozing dark red.

"Jesus," Peter said. "You better come up to the house."

"No. You and Sandy have got to talk this over. I'll be fine."

Peter patted the pockets of his jean jacket, then his trousers. Out of a back pocket he pulled a blue bandana.

"Here," Peter said. Gage laid his hand on his son's. Peter's was as hard as a horn, the kind of hand you earn through ten years of physical labor, yet his touch was gentle. You didn't stab someone to death with hands like this, Gage was sure of it. Peter looped the bandana between thumb and forefinger and then once around the wrist.

"That's not too tight?" Peter asked.

"No, it's fine."

Peter did not look up, focusing on his task, but Gage could see the red rims around his eyes as if he were about to cry. Peter tied the knot once and then twice, a knot that would not easily be

194

undone. Peter had his father's blood on his hands now. A kill-deer shrieked from the brush. Gage lifted his hand away.

"You and Sandy talk," Gage said. Peter stared at him dumbly, wiping his palms on his jean jacket. With his good hand Gage felt for the keys to his pickup. "I'll be waiting for your call."

Sixteen

A MILE FROM HOME Gage saw the nimbus of dust rise on the road, coming toward him, and, a second later, saw it was Amy's car. He stopped and let her pull alongside. She rolled down the window, her face tight with worry.

"Is everything all right?" she said. "I had the radio on, they had the police on the news, but they really didn't say much. I was just going to pick up Jody at school."

"I found Peter," he said. She looked away, as if scanning the dashboard. The dust seemed to catch up, swirl and settle around their vehicles. Amy cupped a shielding palm to her face. A soft putting noise grew louder. Gage glanced in his rearview mirror and saw one of the neighboring farmers on his John Deere, crawling up behind.

"What happened to your hand?" Amy said.

196

"You mean this?" Gage lifted his bandaged left hand from the steering wheel. "It was just a little accident." The tractor rumbled erratically behind them. "Let me pull over. I'll go in with you to get Jody."

It took Gage the entire trip in to explain. They sat in the gravel parking lot, waiting for Jody's class to let out. All around them parents sat in cars. It looked like a prairie-dog town, a head popping up now and then, a few brave souls perched on the hoods, chatting amiably. Some of the children were already out, lined up obediently against the mural wall with their teachers. A couple of boys raced in circles around the jungle gym, swinging jackets at one another.

"So what are you going to do?" she said. "Just wait?"

"Isn't that what parents do?" He could see the brightly painted booths for the school carnival in the far playground, pennants snapping in the afternoon breeze.

"And when he does call? What then?" A yellow school bus wheezed into the lot behind them.

"Are you afraid?" Gage said.

"Of course I'm afraid. I don't know what he's done. I don't know if he's killed someone. Maybe he hasn't. But I don't want him in my house. I have a child to protect."

"And I've got two," he said. Jody's class filed out of the school. Gage pushed open the car door and stood up. "Jody!" She looked up. As soon as she spotted him she broke quickly away from the color-splashed wall, too embarrassed by her parents' presence to say good-bye to her friends. She walked head down at first, then broke into a run, her Strawberry Shortcake lunchbox swinging at her side.

Gage stayed in the house, waiting for Peter's call. The phone rang twice. Once it was a termite-inspection service, then it was a birthday invitation for Jody.

He had put himself in a ridiculous position. This was not the time for anyone to be waiting. Sooner or later the police would find their way to Peter, a line of cop cars would roar across that bridge, if they hadn't already.

He stared out the glass door. Amy and Jody played baseball on the lawn, Amy lobbing an oversized plastic ball, Jody flailing her oversized red plastic bat. Jody ran to retrieve the ball. Gage couldn't hear what she was saying, but he could see her gesturing emphatically, first with one hand and then the other, complaining about the pitch.

He had no reason to trust Peter's judgment. Gage had made a stupid mistake in not taking Peter's number up there. Maybe Peter had called while they'd gone to get Jody and then panicked when he didn't get an answer. A million things could have happened.

Amy had promised she'd take Jody to the Dairy Queen on the highway, Jody raced off to the car while Amy put the ball and bat in the bedroom. Gage stood at the bathroom door with his screwdriver, trying to make himself useful, working away at the loose knob and listening to his wife's every move.

Amy came down the hall searching for her car keys. She spoke without looking up. "We should tell Jody something."

"Yes," Gage said.

"I think it would be better if you told her."

"I will."

"Now?"

"Not now. Let's see what happens first."

"I was wrong to react the way I did," Amy said. "I want you to do whatever you think is best. I put sheets and pillowcases out on the bed. There's the rollaway couch on the porch and we could probably use sleeping bags for the kids."

Gage stuck his screwdriver in his back pocket and reached out a hand. "Amy . . ."

"I should go. Jody's waiting in the car, you know how she gets." She juggled her keys, tears welling up. Playing fair was no small virtue, Gage thought, not at a time like this. "But I just wanted to tell you that it was okay, okay?"

After they'd gone he went into the study and looked up the names of lawyers he thought he might be able to use, then pulled down one of the old albums. It was filled with Peter's grade-school art, crayon drawings made when he wasn't much older than Jody. There was one of Custer's Last Stand, the doomed cavalry leader with his sword raised high while soldiers and Indians battled around him, tumbling off horses, blasting away at short range. Gage thumbed through pictures of Peter with his Cub Scout troop, old algebra quizzes, high school box scores where Gage, P., cf., had gone two-for-four with a double and two runs batted in, and funny crumpled notes Peter had left for them on refrigerator doors. How much Nina had loved him. Gage too. Everyone had loved Peter. Other kids, his teachers, they took to him, his gentle smile could win anyone over. What the hell had happened? Something incredibly precious had been lost and it was Gage's fault. Somewhere in the distance the dogs barked.

A soft pounding on the sliding glass doors made him whirl around in his chair. All that registered at first was the blue uniform, the badge, the holstered pistol at the belt: a huge cop grinning at him through the glass and waving a piece of paper.

"Hey, Gage, how you doin'?" LeRoy Tompkins beamed, one huge white palm pressed to the glass.

Gage slammed the scrapbook shut, his heart pounding, then pushed away from the desk. He flicked the lock and slid open the glass doors.

"What are you doin' here, LeRoy?"

"I thought I'd bring that hunting lease by. Hope you don't mind. I told a couple of the guys in the club about it and they were so damned excited I just couldn't wait."

Gage made no move to let LeRoy in. "Let me see what you got there." Gage took the lease and pretended to scrutinize it, too overwrought to focus on anything.

"I knocked at the front, but I guess maybe you couldn't hear me."

"I guess so."

"Six dollars an acre is what we paid last year. Now if that's not enough, you say so."

"No, that's fine. Let me have your pen there." Gage took LeRoy's ballpoint and signed quickly. "LeRoy, let me ask you something. They ever find out who killed Huerta? You know, I knew that guy for twenty years."

"No. Just another one of those Mexican knife fights. I think they're looking for one of the wetbacks on his crew." LeRoy took the lease back and folded it thoughtfully, slipping it into his back pocket. "Now, if you like venison sausage . . ."

"On the crew? They haven't picked him up yet?"

"I don't think so." LeRoy looked a little miffed. He didn't understand why Gage hadn't invited him in. He wasn't used to being left standing in the doorway like some Jehovah's Witness or encyclopedia salesman. "It's a messy business, to tell you the truth."

"What do you mean, messy?"

"I can't really talk about it. Official police business."

"You're getting the best hunting in the county for six dollars an acre, LeRoy. Now, what's messy about it?"

LeRoy stared down at his gleaming black shoes. "You remember last summer? When they found that truckload of Salvadorans suffocated out in the desert?"

"Yes, I remember."

"It seems the cops had been talking to Huerta about it."

"What do you mean, talking?"

"Huerta didn't have the cleanest record in the world."

"I know that. So what?"

The phone rang. Gage looked back at it as if someone had just jabbed him with a sharp stick. He was caught. The phone ran again. LeRoy seemed confused, his big moon-pie face wrinkling into a frown.

200

"Go ahead and answer the phone," LeRoy said. "I can wait."

Gage looked at LeRoy as if he hadn't quite heard what he'd said. The phone rang a third time and Gage picked it up. "Hello?" he said.

It wasn't Peter, it was someone selling light bulbs manufactured by the blind. Gage let them make their pitch about the extraordinary life of their filaments. When he looked back he saw that LeRoy had come into the room and was stooped over, retrieving something from the floor: a picture that had fallen from the scrapbook.

"I'm sorry, but I really can't, not today," Gage said. He hung up. LeRoy, suddenly somber, handed over the old photo of Peter in his Cub Scout uniform.

"I'll call you later about getting keys for those gates," LeRoy said.

Gage hurried out to the road. Huerta had left one of his pickups overnight, the one with the broken windshield. A tarp had been pulled up to cover the tools in the truck bed.

As soon as Gage opened the door of the truck he could smell something rancid. He climbed in. When he punched open the glove compartment a flood of hardware store receipts and old maps poured out. Gage went through them quickly, but found nothing.

Fumbling under the seat, all Gage came up with was the greasy pieces of the jack. Matín or Martín, Gage couldn't remember the name Huerta had used. Whoever the guy was Huerta had sent to retrieve his cigarettes, he had found something in this truck that had changed everything, Gage was certain of it.

He got up on his knees so he could reach way down behind the seat. A couple of coins slid to the floor and then Gage's fingers brushed something soft. He stretched a couple of inches further, grunting, and got hold of a handle.

He pulled up a soft leather bag, like an overnight case. He undid the latch and stared at the soft silk purple and white stole, folded up like a tie. He set it on the seat next to him, took from it a thin book, riffled quickly through the Latin rituals.

The last thing in the bag looked like a small gold pillbox. When Gage unscrewed the cap the smell of rancid oil was nearly overwhelming. The gold lining in the neck of the bottle had turned black. Gage removed the ball of cotton and poured some of the spoiled oil into his hand.

He stared out through the spider's web of cracked glass. Everything was beginning to fit; almost too well. He wiped his hand on the steering wheel, his fingers slick with a blessing turned sour, absolution gone to waste.

North of Española Gage flashed by a police car camped in a grove of trees, but the cop must have been asleep or not had his radar on, because Gage was doing seventy-five and the police car never moved.

He turned off the highway, rattled across the wooden bridge, rolled up the potholed dirt road and though the orchard. Peter's pickup was gone and there was no sign of anyone.

Gage got out of his truck. The horses in the corral picked up their heads. "Hello!" he shouted. He ran his hand through his hair. Glistening black grackles strutted under the barren apple trees. Peter had taken off. Gage had lost him again.

He walked slowly to the house. The kittens still mewled and tumbled over one another in their cardboard box next to the wall. He shoved open the unlocked door. "Anybody home?" Again there was no answer.

He stepped inside and moved down the long, cool hallway into the kitchen. Breakfast dishes were still on the Formica table, half-eaten waffles on the children's bright plastic plates, a third of a cup of warm coffee on the counter, a napkin on the floor. It was as if everybody has just stepped out of the room a second before, as if they had all gone to hide themselves for a surprise party.

He moved on through the house. In the children's bedroom

one of the beds was made and the other had a Big Bird quilt fluffed up on it like a deflating tepee.

The house was clean, without much furniture, but it had its touches: dried weeds artfully arranged in a pot, an arrowhead collection on one wall, a bright Navajo weaving used to spiff up a worn couch.

He looked through the mail on his son's desk, thumbed through electric bills, seed catalogs, a letter to Sandy from her father in Kerrville, Texas, a dunning notice from a collection agency in Santa Fe for an eighteen-dollar doctor's fee. He tried the desk drawers, hoping for something that might answer his questions. He didn't find it. No one would have known that his son had ever lived here; it was someone else's life, all the mail addressed to some character named Walter Rydberg.

He thought he heard a door open. "Hello?" he called out. There was no answer. He waited a second longer and then walked back into the long outer hallway with its shelves of canned fruit. Through the single curtained window he saw the horse staring back at him, heard the animal bang a hoof impatiently against one of the rails of the corral. At first he thought that explained what he'd heard before, but as he turned back he saw the thin line of sunlight slide slowly across the adobe floor. At the far end of the hallway the outer door was open, no more than an inch or two. Gage didn't remember it having been open when he came in.

He walked to the door and pushed it all the way open. After the darkness of the house the sudden light hurt his eyes, and he squinted at the outbuildings. Wind swirled though the dried leaves in the orchard. The horse trotted along the rail of the corral, begging for attention. There was no sign of anyone.

He walked to the front of the house and stared toward the bridge. He could hear the faint whoosh of traffic on the highway, a half mile away. Maybe his mind was playing tricks; the wind could have blown the door ajar.

He put his hands in his pockets and walked past the tractor and disk, past the oil drums. Beyond the machine shed was an old smokehouse listing seriously to the right, its wooden door rotting and coming off its hinges. He opened the door and stared inside. It caught him off guard. It had been redone as a children's playhouse, the walls painted with bright murals. Gage put a foot up and pulled himself inside.

It was a wonderful place. On one wall, cut-out wooden apples dangled from painted trees. A couple of old screens served as simple dividers and there were buggies and dollhouse, a wooden rocking giraffe and a bin of building blocks. The last surviving wasp of the season bumped sluggishly against the lone window. A couple of bags of potting soil leaned in one corner. Gage heard something move beneath the floor, a rat probably, or some kind of bird. The wind banged the open door against the building.

In the corner was a tiny closet and a bed. On the bed was an open sleeping bag. Gage lifted the corner of it and a couple of coins bounced on the foam cushion beneath. He lifted the cushion and saw the crushed pack of Camel cigarettes.

He held the airy-light pack in his palm. He had been leaning against the rock wall, Huerta had been in the middle of one of his stories, only the last traces of sun in the sky, and the Guatemalan had been no more than ten feet away, holding the crushed pack of cigarettes as if anyone could possibly want it.

The only thing Gage moved was his head, looking left and then right, scanning the room. He heard a car door slam a long way off, but he wasn't interested. He was so close now. If he could just be still enough, he should be able to hear a person breathe. He heard the rat move under the floorboards again, but he knew now it wasn't a rat.

He jerked the closet door open with one swift motion. A man squatted down behind a cluster of rakes and hoes. The closet was narrow as a coffin. He was a small man and, squatting, he looked as small as a child, staring up at Gage with huge brown eyes,

204

staring at the crumpled pack of cigarettes in Gage's hand. Gage remembered the name Huerta had used: Matín.

Matín tried to bolt past him, but the jungle of rake handles made a clean break impossible. Gage tackled him and about three hoes together. The two men fell, landing on the sacks of black loam as tools clattered around them.

"Hello? Hello!" Peter's voice was out there somewhere, but beside the point.

Matín tried to crawl free, but Gage had a firm lock around his waist. The plastic sacks of loam had burst and as the two men writhed on the floor, black clumps stuck to their clothes and skin. Matín grabbed a trowel and hit Gage in the face with it twice.

"God damn it!" Gage let go and grabbed for his cheek.

He heard someone leap into the shed with them. "Just stop it! Just leave each other alone!"

Peter stood above them. Matín tossed the trowel away, still on all fours. Gage sat on the floor, a little stunned, checking the side of his face for blood. Peter offered his father a hand and pulled him to his feet.

"This is ridiculous! Jesus!" Peter shoved a doll buggy angrily out of the way. "How did this happen?"

Neither man would answer him. Matín got to his feet, shame-faced, picking the bits of black soil from his arms. Peter ran a trembling hand over his face. The room smelled of compost or rotting leaves, a fertile rot. *"Matín, este es mi padre. Dad, this is Matín."* The two men exchanged wary nods. Matín held his elbow; he had scraped it pretty badly. Gage sucked for air. Peter gave a disgusted snort, picked up five or six of the hoes and tossed them back in the closet. "Come on, then, let's get out of here."

They stepped outside and Peter closed the door of the smoke-house behind them, fastening the latch with a stick.

They had an audience. Sandy stood at the door of the main house, looking down at Gage with a stony stare. Her eyes were swollen as if she'd been crying. Jason held one of the newborn kittens to his cheek. Shelby clamped a protective hand on her brother's shoulder.

A bronze-skinned woman with raven-black hair stood behind Peter's truck, a Guatemalan shawl wrapped tightly around her shoulders. A slightly built boy of nine or ten, with a Bruce Springsteen shirt, red tennis shoes and Indian features, crouched in the truck bed, eyes fixed on Gage. It was the same boy Gage had seen at the Santuario, the boy who had taken the sacred dirt on his tongue.

"Nothing's changed, has it?" Gage said. He staggered a step or two, shambled weak-kneed, still wiping at his cheek. "Twenty years later and you still can't be straight with me. You know who you're protecting, don't you? The cops know all about him. They're looking all over the goddamn county right now."

"You don't know what he did or didn't do," Peter said. "You've got no idea."

Jason set the kitten down and straddled the tiny animal as it tottered in the grass. Sandy gestured for the woman in the shawl to come up to the house.

"I think I know what he did and I think I even know why," Gage said. "What I don't understand is how the hell you got yourself mixed up in this."

Peter pursed his lips, pondering the leaves scuttling up the aisles of barren trees, then looked back at the house. "Jason, Shelby, you get your things together. We're going to spend the night at your grandfather's."

Matín murmured something to the woman and boy in a language Gage had never heard before. The boy sprang lightly to the ground.

"What about them?" Gage said.

"I don't know. I need to talk to them. They may be coming with us."

"Over my dead body they are," Gage said.

A door slammed. Sandy and the children had disappeared into the house. A flock of horned larks sailed into the branches of a dead tree. Gage turned away, furious. Matín's son still followed his every move.

"What are you staring at?" Gage said. "You got something to say? Huh? What's the matter? Cat got your tongue?"

The larks fidgeted and fussed in the tree. "He's not going to be able to answer you, Dad," Peter said.

"What do you mean, he can't answer me?" Gage gulped hard; he just about had his wind back. "You shy, boy? Spit it out."

The boy's face colored in embarrassment. His mouth began to move, muscles tightening in his jaw and lips, but no sounds came. The boy's mother put a hand on his shoulder and he ducked angrily under it, but she turned him, hustled him toward the house. The horned larks exploded out of the tree, beat their way over the orchard, veered into the wind and disappeared.

"Why don't you go inside with Sandy and the kids for a minute?" Peter said. He sounded dispirited. "Let me talk this out with Matín."

When Gage entered the kitchen everyone quit talking. The bronze-skinned woman, the shawl still around her shoulders, sat at the Formica table, helping Shelby with one of her workbooks. Jason and Matín's son were on all fours on the floor, gathering up plastic dinosaurs and tossing them into a milk crate. Sandy stood at a curtained closet, pausing to consider Gage, then yanking a suitcase from the rough, unfinished shelf.

Gage nodded at Matín's boy, trying to be friendly. "How you doin'?"

The boy looked at Gage, looked at his mother for help, then stood up and began backing away. His mother spoke sharply to him in Indian dialect.

"Cheppi, it's okay, he's not going to hurt you," Sandy said. It was as if the boy didn't hear any of the adult voices. He turned, and glided into the dark hallway. A moment later the door slammed.

Everyone was silent now. Shelby traced her forefinger across her open workbook. Gage looked over her shoulder; the object of the game was to guide a baby mouse through a maze back to its nest.

"Real convenient, isn't it?" Gage said.

"What's that?" Sandy said. The woman in the shawl had a tight smile now, but it was clear that she did not know English.

"The boy not speaking," Gage said. "I wouldn't be talking either if my father had just killed a man."

Sandy's face got hostile. She unsnapped the locks on the worn Samsonite suitcase and let it fall open. "That's not why he doesn't speak."

"Then why is it?" Gage said. "Can you tell me?" Jason sat cross-legged on the floor, happily clashing a plastic buffalo against a plastic dinosaur as if they were cymbals.

"I can show you."

Sandy walked around the bronze-skinned woman. She gave her a gentle pat, then took one end of the shawl as if it might have been caught on the chair. The woman leaned forward just slightly. Sandy lifted the shawl for just a second, rearranging it, but in that second Gage saw all that he was supposed to see: all down the woman's neck and arms were scars, a maze of raised, shiny flesh.

Sandy looked up to meet Gage's eyes, her gaze insolent. Gage could say nothing. The only sounds in the room were the clacking of plastic dinosaur against buffalo and the five-year-old boy's warlike and exuberant hisses.

Sandy tucked the shawl around the woman's shoulders. The woman pulled it tighter and leaned forward to help Shelby with her puzzle. Shelby's finger curved back and forth across the page, retracing old paths as she tried to find her way out of a cul-de-sac.

"I need to pack. You can help me," Sandy said.

Sandy picked through the bureau drawers, tossing children's pajamas and socks into the open suitcase on the bed. Gage stared

208

out the bedroom window at Matín and Peter arguing near the corral.

Sandy told the story with a stubborn insistence, going on with her packing. She talked without looking at him, in a husky Tammy Wynette voice. Gage saw that he had underestimated her; nose ring or not, she was nobody's fool.

Matín was from the highlands of Guatemala, from a village ten miles outside Chimaltenango, where Peter had worked twenty years before. He had a small plot of corn and beans and sometimes he worked in the big coffee plantations on the coast, but he was a respected man in his town, the head of his *cofradía*. One day twenty or thirty guerrillas showed up in the village square. Everyone stayed in their houses, except for a few young foolish ones. But the guerrillas didn't really bother anybody, just bought soda and white bread at the store and washed themselves. They took down a government banner in front of the church and put up their own. Then they left. No one was brave enough to take the banner down; they were afraid the guerrillas might come back at any time. The next day the army showed up, searching for guerrillas. When they saw the banner they tore it down and set fire to it, using it as a torch to set fire to some of the houses and fields. Twenty people they claimed were collaborators they marched into the square and shot through the head. They took Matín's wife, Consuelo—the woman who now sat in the kitchen with Shelby. They said they knew her brother worked for the radio station that broadcast Communist propaganda.

They tortured her with cattle prods, burned her face and arms with lit cigarettes in front of everybody. They held rifles on Matín and his son, Cheppi, making them watch. The boy, only five then, fought his father like an animal, crying out, trying to run to his mother. Matín held tight, covering the boy's eyes and his mouth too, trying to shush him. All around them the fields and buildings blazed. Finally the soldiers grew disgusted at what they'd done and just left her. When they did, Matín ran to her. Burns covered her body. He was afraid to touch her. When he

209

looked back for Cheppi, the boy had not moved. He had not said one word since that time.

Matín took his wife and son into the jungle and for a month they lived like wild animals, eating roots and fruit from the trees, afraid that the army would come back to kill them. When his wife's wounds healed enough for them to travel, they went north across the border into the refugee camps in southern Mexico.

Sandy told the story deliberately, as if she had all the time in the world. She wasn't going to let Gage rush her. She was in no hurry to finish packing either, trying to match up stray socks. Gage made no attempt to interrupt her. He wasn't going to argue politics with the woman. Atrocities were not something you could argue about. He doubted that Sandy was political anyway. She was loyal to her friends, she was pissed at Gage for making her leave her home and she was stalling.

For five months Matín and his family lived in the camps, a long green plastic sheet their only protection against the rains. At night Cheppi writhed and lashed out in his sleep, but when Matín shook him awake he would stare and not see. In the day the boy sat without moving or speaking, refusing food.

Matín found a shaman in the camp, a man from El Quiche whose wife and daughter had been killed. He brought Cheppi to the healer. The shaman counted out the seeds in his bundle, trying to find the source of Cheppi's sickness, but the seeds would not answer, the blood would not speak. The shaman made excuses: he had no power here, away from his own place, there were no shrines in the mountains for him to do his ceremonies, but Matín believed he was just afraid. The shaman knew that if he went into the mountains he would probably be shot.

One of the relief workers, a nun, took pity on Cheppi. She was the one who found them a way north. It was Father Ortiz who met them at the border and took them across, found them a place to stay with a family only two miles away from Peter and Sandy.

Gage sat on the edge of the bed. "So it was all an accident?"

He swept his hand over the nubbly spread. "Your meeting them?"

"If you believe in accidents. Walt . . . excuse me, Peter to you . . . walked into the Dixon bar one day and there was Matín, sitting with the three Mexicans who do the weeding for the local fruit growers." Sandy opened the closet and flipped quickly through the hangers until she found a child's sweatshirt decorated with puff paint. "Just on a hunch he said three or four words to him in Cakchiquel. You can imagine the effect it had."

Gage glanced toward the window. Matín leaned against the top rail of the corral, his arms around his ten-year-old son. Peter was pointing toward the highway. Gage felt his anger returning. There was no time, traps were closing all around them.

"Why are you telling me this?" he asked.

"Because I want you to know what sort of man your son is. Because there are things he would never tell you himself."

For a moment they were both silent. The room smelled faintly of wet ashes. Through the open door Gage could see Shelby and Consuelo still hovering over the kitchen table. Sandy folded the sweatshirt across her arm.

"When Walt told me he'd met Matín, I told him not to see him anymore, it could only lead to trouble. One of the things he had learned about living underground was to pay every parking ticket, walk only when the light said 'Walk.' The last thing he needed was to get involved with a political refugee from Central America."

Sandy tossed the folded sweatshirt onto the other clothes and slammed the suitcase shut.

"A couple of weeks later we ran into Matín and Consuelo at the post office. Matín just lit up. Then one afternoon, on his own, Walt went over to Matín's house with some old mattresses we weren't using, some garden tools and hoses. The week after that Matín was over here helping Walt dig postholes and clean out irrigation ditches for spring planting. Next thing I know, Walt is showing Matín how a fuse box works, finding him a truck he

211

could buy for a hundred dollars, helping him get it in running order."

Sandy bent down to look under the beds, then scanned the room. "Here they are, the two of them speaking in this Indian dialect no one else understands. They had their own private language. But it was more than that. It was like they were brothers, they were both officially invisible; it was as if they became each other's shadows. You like it? I sure didn't. It scared me. It changed Walt. It made him freer than I'd ever seen him. He stopped being so careful . . ."

Jason burst into the room with a fistful of toothbrushes wrapped in toilet paper. "Here, Mommy!"

"Thank you, sweetie. Why don't you go out and get in the truck? We'll be going in a minute."

Jason did as he was told. Gage ambled to the window. Matín's son tried to feed the horse without getting his fingers nipped.

"Matín's kid. What did you say his name was?"

"Cheppi."

"He still doesn't speak? At all?"

"Not a word. Matín's been taking him over to the Santuario every week. He smears the holy dirt on Cheppi's throat and prays to God to give his son's voice back." Gage snorted and she caught him at it. "You think it's funny?"

"More sad than funny. I just don't put that much truck in miracles."

"No? Your son's coming back from the dead isn't good enough?" Gage just let it go. "We took him there, you know. You should have seen him. When he saw the crucifix at the front of the church, I mean, golly, it was the most remarkable thing. It turns out the crucifix is the Black Christ of, oh, I still can't pronounce it, but it's the most holy object in all of Guatemala. I don't believe in miracles either, but if you'd been there, it would have made you believe in something. There was an old man there. I guess he must have been the caretaker. He told us stories about some old tunnels. . . ."

"Oh, yes," Gage said. "He told me too."

The heavy scraping of boots made them both turn. Peter filled the doorway.

"So what did you all decide?" Gage asked.

"They're not going to come with us," Peter said. "Partly he's still not convinced you're not going to turn him in, but really, it's taking too big a chance. If a cop spotted him on the highway . . . well, it's just too big a chance. For everybody."

"So what is it he wants to do?" Gage said.

Matín and Cheppi entered the room silently, staying at Peter's back.

"What he *wants* to do is go to the Santuario and pray for forgiveness," Peter said. Gage could see, over Peter's shoulder, Consuelo rise from the kitchen table, her face grave, heavy with fear. "He's sure that God will put words in his son's mouth."

"I don't know what God will do, but I know what those cops will do." The room had filled up awfully fast; one way or the other, they were all waiting on Gage. "You tell him he can stay here, but there's no time to go running around to any damn shrines."

Peter negotiated with Matín in a language that sounded more Chinese than Indian. Matín frowned, resisting; Peter became more forceful. Sandy swung the dented Samsonite suitcase off the bed. Cheppi squatted down to peer in the windows of Shelby's freshly painted dollhouse.

"There's a hunting camp a quarter of a mile down the river," Peter said. "They can stay there; no one will find them. I promised him that we would be back as soon as we can."

Gage was not perfectly convinced. "Okay," he said. "And you give him the phone number at my house. If anyone shows up here, I want to know about it." Gage put a hand on Cheppi's shoulder. The boy pulled back as if a snake had bitten him, but when Gage cuffed the boy's dark hair, there was the flicker of a smile. "And let's just leave the shrines out of it."

They had sung the children to sleep with round after round of "Froggy Went A'Courtin' " and now they were left with silence and headlights boring into the darkness. Sandy played with her daughter's hair.

Gage leaned forward on the steering wheel, stretching out a kink in his back. "So it was Matín, then, who introduced you to Father Ortiz?"

"Yes," Peter said. The river was to their right, roiling and ghostly in the moonlight, the walls of the gorge rising up on their left. Tires squealed on one of the sharp curves. "He dropped by one morning when I was helping Matín fix a busted pipe. He started sounding me out. Matín had told him that I had worked in Guatemala. He wanted to know if I would be interested in meeting some of the people working with Central American refugees. I told him I wasn't political. But it wasn't a political issue, he said, it was a moral one. Maybe so, I said, but I wasn't into causes."

Headlights from an oncoming car flared across their faces. Shelby whimpered in her sleep, threw an arm across her mother's chest. "Are we there yet, Mommy?"

"Almost, darlin', almost." Sandy began to hum "Froggy Went A' Courtin'," caressing her daughter's back.

"A couple of weeks later we had a birthday party for Cheppi. Father Ortiz came. Everybody drank more wine than they should have." Peter put a steadying hand on the dash as Gage braked for a slow-moving stock truck.

"Matín started talking about Guatemala, about the people who had disappeared, about finding bodies in ditches when he went out to work in the fields. I couldn't take it. I went into the bedroom. A few minutes later Father Ortiz came in and asked me if I was all right. I said I was. I guess I was a little drunk myself. I remember the kids whacking away at the piñata in the other room."

Peter was silent for a moment. The stock truck turned off onto a dirt road. They came out of the gorge, sped by the soft lights of

214

the roadside fruit stands in Velarde. Jason kicked out and Gage pulled his sleeping grandson's leg onto his lap.

"I still don't know exactly why I did it," Peter said. "But I went to the closet and got this old copy of *The Fargo Forum,* it was the only copy of anything about it that I'd kept. And I gave it to Father Ortiz."

Gage leaned over, flicked the lever for the heater, but it wasn't working. Peter turned up the collar of his bulky blue barn coat.

"I remember while he was looking at it, somebody broke the piñata. I remember the sound of all that hard candy hitting the floor, the kids all shouting and scrambling, and I thought, Jesus, I've made a terrible mistake. I took out a ballpoint pen. That was me, once upon a time, I said, a long time ago. And I scratched the face out. Take it, I said. Burn it, wrap the garbage in it, just get rid of it. Just don't talk to me about things being moral issues."

"And that was how it ended up in the trunk of his car."

Peter didn't answer. Shelby snuggled into her mother's chest. Sandy pressed her cheek to her daughter's sleeping head, singing softly. "A sword and a pistol by his side, uh-huh, uh-huh." Her face filled with a terrible sadness.

"Will you tell me one more thing?" Gage said.

"Yes."

"Do you know what happened last night? Between Huerta and Matín?"

"Yes."

"Will you tell me now?"

"Yes."

Seventeen

GAGE SWUNG THE GATES WIDE, headlights at his back. When he turned he saw Peter and Sandy framed in the dark windshield of the truck, each cradling a sleeping child, each with the stunned look of an immigrant.

He climbed in behind the steering wheel and coasted the truck up next to Amy's Datsun. He got out, yanked the two suitcases from the flatbed of the pickup and opened the door on Peter's side. "One day I'm going to get the heater fixed in this truck. Come in, we'll get you warmed up."

He heard a screen door slam and Amy's footsteps on the walk. She came around the corner of the house with a recycling bucket full of glass jars on her hip. She stopped when she saw them all. The light on the corner of the garage was right behind her and it was impossible to read her face. The dogs began to bark, somewhere out in the pasture. The coyotes on the mesa picked up the challenge, chorusing back.

"This is Amy," Gage said. "Sandy and Peter."

Peter elbowed the door to the pickup shut, Jason scrunched up against his chest. "Nice to meet you," he said.

Amy didn't answer at first. As she set down the white plastic bucket a glass jar fell to the gravel, but didn't break. Sandy rocked Shelby from side to side, murmuring a song. The handles of the suitcases cut into Gage's palms. Amy seemed so tired, so wary. Gage watched her; what must it feel like, he thought, to be told that this family of strangers was her family.

"Nice to meet you too," Amy said. She turned to Gage. "You should close the gate, shouldn't you?"

Jason shifted in Peter's arms and the quilt slipped from the little boy's shoulders. Amy came forward to tuck the quilt in again and Gage saw her face soften. She rubbed a hand on the sleeping child's back and looked over at Sandy.

"It's nice to meet all of you," Amy said, her voice filling out, like a sail catching wind. "I've fixed a place for the children to sleep. We can put them down." For the first time Gage noticed the sweet smell of piñon smoke in the air.

Amy and Gage stood in the hallway watching Peter tuck a pillow under Shelby's head. Jason lay dead to the world on a coat next to his sister. Gage held Amy's hand.

Amy had prepared herself for this. She had fixed up the spare room, moved the boxes of Gage's photographic equipment, brought in a rollaway bed, two cots and the good reading light from the study, laid out towels and washcloths and even found an arrangement of dried flowers to stick in an artsy ceramic pot. She moved away from Gage's side and went to close one of the windows. Even after a couple of hours of airing out, the room still smelled of dust and old chemicals, but it was too cold to be leaving the windows open.

"Is this your little girl's room?"

Gage turned at the sound of Sandy's voice. She had her hand on the door of Jody's bedroom. A purple backpack was draped on the knob.

"Yes," Gage said.

"Do you mind if I look?"

"Not at all."

Sandy opened the door quietly and Gage followed her in. A vaporizer hissed in the middle of the room and in the glow of the Mickey Mouse night-light Gage could see his daughter's school clothes laid out for the morning, tiny Barbie Doll paraphernalia scattered about the floor. Jody lay asleep on her stomach, her mouth slightly agape, Babar in a stranglehold under her left arm.

"She's lovely," Sandy said.

Gage felt a hand on his back. He looked around and saw that it was Peter. "Come in and look at your sister," Gage said.

Peter came forward and stood over the sleeping child. The luminescent plastic constellations on the wall above her head had faded, the cloud of vapor struggled, never rising more than a foot above the floor.

"It must be nice having a little girl," Peter said.

"It's nice having both," Gage said.

Peter showed no sign that he heard. Amy came to the doorway, but didn't enter. Peter traced his hand along Jody's arm. Her hand reflexively closed around his finger.

"Does she know that she has a brother?" Sandy said.

"No, but she will," Gage said.

Peter pulled gently out of the sleeping child's grip and straightened up. He scanned the dimly lit room, the unicorn rearing up from the stuffed toybox, the dolls leaning together on the bureau. Peter's face filled with the shadows of such undisguised sadness, with such yearning, that Gage felt as if he couldn't breathe, the cold damp vapor had settled into his chest and was choking him.

"Why don't you all come into the kitchen?" Amy said, her voice wiretight. "I just put the water on for coffee."

218

Gage, on his knees, rummaged through the refrigerator. "Now, I know you all are hungry. Amy, isn't there some of that apple pie left from the other night?" He undid the tinfoil covering a promising-looking platter only to discover a decimated chicken carcass. "Hey, we've got some bagels here we could heat up."

The room was silent behind him. Amy poured hot water through the coffee filter. Sandy was in the doorway, staring at the movie pictures and awards lining the hall. Peter leaned against the sink. Gage saw that he was drinking in everything: the microwave, the Cuisinart, the electric juicer, the washer-dryer behind louvered doors. To Peter, used to living with nothing, this had to seem like a technological palace.

Gage pushed a Ziploc bag of bran muffins to one side and pried open an old yogurt container. The smell of mold was enough to make him blanch. "Whew!" As he turned to pitch the container into the garbage he saw Sandy looking back at him with a question in her eyes.

"That's Burt Lancaster, isn't it?" She pointed to one of the framed pictures on the wall.

"It is, uh-huh."

"My mother loved Burt Lancaster. She always wanted to go to Hollywood and take the bus tour so she could see his house." Sandy smiled brightly. Gage pulled himself to his feet and slammed the refrigerator shut.

"The first time Peter told me his father was a famous director I thought he was lying." Sandy moved back into the kitchen. Peter watched her distrustfully, but didn't try to interrupt. "I was just this runaway kid from Texas, what did I know? I was still worried about whether the Devil existed or not and everybody was laying these heavy raps on me about how they'd just come back from seeing the Dalai Lama with a message for the Hopi Nation. I had no way of sorting it out. But Peter was the first person I'd ever met who actually listened to me." Sandy ran her hand down

Peter's sleeve. "I didn't know two beans about Vietnam. When he told me what he'd done, it just seemed impossible. I mean it was a heavy thing for him, so I took it seriously, you know what I'm saying? But still it was like a story. I never quite believed it was real." She glanced back, pondering the Burt Lancaster photograph. "Until now."

Gage broke the silence. "You know what we've got that you'd like? We've got some quail out in the freezer. We'll take 'em out tonight and tomorrow we'll have a real homecoming breakfast." Amy's eyes were on the unsteady stream of coffee pouring through the filter. Peter stared at Sandy for a long, measured minute. Sandy did not back off. It was a married look, full of blame and love. Peter finally scooped up a sheet of used tin foil on the counter and crumpled it into a tight, glistening ball.

"Amy makes this great spoonbread," Gage said. He turned to Sandy. "When Peter used to come home from college, we'd always have a special quail breakfast. Remember that, Peter?"

"I think we need to make a phone call, Dad."

"It can wait," Gage said. "You haven't even had your coffee yet." Peter pressed the ball of foil even tighter in his fist, the skin turning white across his knuckles. "Sandy, go on, sit down here." Sandy looked to Peter for help.

"No, I don't think we can afford to wait," Peter said.

Gage led Peter into his study and shut the door, then picked up the list from the table.

"So what's that?" Peter said.

"Names of lawyers. When I came back this afternoon I looked them up."

"So who are they?"

Gage handed Peter the list. "The guy at the top lives in Albuquerque. Barry Nass. He's an old ACLU lawyer, his wife's an artist-friend of Amy's. I thought he might be a good place to start."

"Why not?"

220

"No discussion?"

"What's to discuss?" Peter scanned the books on Gage's shelves. "What else can we do? Drive to Mexico and start a new life?" He spied the photo on the desk of himself, Gage and Nina, reached across and picked it up. "You didn't just put this out?"

"No. It's always been there."

Peter stared at the picture. "I like her. Amy. She seems like a very decent person. I can see what you saw in her."

"Thanks. I'll call the lawyer and then I'll put you on. You can say whatever you want to say. I don't know if he's handled cases like this before, but he's a very bright, meticulous guy. . . ."

"Sure."

Gage dialed quickly and Nass's wife answered on the fifth ring. "Hello, Chula? This is Jeremiah Gage. Is Barry there?"

"No, Jeremiah, he's not. He's out of town. He'll be flying in from Phoenix tomorrow morning."

Gage twisted around at the sound behind him. Peter had picked a glass jar off the shelf. It was Jody's science project at school, a green lizard sustained by a few sprigs of grass.

"Listen, Chula, I really need to talk to someone tonight. Do you have a number where I can get ahold of him?"

Peter rotated the jar slowly. The imprisoned lizard tried to scramble up the smooth glass toward the pierced metal lid, sensing freedom, its throat pulsing red.

"Here it is," Chula said. "This is the Hilton in Phoenix. Area code 602-555-7171."

The sudden cry made the two men turn at once. The cry turned to wailing. It took Gage a moment to realize that it wasn't Jody.

"Thanks. I'll call him there." Gage could hear the hurrying adult footsteps in the hallway. Peter put the glass jar back on the shelf. "But if you hear from him, would you have him call me in Santa Fe? It's very, very important."

Peter went to the door and opened it. The crying was louder now. Gage hung up the phone.

"He's out of town," Gage said. "He's in Phoenix and he'll be back in the morning. Maybe I'll call him there. Unless you want to try someone else."

"What about Matín?"

"What about him?"

"The guy is up there, waiting for us."

"You're getting a little confused here, aren't you, Peter? If what you've told me is the truth, what happened to Huerta and Father Ortiz had nothing to do with you."

"But we told him—"

"Don't pull this bleeding-heart crap with me! This once you'd better think about saving yourself. Remember what that other lawyer said? The guy back in Madison? The first thing you do is circle the herd. . . ."

"And Matín isn't in the circle, is that what you're telling me?" Gage said nothing. "And my mother wasn't in that circle either, was she?" Peter turned away, focusing only on the inconsolable child. "You call. I put myself in your hands. Now just let me check on the kids."

Gage walked out onto the dark lawn. "Peter?" he called. There was no answer. As he moved toward the fruit trees, into the tangle of shadows and away from the pale light of the house, he stumbled into one of the lawn chairs. He snapped on his flashlight. The stars had just started to come out; it was a crystal-clear night.

He fanned the beam of light slowly through the gnarled branches. Light glared back at him, reflecting off metal. The gate to the pasture was open.

He walked to the gate. The beam of the flashlight fell short, but he could still make out the shadows of horses milling uneasily in the barn.

He trudged down the uneven slope. "Peter?" he called out softly. A wraithlike figure leaned against the ladder to the loft, a child asleep on its shoulder.

222

The pipe to the water trough was broken and Gage splashed through mud as he entered the barnyard. He waved off the expectant horses. They tossed their heads, shying away. Peter rose to greet him, one hand on Jason's back.

"Are you okay?" Gage asked.

"I'm fine. He was just a little disoriented, he woke up and didn't know where he was." Peter pulled the quilt over the top of Jason's head. "He said he wanted to see the horses, but he was asleep before we even got down here."

"Do you want me to carry him back up?"

"No, that's all right," Peter said. "You get ahold of the lawyer?"

"No. I left a message at the hotel for him to call. But we can try some of the others. We can do that right now."

"No."

"No?" Gage pushed the nose of one of the curious horses away. The horse smelled of dung and dust and hay. "Here, why don't you put him down? Hold on."

He jerked the rusty nail from the tack room latch. As the door swung open, rodents scurried for cover in the darkness. Gage swung himself up into the dusty cell-like room. He waved the flashlight across the rows of saddles and bridles, yanked a stiff saddle blanket from one of the posts and laid it on the plank floor.

"Just set him down here. He'll be fine."

Peter laid Jason down carefully, then tucked the quilt under his chin. Jason sighed, threw up an arm, but never woke up.

Gage set the flashlight down and squatted above his grandson, ran his hand over the blond hair. "So you're getting cold feet, huh? I thought you and Sandy agreed."

"Sandy doesn't really know. There are things about this I've never told her. That I've never told anyone."

"And if you call a lawyer . . ."

"It'll have to come out."

A bridle lay on the floor in a tangle of reins. Gage picked it up,

223

tested it, felt the rotten leather tear in his hands. He was going to have to get down here and do a little work; all this stuff was going to need to be replaced.

"So tell me," Gage said.

"Tell you?"

"Yeah." Gage tossed the bridle aside.

"Where would I start?"

"I said good-bye to you in the airport in Madison. Start there."

A horse butted its broad head against Peter's shoulder, but Peter didn't move. The animals had gathered around the tack room, nosing in toward the sleeping child, looking for sweet feed. Gage hopped down and waved his hands over his head.

"Goddamn it, Red, get on back!" The horses retreated, truculent, muzzles tossing in the air. Gage looked over his shoulder. "Do whatever you want."

"What I want? For seventeen years I've wanted to tell you. You may think you know, but you don't. What it was like." Peter was quiet for a moment. Gage couldn't see his face. Pigeons cooed in the loft overhead, awakened by the light.

"After you flew back to L.A., Jesus, it was surreal." Peter picked up the flashlight and snapped it off and on again. "I'd been five minutes from signing up for the Navy and now I was this radical hero. I hop on a policeman's back and suddenly I stood for something."

The massive shadows of horses drifted in and out of the stalls; it was like being in a cave of restless bears. Peter sat down in the doorway of the tack room, next to his son. Gage leaned against the wall, one boot up on the lowest rung of the loft ladder.

"I'm a walking allegory, I'm everything that was wrong with America, or right with it. Here there's a war going on, people are dying, and I'm playing Charades. People wouldn't leave me alone. They wanted me to address rallies, appear on panels, these crazy women would call me up. . . . It was insane."

There was the sound of wings beating in the rafters. Peter

swung the flashlight up, the light flitting across the bales of hay, the high beams, stirring shadows, dislodging old ghosts.

"The first time somebody suggested I go underground, I thought they were nuts. What had I done? Jumped a cop? What were they making me into? But the trial got closer and I kept hearing more stories, about some ex-Eagle Scout and all-state wrestler who'd been smuggling guns to black revolutionaries in the South and the guy was supposed to be holed up in a barn outside of Oconomowoc. Someone had gone to Canada, someone else to the Lower East Side. And the whole time I'm in the lawyer's office, rehearsing what I'm going to say. I realized that I was going to have to declare myself, one way or the other, and I realized what an impostor I was. People were going to find me out."

Peter brushed the hulls of sweet feed from the tack room floor. "So two days before the trial I gave away my clothes and all my records, cut my hair, emptied out my bank account and this guy picked me up out on University Avenue. This farmer named Meinhardt."

"I know. I met him."

"I figured you had. He was a good man. The champion of lost causes. He was an old socialist, the kind that had been trying to organize farmers' unions for years. He loved to talk about the fat cats. He was against the war. He had a dairy farm and a part-time welding operation."

"Yes," Gage said. "I was there."

"So you know about Richard. A nice kid, but not a political bone in his body. As far as I could see, all that Richard really cared about was the Packers, squirrel hunting and his snowmobile. He worked as a rigger at the powder plant, cleaning out tanks, cutting grass, whatever they asked him to do. It was a little strange, the son of the old socialist working in a munitions plant. It bothered his father a lot, though neither of them ever said a word about it.

"Both of them were great with me. Benny Meinhardt never

225

asked me what I'd done, though there was no way he couldn't have known. My name with them was Philip, that was how they introduced me to people. I was the hired man. The one with no calluses on his hands, at least to start. The first couple of weeks all I did was hop out of the truck and open gates. But I learned. I got to be decent on a tractor, I helped with the haying.

"We got along. We'd sit and watch the news together. Benny would tell me about Fightin' Bob La Follette and the old battles, all the stuff his own son had heard a hundred times.

"The first few weeks I was so paranoid, I'd wake up in the night, sure there was someone in the room with me. When we passed anyone on the road and they stared a second too long, I was convinced I'd been recognized. At first I refused to even go into town, but after a couple of months I realized how crazy that was, I was only going to create more attention. So I made myself go in, I made myself act normal and I got pretty good at it. I even started going to this Baptist church in town that Benny and Richard went to, can you believe that? I figured if I could get away with that, I could get away with anything." Peter put his hand over the flashlight and light glowed through the flesh between his thumb and forefinger.

"Richard and I became better friends. He wasn't quite the unthinking slob he liked his father to think he was. Every now and then he'd get ahold of a little dope and we'd go up on the hill above the house after work, swat mosquitoes, watch the cows come home, get stoned. In the fall he took me squirrel hunting, on Friday nights we'd drink beer and go to this polka parlor, when the ice froze we set traps for muskrats on the river. We really got to be like brothers. I told him about Guatemala, we started to talk about Vietnam. He wanted to learn, he just didn't want to learn from his father. It bothered him some, working at the powder plant, but it wasn't like he was going to work there all his life, and no one paid as good as they did."

Jason moved in his sleep and Peter took the boy's soft arm and slipped it back under the quilt.

226

"Sometime in the middle of the winter Richard started to get quiet. I wondered if it was something I'd done, something I'd said, but when I asked him about it, he said no, it was just February, February always brought him down.

"The spring came. And the invasion of Cambodia. Four days after that came Kent State. I remember watching it on the news with Bennie, I remember holding on tight to this old rocker he had. I saw the guardsmen firing into the students, I heard the shots and I started to cry. No one was playing anymore. Nobody was acting. Richard came in. He was just back from work. He stood in the doorway to the kitchen, he wouldn't come all the way in, he was in his gray uniform and those big steel-toed shoes.

"Benny started to shout at him, 'You get in here!' "

" 'My shoes are muddy!'

" 'I don't care! You get in here and sit down! I want you to see this! I want you to see just who the hell you're working for!'

"Richard never said anything, just walked out of the house, got in his truck and took off. At nine he still wasn't home and I went into town and found him at a bowling alley, drinking himself into oblivion. I sat with him and we watched the Kent State footage all over again on the ten o'clock news. A couple of drunks started shouting back at the newscaster, 'Yeah, those fuckin' kids are finally getting what they deserve. . . .' I hauled Richard out of there and drove him home. I thought he was asleep in the truck and it made me jump when he said something. 'I got to talk to you, Philip, I do, man.'

"The next afternoon we went back to our old spot on the hill above the house. It was all muddy, it was May, but there were some newborn calves down below us, the pond had flooded over its banks. And Richard began to talk.

"He had been bothered for months, but he'd been afraid to say anything to anyone. All those rifles had been jamming in Vietnam. It was no secret, it had been in and out of the news for months. Seventy percent of the rifles in some units were blowing up in soldiers' faces. The papers were saying it was the rifles, but

227

it wasn't just the rifles. It was the wrong powder for that gun, slow-burning ball powder that just gummed up the works and the worst thing was that enough people knew and no one was talking. There were factions within the Pentagon, Richard had it all down, it was amazing, and each side had their pet contractor and one side wanted the M-16 to fail, it would prove that they'd been right all along. Even if American soldiers died because of it.

"Richard couldn't take it anymore. He was shaking and crying like he was the one who'd done it. We smoked more dope.

"It was so beautiful up there, with the soft spring light and new grass and young calves. There was even a heron in the pond, the first we'd seen. It was strictly Norman Rockwell if you were just looking at it. And at the same time everything was so fucked up. Nothing worked the way it was supposed to. The bad powder was the capper. We weren't just killing Vietnamese and students, we were even killing our own soldiers. It felt like everything was coming to an end. I don't know how I can make you feel the certainty I had then, that society was blowing itself apart. We both felt, Richard and I, that we had to do something. I think I was the one who said it first. I said, 'Well, maybe we could stop it somehow. At least stop part of it.'

" 'What do you mean?' he said.

"And I said, 'If you could get us in there some night, maybe I could come up with a way to really stop it.'

"We talked some more. When I went back to the house I called my friend Cobb in Madison, one of the guys in the movement, a real talker, but totally fearless. Every night that week Richard drove over to the plant, checking it all out."

Gage leaned back against the ladder, the wooden rungs cutting into his back.

"I remember that Sunday morning I went to church, same as always. Since it was a Baptist church, about every other week the minister wound up everything with a call. He'd raise a hand. 'Look into your soul, let the light in, let God speak to you, let all those yearning for forgiveness come forward now.' I remember peeking out at all those decent German farm folks scrutinizing their souls, doing the best they could. What did they have to do with this war? I looked over at Richard and then this twelve-year-old girl named Mary Ann slipped into the aisle. She caught her parents by surprise and started toward the altar and then hesitated, looking back to make sure she wasn't doing something wrong.

"The minister brought her down front, took her hand for the final prayer, gestured for her parents to come down to stand beside her. I remember her father, this stocky, thick-necked guy who worked at the plant, Otto . . . I'd gotten to know him a little through church. He was the kind of guy you'd see adding up his hours for the week on the back of a church envelope during the sermons. Here he was up front, trying not to seem embarrassed, shaking hands with everyone, going through it all for his kid.

"That afternoon Richard and I told Benny we were going to see a movie with some friends up at the Dells. We met Cobb at a restaurant on the highway. I think Richard thought Cobb was pretty weird with the long hair and the Day-Glo peace symbols painted on his tennis shoes. I don't think Richard had ever heard anybody talk so fast and every other word was fuck this and fuck that. But I guess Cobb had reason to be wired up, driving all the way from Madison with a bomb in his trunk.

"We parked on top of a hill, changed into work overalls in the car, then walked through the woods and found a perch on a rocky ledge where we could see the whole plant below us. It went on for miles. Richard pointed out everything, the patrol roads inside the fences, the green powder areas, the still house, the acres of pipeline, the underground magazines, the small trucks hauling things back and forth. He explained the process to us, how some of the elements were so unstable they had to be mixed with water into what they called a slurry, how they kept them separate until the very last. When you saw it, it all became so clear. It was like looking at the inside of a watch, or some huge system of intestines. You know what it made me think of? Those Guatemalan shamans who are supposed to be able to reach right into the chest of a sick person and pull out the infected part. They'll show it to you, probably it's chicken guts or a little stone. Maybe that's what we thought we were doing, reaching right down into the guts of the sickness.

"Beyond the fence a farmer plowed his fields, using the last bit of daylight, going up and down the mile-long rows, birds following, rising and falling, scavenging whatever insects he turned up.

"Night came. We waited some more. We timed the patrols that ran inside the fences. The shifts changed, car lights pouring over the hill in long lines. We were all getting edgy. Cobb talked about the firebombings that had been going on every night since Kent State, about the shootings at Jackson State, the campuses going out on strike. Richard got real quiet then, I thought maybe he was getting cold feet. But when it was time to move he was the first one up.

"We crawled through a drainpipe that went under the fence. That's when I first started to get panicky. The pipe seemed to go on forever. We padded along on one another's heels, our knees were sliding through this slime, it felt like we were never going to get to the end of it. You wanted to hear this, right? You said you wanted to hear this."

"Yes," Gage said, barely audible.

"Once we came out we ran through huge dark grassy distances, staying away from the light. We climbed through a maze of pipelines that delivered the alcohol and the ether. We saw one of the patrol Jeeps pass behind us without ever slowing up. All this time Cobb carried the bomb, holding it to his chest like a guy carrying a birthday cake home.

"We came to the finishing area. Richard had made sure the door to the building was open. We slipped inside. In front of us was a gigantic rotating drum. It was at least two stories high and a catwalk went all the way around. We stood staring at it. Remember how they used to talk about living in the belly of the beast?

230

Well, we were looking at it, this huge, rumbling metal belly, turning real slow, like a whale rolling in the ocean.

"It was the place where everything was finally brought together, it was where it became live powder. It was like being in a goddamn cathedral or something, it doesn't matter whether you believe or not, you feel awe, you do."

Peter smoothed the forehead of his sleeping son, but it was his own face that needed comforting, it was his face that was filled with grief and Gage could not bring himself to move.

"I thought about guns blowing up in soldiers' faces and students shot on green lawns and bombs falling over Vietnam and Cambodia and this was where it was born, this was the cradle and I thought we were doing the right thing. I did.

"The drum looked so massive, I asked Cobb if he had enough explosive to blow a hole in it. He didn't need that much, he said, all he needed was enough to just rock it once, hard.

"There was a huge box against the far wall. I asked Richard what it was. He didn't know exactly, some sort of control device, he thought. I thought I should ask him some more, but, really, I just wanted to be done with it and get the hell out.

"We checked the timer. It was set for just a little after one in the morning, when no one would be in the building. We had gone over and over that, Richard had checked it out every night for a week.

"It took Cobb no time at all to slap that packet of explosives on the underside of the tumbler. 'Let's go,' he said. We started to move toward the open door when he heard another door slam somewhere at the far end of the building. We froze, crouched down behind some racks. We could hear someone up on the catwalk. I don't think any of us took a breath. I heard the steps coming around, saw the flare of the flashlight, some figure behind it. I could see the bomb sticking to the wall of the tumbler like a fluke dangling on the belly of a whale. It kept rising higher and all I was thinking was, he's going to spot it.

"But he didn't. The flashlight waved once around the building, over our heads, across the control box. Then he switched off the light.

"I had my head down, but I saw Richard staring with his mouth open and I looked up too. The guy had taken a pack of cigarettes out of his pocket and he was lighting up, the match cupped close to his face so I could see the face, it was Otto. Otto whose daughter had been saved that morning. Here we were in the belly of the beast, right? And what do we find? Somebody sneaking a smoke. He shook out the match and there was just the glow of the cigarette.

"Richard made a move to get up, but Cobb grabbed him by the arm. 'What the fuck are you doing?'

" 'It's Otto, I've got to get him out of here,' Richard said.

" 'Nothing's going to happen,' Cobb said, 'It'll be all right. He'll be out in time.'

"I watched the bomb rise and then Richard pulled away from Cobb and ran onto the floor.

" 'Otto! Otto! What are you doing in here?' His voice echoed in that place.

"The first thing Otto did was pull the cigarette out of his mouth and try to hide it, cradling it in his palm. What a joke. He thinks *we've* caught *him*.

"Cobb ran and grabbed Richard, the two of them battled each other. Suddenly Otto had the flashlight on again, light waving over everything, and I got just a glimpse of the bomb rolling out of sight. All I was thinking was that I had to get out. I ran. I was maybe two steps outside the door when the explosion went off. It was unbelievable. It was as if the light went right through my eyelids. I was thrown into the air. I must have been out for a while. The next thing I remember was someone pulling me to my feet and flame and smoke and sirens. They started walking me toward an ambulance, but there was so much confusion, people shouting and running, they just let me go. I kept walking. Nobody stopped me. I was wearing work overalls, right? I stumbled over pipelines, over bunkers, trying to remember the way we'd

232

come in. I had burns on my back and on my arms, a big gash on my forehead, it felt like one of my eyebrows was burned off, it stung so bad. I must have looked like Frankenstein lurching around out there. But I found the drainage pipe and crawled back through. I remember the feel of that slime on my burned hands and arms. I climbed back up the hill and I wasn't worried about who might be dead or who might be alive, all I was worried about was whether Richard had left the keys in the car or not. I turned that car inside out for fifteen minutes, really went nuts, but I found them, in the glove compartment, in the most obvious place."

For a moment he was unable to continue. Rats rustled in the walls. "I drove all that night. My hair smelled of smoke, my clothes smelled of smoke, I was afraid to stop anywhere. I slept that night somewhere along the Mississippi. All of Richard's and Cobb's stuff was there on the seat next to me. The next morning I took the money out of their pockets, tossed the clothes into the river, rolled the car in after.

"I finally got enough nerve to go into a bus station and buy a ticket. Somewhere in the middle of North Dakota I looked across the aisle and on the empty seat was a newspaper. There was the story, all our pictures, all except Cobb. I picked it up, I didn't want anyone else on the bus to see it. I must have read the thing ten times, how they'd talked to Benny, who'd told them everything about me and Richard.

"At first I thought it was only a matter of time before they realized their mistake, realized that it was Cobb and not me that they'd found. I thought someone would come forward, but no one ever did. Cobb was this kid from Worcester, Mass., who hadn't talked to his parents for ten years and I guess all his friends in Madison figured that Cobb was off on a mission, who knows? But it was very strange. To realize that no one was after me. No one was looking."

Peter stopped speaking, pulled himself up, slapped at the

doorframe of the tack room. "We should go back up. Maybe your lawyer has called."

"Did you ever figure out why that explosive went off when it did?" Gage asked.

"I don't know. I've thought about it a lot. The only thing I've been able to come up with is that it was some sort of magnetic control device on the wall and that it tripped our timer, set up its own magnetic field. We weren't as smart as we thought."

An owl hooted somewhere in the piñons. Gage stared into the barnyard. There were a million stars out, Gage could see them above the cottonwoods at the far end of the pasture. He tried to remember how many lifetimes it took that light to reach them, someone had told him once.

"Can I ask you something?" Gage said.

"Yes."

"Did you ever call me?"

"Twice."

"And hung up."

"I had to hear your voice. I had to know that I existed in some way."

"And yet you couldn't speak?"

"Speak? What was I going to say? That they'd died and I'd lived because I was the only one who'd lost his nerve? How could we have believed no one was going to get hurt? You talk about magical thinking. As if we were going to stop the war with one symbolic act. Sure. Just like they levitated the Pentagon through meditation. A guy sneaking a cigarette walks into the ceremonial circle and it screws up everything, all the magnetic fields reverse, the blood's on our hands now."

The flashlight lay on the corner of the quilt. Peter picked it up, tried to tighten the cap. The beam flickered as if it was ready to go out, but there was enough light left for Gage to see the self-contempt in his son's face.

"But how did you live? After that?"

"I took the bus as far as my money could take me and in some

234

town on the Montana border I washed dishes at a truck stop for a week. Then I ran into a man who had a combine crew heading down to Texas to start cutting winter wheat and they needed an extra man. I was introducing myself to people as Charles then. I went to Texas and just followed the harvest north.

"There were nice decent kids on that crew. We'd cut wheat till midnight, it was good money, I saved what I could. I'd drive the trucks into the granaries and wait in line sometimes as long as an hour, and it would come over me, what I'd done. I came close to turning myself in a dozen times. One day I was sure I saw somebody I knew from Madison in an Arby's in Rocky Ford, Colorado, and I just took off."

He took a deep, exhausted breath. He bent over, scooped some knotted baling twine from the dust and twisted it around his palm.

"I shelved books in the library in Berkeley, did a month in a commune outside of Eugene, hung out part of the winter with these insane rock climbers in Yosemite. Total fanatics. Everybody living on peanut butter and raisins, living in tents at twenty below, in the middle of this incredible beauty. It was a remarkable thing, but in a way it was as if I wasn't really there at all, I was so blasted away inside.

"I drove a doughnut truck in Albuquerque. All this time I'm going through the names. I called myself Duke for a while, and then Montana and Vito and Rey. I'd rechristen myself every other month. One December I went with a couple of freaks out to the Superstition Mountains, dropped mescaline, walked around for three days, around where Mother died. . . ."

"What did you do that for?"

Peter picked up on the bite in his father's voice. He jerked the knotted twine from his hand and tossed it away. "I don't know. I suppose I wanted to touch base."

"You want to touch base, you touch base with the living, not the dead. Unless you want to drive yourself crazy."

235

Neither of them spoke. A horse sucked loudly at the trough. Peter stood up and walked to the front of the barn.

"What's wrong?" Gage asked.

"See for yourself," Peter said. Gage stood up and looked back toward the house. A light swung slowly down the hill, swaying like a lantern on a ship.

Gage pulled Peter back into the shadows of the barn. "You stay here," he said. He walked to the barnyard gate, slipping for a second on the slick mud below the trough.

"Amy?" he called. The lantern kept moving down the hill. "Amy?" he called more loudly.

"Yes."

"Did Nass call?"

"No."

The horses, sensing a trap, thundered through the gate, heavy guts bouncing, spooked suddenly, heading for open pasture.

"But there was a call." The last horse, the three-year-old gelding, kicked and bucked through the gate, whinnying. "It was Consuelo. Matín went back to the Santuario. Someone spotted him. The police are there, I don't know if he's inside the church or what. Sandy talked to her, but it was very hard to understand, but there's been some kind of shooting. . . ."

The lantern was stationary now, twenty feet above him on the hill. Gage turned his eyes away, trying to make out the dark fleeing forms of the horses vanishing into the darkness. He could still hear their hooves, even a couple hundred yards away, and then he could hear the crunch of his son's boots behind him.

Gage half ran, half walked up the slope, Amy at his heels. Peter had run back to retrieve Jason from the barn. Sandy stood waiting in the glass doors, silhouetted against the lit-up house that blazed like a showboat.

Gage hit her with a barrage of questions: how the hell had Matín gotten to the Santuario? Did he have a gun? Was the boy

236

with him? Had either of them been shot? Did you ask? Well, why not?

Sandy, shaken and white-faced, didn't buckle under the assault, as if she understood that he was taking out on her what he couldn't take out on anyone else. There had been no time for questions. Consuelo had been hysterical and hadn't been on the phone more than a minute before someone had ripped it away from her and slammed it down.

Gage surveyed the room balefully. Sandy had been unpacking suitcases and children's clothes were stacked up on the calfskin chair, coats and scarves draped across Gage's desk. The whole thing was a mess. If Consuelo had been able to make the call, it meant that the cop standing over her shoulder had the phone number now too.

"Maybe you could call Rig," Amy said. "Or LeRoy."

"What good would that do?" Gage countered. His car keys, snarled in their ring of coiled blue plastic, lay on the mantel. He gathered them up in one long, slow sweep.

"Gage, I'm not going to let you go up there," Amy said.

"Amy, just let me handle this. I know half the cops in Rio Arriba County. I'm sure one of my buddies will be there. There's gotta be somebody up there willing to be reasonable."

"But why? Why are you doing this? You have your son back. Isn't that enough? I'm sorry, but what is this Matín to you?"

He stared back at her, amazed that he didn't have an answer. All he knew was that the whole house of cards was collapsing, all holy hell was about to break loose and he wasn't going to trust anyone else with it. No one understood mayhem the way he did.

The sound of the sliding glass doors made Gage turn. Peter entered, cradling the sleeping Jason. Amy cleared pillows and newspapers from the couch and Peter set the boy down. Peter straightened up and saw the car keys in his father's hand.

"What are you doing?"

"What do you think I'm doing? I'm going up to get Matín. You

237

want me to bring 'em back, I'll bring 'em back. The more the merrier. Hell, we'll have ourselves a real pajama party."

"I'm going with you," Peter said.

"The hell you are," Gage said. Cold night air poured in through the open glass doors.

"I can talk to him, you can't."

"Right now you're in no position to talk to anybody. Why don't you close the goddamn doors? Unless you're trying to heat up the whole outdoors."

Expressionless, Peter turned back and slid the glass panels shut.

"Nothing's changed, has it?" Peter said. "You still go right on rolling over people."

"There are times when I've got no choice," Gage said. Sandy ran her hand over Jason's forehead, her eyes averted, caged. Amy stared into the fireplace. No one wanted to watch this. "Didn't I tell you to tell Matín to stay put?"

"Yes."

"And did you tell him?"

"Yeah, I told him."

"Well, then, what the hell is going on here?" Gage paused for a moment, trying to get hold of himself, but it was no good. It was a terrible thing to discover: you could pray for twenty years for a second chance and then when you get one, turns out you're the same irritable bastard you always were. How could Peter go back to visit the site of Nina's death and not be bothered to come see Gage, not once? The whole thing was screwed. "Everybody's got to go back to pay their last respects to just one damn thing after the other, don't they?"

"You didn't understand one thing I told you, did you?" Peter said. "Not one thing."

"I may be a son of a bitch, Peter, but I know how to survive and no one else around here seems to have the attention span for it. You just do me this one favor. You stay put. All right?" He shouldered his way toward the door. "All three of you."

238

Eighteen

A S HE CAME DOWN the long, curving hill Gage could see the Santuario below bathed in light, bright as a movie set. He pumped the brakes and slowed to a crawl. Pickups with mismatched doors and a half-dozen cars were parked along the pavement edge. His headlights flared across trudging silhouettes, pilgrimlike groups moving down the long dirt road into the church.

A cop stepped out with his hands raised, motioning him to stop. Gage rolled down the window.

"I'm looking for Captain Trevino," Gage said. "I've been trying to get him on the radio for the last half hour. You don't know? But you must know Trevino, right? No? Forget about it, then. You need to see identification or what?"

The officer waved him on. Gage nosed his pickup toward the

239

long, sloping parking lot, the crowd parting and then closing behind him like a trap.

Four patrol cars were stationed around the church with their spotlights illuminating the ancient adobe walls. One of the cars was pitched forward in the irrigation ditch, its windshield shattered. A trio of policemen crouched behind it, heads together, conspiring. Off to the left a rail-thin deputy leaned against a sawhorse looking bored, the butt of his rifle resting against his thigh.

A hundred or a hundred fifty people had come out to watch, most of them huddled in the doorways of the souvenir shops and the surrounding buildings, out of harm's way, but there were those who seemed oblivious to any danger: a low rider sitting on the hood of his car with his girlfriend, a knot of men arguing around a rusted-out blue truck with cattle racks, a pair of teenage boys slouched on a spavined old mare under the trees.

As Gage rolled his truck through the parking lot he could feel heads turn. He stared at the low, barred windows of the Santuario, the flickering candles inside, the silhouettes of the tiny black plaster statues. There was no sign of Matín.

The deputy pushed up from his sawhorse, but made no move to stop him. A few more policemen sat on the low wall behind the Santuario, trying to get a walkie-talkie to work.

Gage drove down the steep concrete embankment behind the church, his headlights picking up the half-dozen cobblestone shrines among the cottonwoods. He parked in the shadows beneath the wall and got out.

The cottonwoods were ghostly in spilled light and he could hear the river rushing just beyond them. Beyond the river, pastures stretched to the far mesa. He could see the backs of the two policemen who were sitting on top of the wall and the gleaming tips of their rifle barrels.

He trudged up the steep embankment. Hands in pockets, he strolled the thirty yards to the knot of men gathered around the ancient blue truck. A flashy young cholo in a net shirt held forth.

240

"They should storm the place. Twenty cops outside and one guy inside, what are they waitin' for?" Inside the cab, a goateed old man who looked like an Oriental karate master popped a beer. "Let's have a little action, you know?"

A banjo-bellied young man was contemptuous. "Hey, we can't all be Rambito, man." The wizened karate master gestured with his can of beer, speaking rapid and vehement Spanish.

"So what's the story?" Gage asked.

A guy in a dirty ski jacket sat up suddenly in the back of the truck and peered through the cattle rack. "Ahh, it's some *mojado* who knifed a guy last night."

"Plus he shot a cop," the cholo said.

"He didn't shoot a cop!" The banjo-bellied man snorted. "I was there, man! If you'd listen a second. I'll tell you what happened. Somebody sees the guy breaking into the church, so the guard who works here and a couple of the cops come over to investigate, they surprise the guy and his wife and kid inside. They take them out to the squad car and when they get on the radio it turns out this is the guy the cops down in Santa Fe have been looking for. . . ."

Gage was only half listening. He scanned the crowd, looking for an opening, an edge, someone he might be able to use. A policeman in an unbuttoned bullet-proof vest leaned into one of the patrol cars, talking on the radio. Gage could see two dark silhouettes in the backseat. When one of them moved forward into the light, Gage could see that it was Consuelo. His heart leaped. It would not do for her to recognize him now. He turned back to the truck.

"So the guy panics, right?" the banjo-bellied man was saying. "The guard had left his rifle on the hood of the squad car and the guy grabs it and runs into the church." The cholo moved from one foot to the other, hugging his chest. It was too cold a night for a net shirt, no matter how macho you were. "By the time I got here there's a half-dozen cops and some local hero types who are getting ready to storm the place. It's a joke. The first shot that's

241

fired this two-ton traffic cop from Española dives for cover and breaks a rib on a rock, a windshield gets shot out, they roll a car into the irrigation ditch."

"That's not what I heard, man. I heard he blew the cop's face away with a shotgun." The cholo kicked at the front tire. "This is getting boring. I been here two hours, man. I'm going home and watch it on TV."

"So no one was hit?" Gage asked.

"They think they may have hit the guy inside once, but I don't know."

Gage stared at the low, barred windows of the church. The light from the votive candles swelled for a second, then flickered, as if someone was moving inside.

A scrawny old man in an oversized Pendleton shirt limped across the parking lot, dragging a smashed garbage can on his hip. A patrolman yelled a warning, but the old man paid him no mind, going on about his business. It was the caretaker of the Santuario, the teller of the wildest tales, of tunnels and catacombs and miraculous escapes.

Gage stared up at the shadowed, slightly askew bell towers. "But you're sure he's still in there?"

The cholo snickered. "Hey, where's he gonna go?"

The crowd was bored and restless, there was no doubt about it. Some had already started home. A man shook out the blanket he'd been sitting on, folded it over his arm, saying good-bye to his neighbors. Two elderly sisters huddled on the souvenir store steps, sharing hot soup out of a thermos. Danger was still in the air—when a daredevil teenager sprinted past the churchyard, he zigzagged, head low, as if foiling any imagined sharpshooter—but it had the feel of turning into a long night.

The sound of a bullhorn made Gage glance back. A big Hispanic policeman with shoulders of marbled beef leaned across the hood of a patrol car, cradling the horn. *"Tira tu carabina enfrente de ti, y sal despacio con las manos arriba. No te queremos hacer ningún daño."* He tucked in his shirt with his free hand. "Throw

242

the gun out. No one's going to hurt you. Come out nice and slow. Your wife and child are waiting for you."

When there was no response the big policeman shrugged and said something to a second officer. The second officer turned, shook a box of cough drops against his palm. The second officer was Captain Trevino.

Gage stared at the two of them. There was the smell of piñon smoke in the air, drifting wisps of it lit up by the spotlights of the patrol cars. Gage took a deep breath; there was nothing to be gained by waiting.

He trudged across the open parking lot, put his hand on the roof of the police car. It got their attention.

"Hey, fellas, how's it comin'?" Gage said. The officer's black plastic name tag read ESPINOSA; the gaze was hostile. "Listen, I might be able to help."

"I don't think I know you, do I?" Espinosa said.

"No," Gage said. "But the guy you got inside the church there, he worked on one of Huerta's crews. He built the wall around my house." Gage made a point of not meeting Trevino's gaze. "Maybe a familiar face might help, you see what I'm saying?"

"I don't need any more volunteers," Espinosa said. "I'm just holding down the fort until the big boys arrive."

"Big boys? What do you mean, big boys? I'm telling you I know the guy. This doesn't have to be a big deal, okay?"

"But it is a big deal, Gage," Captain Trevino said. "He killed a man. And maybe he killed two."

"Two? Who's the second?" Gage asked. Trevino said nothing, sucking on his cough drop. "Aww, come on, Trevino, no way. You know the story as well as I do."

"What story?" Espinosa said.

"Huerta's been running wetbacks across the border for years. Last year he was driving up from El Paso with a truckload of Salvadorans. . . ." Trevino frowned; Gage had caught him off guard. "Immigration had changed all the checkpoints, whatever,

243

Huerta's old tricks didn't work. He panicked. He left them locked in the truck."

Espinosa looked baffled. "Gage, you're just guessing," Trevino said.

Three men with deer rifles struggled to get through the barbed wire fence behind the souvenir shop and they were having a tough time of it. Espinosa motioned to a young patrolman, baby-faced and tight-muscled as a collegiate rodeo star.

"Get those guys with the rifles out of here," Espinosa said. "We've had all of the vigilante crap we need for one night. If you have any trouble, get Rivera to help you."

The baby-faced patrolman took off. Sergeant Espinosa watched him go.

Gage touched Trevino in the chest, lightly. It was just between the two of them now. His voice slipped down to little more than a whisper. "Every day Huerta waits for the cops to arrive. They never do. It slowly drives him nuts. He finally goes to a confessional and pours out the whole thing. A couple of days later he gets a call from the police. They want to talk to him. How am I doing so far?"

The baby-faced policeman argued with two of the tipsy riflemen. The third still had his foot tangled in the barbed wire and danced on one leg.

"Who you been talking to, LeRoy? LeRoy's got a big mouth. We talked to Huerta, sure, but we talked to a lot of people," Trevino said.

"Maybe so. But Huerta was convinced that the cops were onto him, that the priest had betrayed him. He'd never seen the priest, you understand. All he had to go on was the voice on the other side of the screen. He called the cathedral a half-dozen times until, bingo, Father Ortiz answered and he thought he heard the voice again."

Espinosa waved to the baby-faced officer. "You tell them to get their goddamn guns out of here or I'm hauling them all in!"

Espinosa waited. One of the men flapped an arm in disgust

244

and shouted something, but his friends pulled him back and the three slunk off through the crowd.

"You've got a great imagination, Gage, I'll give you credit," Trevino said.

"Let's not worry about the credit," Gage said. "This is the part you already know. Huerta told Father Ortiz that his mother was dying out in the desert."

"You've got no witnesses. Unless Huerta told you himself."

"He didn't tell me. But he did tell someone."

"Who?"

"Matín. The guy you've got pinned down inside the church."

Trevino laughed. "Nice try," he said. Espinosa looked Gage up and down. He clearly thought Gage was some sort of crackpot. He picked up the bullhorn.

"You hold it, just for a minute," Gage said, putting a restraining hand on Espinosa's arm. "A week after Father Ortiz was killed, Huerta sends Matín to his truck to get a pack of cigarettes." Gage was talking too fast, he could feel it. A mangy yellow dog trotted through the crowd, begging for food. "Matín can't find it, but while he's looking he digs down behind the seat and finds a bag of sacraments. After work he gets a ride back to Santa Fe with Huerta. They buy some beer."

"This all come to you in a vision, Gage? What are you pitching this to me for? What's this guy to you?"

"They get good and drunk under the trees along the river and Matín tells him what he's found." Gage knew he was blowing it, because he was telling the truth and that was reason enough to distrust him, but he was angry now, he couldn't help himself. "Huerta denies it at first, takes a couple swings at Matín, then starts throwing up and crying. He tells everything."

"But why would he tell? He keeps his mouth shut, he's in the clear."

"People tell, Trevino, people tell. You're a cop, you should know that. Huerta tries to get Matín to promise to say nothing. Matín refuses. Huerta threatens to go to Immigration, get Matín

245

sent back to Guatemala. Still he refuses. Huerta has a knife. So does Matín. A stone knife a friend has given him. Trevino, you know I'm right."

"What if you are?" Trevino said. "So what? How does that change anything?"

A shout made them turn. Consuelo was out of the police car, shouting to someone in a bulky coat standing in the shadows of the trees. The policeman had her firmly by both wrists, but she clung to the open car door, pleading in torrents of Indian dialect.

The man in the shadows came forward into the light and Gage saw that it was his son. Peter didn't look at anyone except Consuelo. He came to the car, put a hand on her elbow, tried to comfort her. Sergeant Espinosa squinted, scratching the back of his neck.

Consuelo gestured toward the church, the police car with the shattered windshield, toward Espinosa and Trevino. When Peter glanced back and caught his father's eye there was the briefest flicker of recognition, a quickly contained flash of bravado. He turned away, soothing Consuelo, brushed a strand of jet-black hair from her anxious face. When he reached inside the police car to shake Cheppi by the back of the neck, he said something that made the boy smile.

It was the nerviest thing Gage had ever seen. There was no way Peter could ever pull it off. He ambled toward Espinosa and Trevino with his hands jammed in his pockets. Gage was too furious to speak. His son had just thrown his life away.

The policeman in the bullet-proof vest tried to sit Consuelo back down in the squad car, but she twisted around, her dark eyes filled with fear, shouting out warnings. Peter lifted a hand, his lips moving soundlessly, passing on some wordless assurance.

"Hey, Walt, how you doin'?" Espinosa said.

"Doing all right," Peter said. Gage was stunned. He looked

246

quickly at Espinosa, then back at Peter. "I talked to your cousin at the store, she told me what happened. . . ."

"Oh, man," Espinosa said, "you had to be here to believe it."

Peter looked up at Gage and gave him a good-humored wink, then patted him on the elbow. "How you doin' tonight, old man?" Trevino dug another cough drop out of the Smith Brothers box and crunched it between his teeth. He wasn't committing himself either way.

"You know the guy inside the church?" Espinosa said.

"Oh, yeah. They live in that house back of the Embudo bridge, the one the sheep herders were using for a while." Peter's voice had taken on a real New Mexico lilt.

"So what was his wife tellin' you?" Espinosa asked. Gage leaned against the police car and looked back toward the crowd, afraid of giving anything away. Peter didn't know just how big a chance he was taking with Trevino; Gage needed to warn him, but it was impossible. A huge, bearded reporter and a diminutive Chinese photographer stood under the portal of the souvenir shop, taking pictures and interviewing.

"She says he would give himself up, but he's afraid you all are gonna open up on him as soon as he shows himself."

"Man, I been tellin' the guy for two hours."

"Well, I guess he doesn't understand so good."

Espinosa gave an exasperated sigh. For the moment Trevino and Gage were out of it, onlookers. "You think you could talk to him?" Espinosa said.

"I could try," Peter said. Gage took a sidelong glance at Trevino. Maybe it was just the sourness of his cough drop, but Trevino didn't look like he approved.

Espinosa gave Peter the bullhorn. "So go ahead." A knot of old women near the wall peered out, witchlike and suspicious behind their shawls.

"How does this work, anyway?" Peter asked. Gage tapped the back tire of the police car with his boot. He felt as if he had a

247

lump of raw dough in his stomach. Trevino slipped the box of cough drops back into his jacket.

"You just flick the switch there," Espinosa said.

Peter did as he was told. Drifting piñon smoke trailed off the buildings. "How's your uncle doin'? I heard he was back in the hospital," Peter said. Good God, Gage thought, he's starting to sound like a character in a Thornton Wilder play, let's not overdo it.

"Aww, he's all right. Same old thing. His blood pressure shoots up. But he keeps sneakin' out for his Kentucky Fried all the same. We're gonna bring him home tomorrow," Espinosa said.

Peter was almost making it too easy. It was the most amazing acting job Gage had ever seen, or maybe it wasn't acting at all.

Peter stood up and raised the bullhorn to his lips. "Matín!" he called. The crowd was silent. For several seconds the only sound was the murmuring of the irrigation ditch. "Matín!" The radio inside the police car crackled with static. Peter hesitated, then shouted out several short phrases in Cakchiquel.

Gage stared at the huge wooden door of the church, at the wooden crosses, the glistening gravestones. A gust of wind brought down a flurry of leaves from the cottonwoods. Then, as Peter handed the bullhorn back to Espinosa, a muffled voice rose from the Santuario. The deputy leaning against the sawhorse stood up, shaking out the leg that had gone to sleep, and raised his rifle. Both Espinosa and Trevino instinctively went into a half crouch behind the police car.

Peter moved forward several steps. "Look out, Walt," Espinosa said. "He's got a gun in there."

Peter put a hand to his mouth and called out again. After half a minute the church door opened a crack. One of the troopers sidestepped his way through the dark trees, edging along the wall of the Santuario, but Espinosa motioned him to stay put.

Matín's voice came from the safety of the shadowed wedge of the barely open door, came in short, choking bursts of distrust.

248

Peter pointed back to Consuelo and Cheppi, put his hand on Espinosa's shoulder, answered Matín's questions one by one.

The crowd had become still, realizing that they were watching something extraordinary. A few of the braver ones moved forward, the circle tightening like a drawstring. A man lifted his daughter on his shoulders so she could see. Matín's voice became less hysterical, but he still clung to the narrow slice of darkness like a terrified climber on a ledge. Peter kept answering questions, matter-of-factly, patiently, as if there were all the time in the world.

Gage finally got up the nerve to look his son full in the face. It was a great performance. It was working, not just on Matín, but on the cops and the crowd too. Peter had them all in the palm of his hand, creating the illusion that there were no sides here. A kind of alchemy was taking place.

But when he reached out a hand, inviting Matín to come out, the only answer was a short, guttural outburst. Cottonwood leaves rattled against the gravestones.

Peter looked to Espinosa for help. "He wants me to go in there and bring him out."

Espinosa shook his head. "The guy's dangerous, Walt. People may have been shooting at him, but he's been shooting back."

"Let him come out on his own," Gage said. The other three men looked at him in surprise. Peter tried to pretend he hadn't heard his father's remark. Trevino, still crouched by the door of the police car, looked slowly from father to son, rolling the cough drop around in his mouth, trying to figure it out.

"Arturo, the guy came here to cure his son," Peter said. "He hasn't done anything you or I wouldn't have done."

Espinosa looked around to be sure no one else saw him giving in. "If you're not out in a couple of minutes we're coming in after you."

"Thanks," Peter said. He looked Trevino straight in the eye. "Maybe you should get Pops here out of harm's way." Gage understood that Pops meant him. The remark was made casually enough, but Peter wasn't taking the chance of glancing in his father's direction.

Trevino stood up, straightened out his trouser leg, put a hand on Gage's chest. "Come on, Gage, let's go."

Gage let Trevino back him off, finally brushed Trevino's arm away, conceding, feigning indifference.

The wail was faint at first, a sound so small and insectlike it was impossible to locate, but everyone heard it and was confused. The sound grew into a chorus of sirens. Gage stared through the trees as a string of flashing red and blue lights descended the hill.

"What the hell is that?" Gage said.

"Looks like the big boys have arrived," Captain Trevino said.

"What big boys?" Peter said. "I thought you guys were in charge." Espinosa stared at his hands; he had huge, arthritic-looking knuckles.

The caravan of police cars slowed to make the turnoff, blades of color carving up the dark hillsides. Two huge police vans muscled into the crowd.

"Arturo, I'm going in," Peter said, "I can get him out, we don't need any of this."

"Walt, just hold your horses," Espinosa said.

The door to the lead van slid open and a half-dozen troopers leaped out. They wore camouflage suits and dark goggles and shiny black combat boots. Rifles jutted over their shoulders, gear rattled like silverware as they moved, burned cork streaked their cheeks like warpaint. The crowd was in awe. The troopers seemed half a foot taller than anyone in the crowd and none of them spoke, as if they operated under secret vows.

They huddled around their leader, a lean, handsome middle-aged man with chiseled features, his goggles pushed high on his forehead.

Peter looked as if he'd seen a ghost. He took a step back and then another, like a runner hung up between bases. Gage suddenly realized what his son was going to do.

250

"Peter, don't!" Gage shouted.

Peter froze at the sound of his rightful name. It took Gage a moment to realize what he'd done, that he'd given it all away. Trevino wiped a sliver of cough drop from the tip of his tongue, flicked it away with his thumb. There was something meditative about the gesture. He had put it together in an instant and it gave him pleasure.

Peter backed onto the irrigation ditch, his face flushed. "Hey, Walt, what you doin'?" Espinosa said. He waved his bullhorn impatiently. "Get back here, man!" A masked trooper ducked under the strap of his rifle, held the weapon across his chest.

"I'm bringing him out, Arturo. You promised me, remember?" Peter's voice was shaky now. He kept moving back, feeling his way with one hand behind him, looking toward Consuelo and Cheppi, their faces pressed to the window of the police car, looking toward the commander and his mottled troopers and then back toward his father.

"Walt, goddamn it, have you lost your fuckin' mind?" Espinosa shouted. "I'm ordering you to get back here!"

"You know you can trust me, Arturo." Peter scanned the crowd, wary as a kayaker trying to read a raging river. "You and I, we know each other, Arturo." Peter turned and ran through the gravestones and the shadows and the wooden crosses toward the church door. Gage couldn't bear to watch anymore. He looked up only when he heard the sharp creaking. The door to the Santuario opened another six inches and, once Peter had slipped behind it, closed tight again.

"Aww, shit!" Espinosa threw the bullhorn and it bounced off the hood of the police car and landed in the dirt at Trevino's feet. Espinosa turned on Gage. "So what the hell did you call him?"

Trevino pried Espinosa away gently with a hand on the larger man's shoulder. "Come on. I think the new commander here is waiting for his briefing."

"Trevino," Gage said. "I can explain."

"I'm sure you can, Gage. And there will be time for that."

251

Trevino bent down to retrieve the battered bullhorn and handed it back to Espinosa. "Meanwhile, I wouldn't go away if I were you."

Trevino escorted Espinosa toward the commander, Espinosa tucking in his billowing shirttail. The leaves of the cottonwoods seemed unreal, golden filigree illuminated against a black sky.

Gage watched the three police officers confer. Trevino did most of the talking. For a moment it seemed as if Espinosa was registering some kind of vehement protest, but Trevino overrode his objection. Espinosa put his hands on his hips, quickly sliding from confusion to morose silence. Trevino and the commander turned their attention to the bell towers, the surrounding walls, the sheltering trees.

Gage pivoted away in disgust. In front of the van, troopers passed tear gas canisters from hand to hand like batons. Flames flickered in an oil drum behind one of the buildings; a half-dozen men gathered around, warming their hands in the smoky light. The crowd had moved back again, lined up against the far walls, silent and faceless as cornhusk dolls at a country fair.

The only person paying Gage any mind was the milky-eyed caretaker, squatting by the souvenir shop. He watched Gage as if aware of his distress; his gaze never wavered, as if he were trying to tell Gage something.

Out of the corner of his eye Gage caught motion. He turned. The comander sent his troops into action with one quick nod. They ran, bent low, heading around the church in long, looping curves, reconnoitering. They were as perfectly drilled as dancers, vanishing into darkness.

The commander took the bullhorn from the deflated Espinosa. "This is Captain Hancock of the state police." His voice had air-terminal quality. "The two of you have exactly fifteen minutes to throw out the rifle and come out with your hands up."

Hancock put his hand on the shoulder of the one remaining trooper and gave last-minute instructions. The goggled trooper was young, strapping, soft cheeks slashed with burned cork,

252

hands big as a wide receiver's. Hancock patted the boy warrior on the back and the trooper sprinted toward the rear of the church.

Gage moved across the open lot toward the three officers as if he were crossing mined waters. He could feel the wary eyes of the crowd on him, the eyes of a hundred witnesses.

Hancock raised the bullhorn again. "If you are seriously hurt, we have medical assistance on hand. Your family is safe and waiting for you. You have fifteen minutes to decide."

"There's nothing to decide," Gage said. The commander lowered the bullhorn and regarded him evenly. "Everything's already been decided. Maybe my friends here didn't explain it to you." Espinosa, overcome by gloom, refused to meet Gage's glance. "My name's Jeremiah Gage and my son is in there."

"I know who you are," Hancock said. "And I know who's in there. Looks like we hit the jackpot tonight, didn't we?" Two blinking red lights drifted over the mesa.

"Listen, my kid has nothing to do with this."

"No?" Hancock said. His eyes were an unflinching blue. When he spoke, he spoke in measured tones. "Then what's he doing here? Or is it just chickens coming home to roost?"

Espinosa blew into his fist, trying to warm his fingers. He had lost face. The blinking red lights above the mesa disappeared for a moment and then appeared again, lower down and moving faster.

"Just how slick do you think you are, Gage?" Trevino said. "You must have thought you could finesse anything." In the shadows to the right of the church two of the camouflaged elite troopers ran together, exchanged a word, sprang apart, mystic warriors disappearing back into the darkness as if they were swinging on strings. "We may be slow, but we're not that slow."

Gage ran his tongue over his lower lip, stared at Trevino and saw there was no point. He turned back to Hancock, who caressed the bullhorn with his fingertips, wiping some of the dirt away.

253

"Captain, the man who killed Father Ortiz is dead. The man who died last night was killed in self-defense and Trevino knows all this. My son had no part in any of it. So you can just call off your dogs." Hancock's choirboy eyebrows rose. "I thought you guys were interested in justice." Somewhere above them was a thick whirring, a pulsing of the air.

Trevino held his tongue for a moment, his face tightening with ancient grievance. "Don't you talk to me about what's just. My son didn't come back from the dead."

The thudding grew louder, drowning out Trevino's voice. A helicopter rose above the trees like a huge sea creature emerging from the deep.

Gage looked wildly at the trio of cops. "What the hell is this?"

Hancock shielded his eyes, teeth clenched, staring upward. Gage spun around, saw the panicked horse rear up, the boy sliding off, yanking at the halter rope, trying to calm the huge animal. The trooper with the big hands ran out of the darkness and leaped the ditch.

The helicopter hovered dreamlike above the church. Everything was dark behind the glass. For one moment Gage entertained the wild hope that there were just cameras inside, not guns, maybe it was just some Albuquerque news team.

He glanced back at Trevino. The detective had turned his back, his head down, as if to protect himself from the battering wind and the blowing dust. If it was the death of Trevino's son they were trying to solve, there was no hope for any of them.

"So who cooked this up?" Gage shouted at the three of them, but the whomping of the helicopter obliterated everything.

Gage spun around again. One of the SWAT team boosted his partner up the wall of the church, watched him wriggle onto the low wall of the narthex.

Espinosa took Trevino by the elbow and led him away. Hancock and the trooper with the big hands huddled, the younger man pointing toward the back of the Santuario. The churning

254

blades of the helicopter drowned out all other sounds. Neither man heard Gage's approach.

"He's in place, Captain, everything's set," the trooper said. "As soon as you give the signal, it will take ten, twelve seconds, max."

"What signal?" Gage said.

The trooper's mouth sagged, but Hancock didn't miss a beat. "There's no signal," he said. "I don't know what you're talking about."

The elite commander scanned the church. The goggles on his forehead gleamed in the half light like reptilian eyes, giving second sight. Gage followed his gaze and saw, for the first time, the camouflaged trooper perched in the bell tower, slouched and patient as a duck hunter in his blind.

"What signal?" Gage said. The yellow dog scampered across the parking lot, tail between its legs.

"I'm here to protect lives, Mr. Gage."

"You promised them fifteen minutes. You lied to them. My son is turning himself in, goddammit."

"Your son had years to make up his mind, fifteen more minutes isn't going to matter. He slipped through once. He's not going to slip through again. You can't call, 'Cut,' now, Mr. Director. It's not your movie anymore." Hancock glanced up at the copter with his hero's face, turned to the big-handed trooper. "Get the pilot on the radio, would you? I don't want any more interference."

Gage turned, looking for help. The caretaker was gone, Trevino had retreated under one of the portals, Espinosa waved his arms at the regular police. The gravel of the parking lot, under all the lights, shone like raked sand. Gage stared up at the massive, gleaming machine. The blades whirred like the reel of a projector, hypnotic and endless. Hancock and his young trooper were already on their way back to one of the vans.

"Hancock!"

The commander never looked back. Peter had no chance. He didn't know that. Gage was the only one who could tell him.

Gage had trotted halfway across the parking lot before anyone seemed to notice.

"Hey, mister, get back here!"

He never stopped. Looking back over his shoulder he saw Hancock spring away from the police van, barking orders. Gage began to run, his shadow flickering across the bright gravel, marring the frame of perfect, pitiless light. He was across the irrigation ditch, through the arch, among the slick gravestones. The masked trooper in the bell tower rose up, taking aim, but Gage knew he wouldn't dare.

Gage hammered at the door of the church. "Peter! Let me in there!" He heard feet running behind him.

He slammed his shoulder against the wooden door and it gave almost at once. His momentum carried him inside, a blade of light flaring across the linoleum floor. He stumbled, caught himself, heaved the door shut, restoring darkness. He slid the bolt in place.

He leaned against the rough wood of the door, trying to get his breath back. After a moment his eyes adjusted enough to make out the clusters of candles flickering at the far altar.

"Peter?" he whispered. He waited and then called more loudly. "Peter!" Still there was no answer.

He groped his way down the uneven steps, running a supporting hand along the cool wall. Everything was hushed inside the church; even the thudding of the helicopter was eerily muffled.

Gage turned slowly, scanning the sanctuary; candlelight reflected off the glass panels in the wall. "Peter! Matín!" he bumped against one of the pews. "This is no time to play games!"

He felt his way up the aisle and yanked one of the candles from the altar, trying to fight back the panic. They couldn't have just disappeared and they weren't big enough idiots to try to hide from him. Using the candle to light his way, he ducked into the side room and surveyed the crutches and braces hanging from the flaking walls. Hot wax dripped onto his hand; Gage cursed softly and sucked at the flesh between his thumb and forefinger. An ancient wooden door at the far end of the room had been braced shut with a pair of benches: the first sign that Peter and Matín had been here.

A flashlight hung by a leather thong above the door. Gage took it off its hook and snapped it on and off to be sure it worked.

The helicopter sounded as if it had just come down another ten feet, was settling around his shoulders. With the steady roar there was no way Gage was going to hear someone working open any of the barred windows.

He snuffed out the candle and set it aside, shone the flashlight through the narrow doorway of the *pozito*. Light rolled in the sacred-red-dirt hole like a heavy liquid, the hole was a socket. The whole thing was nuts. Was it some kind of prank? Did they think they could escape by squirreling themselves away in some nook or cranny?

He moved back into the sanctuary and glanced up at the sound of a rope, slapping against the outside of a wall. There was a trickling of adobe, the dull scraping of climbing boots. Fear ratcheted upward. He shone the flashlight across the scalloped beams of the ceiling. He still hadn't found the entrance to the bell tower.

He waved the light along the walls, across the bultos and reredos, blue-robed saints in faded red and gold cases. It gave Gage the willies. It was like being in a caveful of bats, a thousand tiny figures out there in the darkness with their eyes full of mildness and surrender.

As the light swept across the pews, Gage saw the jagged fault line in the linoleum floor. The caretaker's story came back to him, the story about the tunnel, the legendary escapes, but he quickly pushed it out of his mind. Some things were not possible.

"Peter!" He was angry now. There was no time for hide-and-seek.

257

Heavy curtains draped the confessionals near the front of the church. He moved quickly down the aisle and then he saw, under the back pew, a series of glistening circles, some of them the size of quarters. It was a trail of blood, leading to the equipment room.

He was there in a second. He swung open the door. The flickering beam played across a scarred desk, a low sink and, in the corner, an open closet. The dirt floor of the closet had hard-packed shoulders a couple of feet wide, like an animal burrow or the shallowest of graves. He moved closer and saw the three or four steps leading down into a narrow tunnel.

Gage went to one knee. At the bottom of the tunnel was a blood-soaked rag.

He muttered a curse, then looked back suddenly over his shoulder, as if he sensed someone there, some witness to his shame, but there were only coffee cans full of nuts and bolts, dirty towels hanging above the low sink. He had lost his son again.

There was no time for strategy now. He lowered himself into the tunnel, reaching back to pull the closet door shut behind him. It was a tight fit. He had to corkscrew his way in as if he were pulling a shirt over his head.

He moved on his hands and knees, sliding his flashlight ahead of him in the dust. The only sounds were his own breathing and the slithering of his own knees through dirt. He was totally cut off. They could be storming the church above him and he would never hear it.

The feeble beam of light bobbed in front of him as he crawled, picking up what seemed to be roots, twisted bits of chewed animal fur, rocks, the shattered skulls of mice. The tunnel smelled of resin and smoke and old skunks' nests.

He accidentally brushed against one of the ancient cedar crossbeams and dirt fell, first in a trickle and then more. It caught him by surprise, got in his eyes and mouth.

He rubbed his eyes with the back of his hand, but that only made it worse. The taste in his mouth was acrid.

He began to crawl, eyes watering, scarcely able to see. Peter would never make it. The tunnel could be collapsed, who knew where the hell it went; not in a million years could a stunt like this work. Now it really was the blind leading the blind.

Gage thought he heard the sound of someone breathing ahead of him in the tunnel, but when he called out, no answer came back. He crawled faster. There was the faintest glow of light.

The tunnel flared into what seemed almost a room, a bear's den of the miraculous. Two ancient stone caskets, looking black and heavy as lead, sat up on cinder blocks, a few plastic Woolworth's flowers scattered around them. A monstrance lay half-submerged in the dust like a buried horseshoe crab shell, and near it, an empty Hi-Ho cracker box. There were animal droppings and one curled-up cracked leather shoe and carved wooden icons, some painted, some not, some broken and charred, sacred vestiges and remnants Gage didn't know the names for.

Matín sat curled up in the corner, arms wrapped tight around his knees, almost indistinguishable from the broken and charred icons around him. He gave no sign of surprise at seeing Gage. When he turned his head to one side to protect his eyes from Gage's flashlight, Gage could see blood glistening from his shirt. The two men did not exchange a word.

Gage moved past him; the tunnel curved to the right and pitched downward. The light ahead was stronger, but wavering, reflecting off the walls, and Gage heard the sound of blows.

Peter gave no sign of hearing his father's approach. A massive wooden figure blocked the end of the tunnel and Peter dug furiously around it, banging at the dirt wall with the butt end of a flashlight, using it as a trowel. He set the flashlight aside, tried to get a fingerhold on the statue, tugging on one spot and then another. His knuckles were bleeding.

259

"Peter!" Gage whispered. Peter still did not turn, working like a trapped animal.

The figure blocking the tunnel had a painted crown of thorns and painted drops of blood streaking its face, but the shock of black hair on its head was human. Its limbs were jointed like a puppet's, bound together by leather. The lower half of the torso was charred and it was wedged in as tight as a log.

"Peter!" Gage shook the heel of Peter's boot. Peter glanced back, startled, with the look of a man afraid of being yanked off a pitched roof.

"Just leave me alone." His voice was hoarse, his face streaked with soot.

"It will never work. You don't have a chance."

Peter turned sideways, supporting himself on one elbow in the cramped space. He sucked on his lower lip, still breathing hard. "Maybe not. But you think I've got a chance with them, up there? I've been through that once. . . ."

Peter grabbed hold of one of the jointed legs of the statue. He gave it one hard yank and it tore loose at the knee. He tossed it aside. Gage heard a low rasping sound behind him. Looking back over his shoulder, he saw Matín dragging himself toward them.

"Even if you make it out of this tunnel, how far are you going to get? Unless you've decided to leave him behind. He's hurt bad. You'd be lucky to make it a hundred yards."

Peter didn't answer. He got a good fingerhold on the shoulder of the statue and tugged once, twice, three times. Some of the earth above broke loose and showered down on them. Peter cleared away the clumps of dirt.

"Don't worry about us. I've gotten lost before."

Matín lay on his side behind Gage, listening to them, not understanding a word.

"But it's not like before," Gage said. "You've got a wife and two kids sleeping at my house." The two flashlights created bright webs on the dirt walls. "What do you want me to tell them in the morning? That you cut and ran?"

Peter yanked harder at the statue, forward and back, like a rower straining against rusted oarlocks. "Don't you tell me about running." Peter looked over his shoulder, his eyes wide with fury. "You ran out on my mother. You knew she was sick, you knew she was lost, and you just waltzed right out of there. . . ."

Peter turned away. He slashed at the dirt wall with the blunt end of his flashlight, and with every second or third blow there was the sharp sound of metal striking wood.

Gage sat back on his knees, too numb to speak. So all those years, that's what Peter thought. Gage brushed the dirt from his hair. The unfairness of it all welled up inside him. Son of a bitch, think what you want, but nobody turns their back on me.

With a cry, Gage threw himself at his son. They fell together. Gage tried to pin his son's arms, but Peter was too strong for him. As they rolled over, Peter worked one arm free. Gage raised a hand to shield his face from the blow, but Peter struck him flush on the cheek with the flashlight.

Gage fell on his chest in the dust. The salty taste of blood was in his mouth and somewhere above him he could hear thumping blows. Gage tried to push himself up with his hands, but failed.

Something gave. There was a shower of dirt, light from the outside, and Gage could hear the thudding of the helicopter; it was as if a fist had been removed from the bell of a horn.

Gage lifted his head. Peter had fallen on his side, the statue sprawled across him like some double-jointed drunk. All that separated them from the outside was a metal grating. Peter shoved the statue aside and heaved against the metalwork. It gave at once, falling into some tall weeds.

Blood pooled in the back of Gage's throat. Peter leaned back on his heels in the open tunnel mouth, hands resting on his thighs. Beyond him, by a good thirty yards, were cottonwoods and the faint outlines of cobblestone altars. It took Gage a couple of seconds to put together exactly where they were: below the wall, at the back of the church, and beyond the circle of police and onlookers.

Gage felt a gentle hand on his shoulder, Matín's hand, but he brushed it away. Peter still had not moved, staring out at the ghostly trees and the dark pasture like a man in a trance. Gage was afraid to utter a word. He wiped blood and dirt from his mouth.

Gage's pickup was off to the right and a couple of cars had come in to park behind it. A sprint would be crazy, he'd be gunned down in a minute, but if Peter had the nerve and strolled out like someone wandering off for a leak in the woods, it could work. If Peter wanted it, there it was, laid out on a silver platter.

"So go then," Gage said. "Go if you're going to go."

Peter turned his head, but in the darkness of the tunnel Gage couldn't see his face. Peter's shoulders began to rise and fall, as if he were gasping for air, but it was not the same as before, now it was a sound Gage had not heard for twenty years, not since that morning in the Madison airport when Gage had said good-bye for the last time. It was the sound of a boy's crying.

Gage crawled to Peter and put his arms around him. The smell of dust was on them both. He took his son's face in his hands and pulled him to his chest. Cradling his son's head, Gage gazed out at the dim altars, the cottonwood leaves golden, shaking with light. The thudding of the helicopter became one with the pounding of Gage's heart.

"I'm going to take you home, Peter," Gage said. "Just hold on."

Gage stuck his head out, peered left and then right. The helicopter whirred somewhere above, but he couldn't see it. He slipped out, like a swimmer sliding silently into a pool. He was in shadow at the base of the wall, at the corner farthest from the parking lot.

He reached back for Peter's hand. "Come on," he said. "Now." Peter's fingers locked into his father's and Gage pulled him to his feet.

Gage shook dirt out of his trousers as Peter reached back to help Matín. Peter stared up at the thumping of the helicopter. His face was pinched, squinting in the sudden light. Matín plucked his bloody shirt away from his skin, his dark, lustrous eyes darting from father to son.

Gage put his hand on Peter's shoulder, talking fast and low. "We do this right, we're going to be fine. We're going to go up there. Like we belong. Once we're in that crowd, they can't touch us. They don't have the nerve. It's the only shot we've got. All right? All right?" Peter raised his eyes, his gaze grave, heavy as lead. He nodded. "Okay," Gage said. "So let him know what we're doing."

Matín's eyes widened as Peter explained quickly in Cakchiquel what they were doing. He puffed out his cheeks in disbelief, plucking at his bloody shirt.

Out of the corner of his eye Gage saw something moving up on the concrete ramp. For a second it froze them all. The mangy yellow dog stood staring down at them and wagging its tail.

The dog trotted happily toward them. Gage caught the mongrel by the collar and patted it, trying to calm it.

Peter slipped out of his heavy blue barn coat and held it out for Matín. Matín winced as he tried to raise his arm into the sleeve. Gage glanced up and for the first time saw the tips of helicopter blades.

"So let's go," Gage said.

The three men moved slowly up the concrete ramp, Peter putting a helping hand under Matín's elbow. Halfway up, Matín had to stop, squatting down for a moment in pain, but never uttering a sound, regathering his strength. A middle-aged woman and her son sat at the top of the incline, staring toward the church, utterly hypnotized. Gage could see the helicopter clearly now, hovering twenty feet above the church in a smoky yellow gravy.

They moved again, the backs of the crowd coming into view. Gage caught sight of the knot of men gathered around the an-

263

cient blue truck. Barricades had been set in place and the onlookers pushed even further back. Gage glanced at Peter, but
couldn't catch his eye.

They came to the top of the incline. A boy looked idly back at
them for a second, but nothing registered. His mother shook
him by the shoulder, pointing toward the back of the church.
Members of the SWAT team had pried loose a couple of the bars
at the back window and one of the troopers tried to squeeze
through while his companion crouched alongside, rifle balanced
on one knee. The sniper still squatted in the bell tower and there
was at least one man on the roof.

Gage and Peter and Matín stood five feet back of the crowd,
uninvited guests. The man in front of them ate grapes out of a
cellophane Baggie, spitting the seeds on the ground. Gage
scanned the parking lot for Trevino or Espinosa or Hancock, but
the only face he recognized was that of the caretaker, who had
rejoined the crowd under the portal of the souvenir shop.

No one saw them. It was as though they had wandered in
through the back door of an arena during some championship
match; all eyes were riveted on center ring. The rail-thin deputy
leaned against a barricade fifteen feet away. A woman cringed
against her husband's chest, her hand to her mouth.

If a signal was given, Gage missed it, but suddenly things were
in motion. Once the first trooper slipped through the bars of the
window, the second quickly followed. Gage glanced back at the
bell tower. The sniper was gone. Espinosa, crouching low, arms
trailing behind, ran out from behind the big cottonwood by the
irrigation ditch.

Gage tapped the shoulder of the man with the bag of grapes.
"Excuse me," he said. "If we could just get through here."

There was a muffled shot inside the church and then, after a
moment, two more. A woman in bright polyester pants and
running shoes broke into a wail, "Oh my God, oh my God." The
banjo-bellied man winced, rubbing the side of his face as if he'd
been struck. Someone near Gage wept.

Gage stood in stunned silence. It wasn't hard to figure out what had happened: a trigger-happy trooper firing at the first thing that moved, a shadow, a reflection, one of his own men. What was hard was standing outside, looking in. The three shots had been meant for them. It was like being an onlooker at your own funeral.

Gage heard someone fall behind him and then a woman's scream. He looked back and saw Matín down on one knee. Peter tried vainly to help him up. Blood had soaked through the heavy blue barn coat, plain as day. People backed off in a hurry. A mother scooped her child up, an old man stumbled and spilled his beer.

"Hey! They're over here!" The man with the grapes shouted.

Gage grabbed Matín under the left arm, helping Peter to get him onto his feet. People scrambled for cover, pushing and shoving, a couple of the younger ones hurdling the low stone wall. An old woman gaped at them, then crossed herself. The deputy shouted at her to move, but she was confused, starting in one direction, then heading back in the other, until the deputy came to pull her away.

A pair of the local cops had their guns drawn and pointed in Gage's direction, but they lacked conviction. A spotlight swept around, glaring in Gage's eyes and then a second light did the same.

Gage put a hand up, glanced at Peter. So he thinks I ran, Gage thought. They had all run, one way or the other, but no one was running now. They were a total mess: Peter with soot on his face and bloody knuckles; Matín bent over, clutching his blood-stained jacket; all three of them covered with dirt.

Gage heard someone barking orders. It was almost impossible to see in the intersecting beams of light. Someone came out of the churchyard. Gage cocked his head to one side, shielding his eyes, trying to make out who.

"Hey, Hancock!" Gage shouted. "We're turning ourselves in!

That's what you wanted, right? Tell them to put their guns away!"

The crowd was hushed. Gage heard the helicopter directly overhead. He swung around slowly, like a needle in a compass, trying to get a reading. He could make out the goateed old man who looked like a karate master, kneeling in the flatbed of the ancient truck; he could see a woman pressing a dark blue shawl tight to her throat. He could see the awe in their faces. No one knew if they were witnessing a miracle or a brilliant trick. They'd all heard the shots. Now they had the three who'd been gunned down walking in their midst.

The door of one of the police cars swung open and a small figure leaped out and ran toward them. It was Cheppi. An officer grabbed for him, caught him by the wrist, but Cheppi pulled free and darted past the armed men.

Matín went down to one knee and caught his son in his arms. At first Gage thought the sounds the mute boy was making were just sobs, but then it dawned on him that Cheppi was forming words, in a language Gage didn't understand.

Matín tried to stand with Cheppi in his arms, but it was more than he could handle. He staggered and fell, the father and son landing in a tangle. Cheppi scrambled to his feet, one hand still clutching the collar of his father's coat and crying out.

The woman in the blue shawl was the first, running out to protect the boy, but behind her came the cholo in the net shirt, and then, in a great surge, everyone.

A couple of the cops tried to stop them, shouting to the crowd to back off, but it was too late. They'd lost whatever hold they'd had. It was like trying to stop water from pouring over a dam.

Gage and Peter were engulfed in a sea of strangers. Someone yanked at Gage's wrist, another whispered fervent advice. Across the bobbing heads Gage could see the banjo-bellied man standing over Matín and shouting for a doctor.

Gage glanced back at his son. Peter looked stunned. He was a head taller than most of the jostling and prodding crowd around him and he had his elbows up like a man trying to keep his balance in a rushing river. There was a dull pop and a flash of light; the Chinese photographer hustled along the periphery of the crowd, her camera held high.

The butt of a rifle caught Gage in the back. He spun angrily and saw the begoggled trooper about to deliver a second blow, but the cholo in the net shirt shoved the trooper first. Both cholo and trooper squared off, but quickly there were three or four others, cops and noncops, breaking them up.

The baby-faced patrolman got hold of both Peter and Gage and hustled them through the crowd. There was the sudden yipping of a dog getting stepped on and, from behind one of the walls, the sound of breaking glass. A woman trotted at Peter's side, taking his hand, pressing a wet rag to his bloody knuckles until the policeman in the bulletproof vest pulled her away. Some of the crowd pushed forward, reaching out to touch their hair, their clothes, their faces, and others pulled back, afraid. The goateed karate master stood in the back of the truck, pointing at the police, laughing his head off, slapping his thighs, having the time of his life.

Espinosa waited for them at the police car at the upper end of the parking lot. "Okay, leave 'em alone, dammit. I'm in charge here." He jammed his shirt back into his belt, then waved off the baby-faced patrolman and a pair of baffled county policemen. He waggled a finger at Gage and Peter. "Go on, get up against the car."

Father and son spreadeagled against the squad car while Espinosa, frisked them. In the midst of the milling crowd Hancock stood alone, looking like the spurned suitor at a wedding, a man cheated of his moment. One of the snipers had come out of the church, shamefaced and a little shaken, not wanting to talk to anyone, but the caretaker bird-dogged him, berating him. Steam rose from an overheated police car like steam from warm bread.

Espinosa fumbled with a pair of handcuffs at his belt. He glanced up darkly. "So how long have we known each other? Ten years?" He gave a short puff. Hancock strode toward them, shouldering through the knots of people. "That goes to show how much I know. Let's have your hands. Both of you."

Gage and Peter held out their wrists. A sullen semicircle of fifteen, maybe twenty people had gathered around the car. The hefty sergeant clamped one handcuff on Peter, the other on Gage. Gage felt the metal bite into his flesh. A priest stood in the middle of the parking lot, trying to wave off the helicopter, which finally rose slowly and then veered over the trees like a dragonfly.

Espinosa opened the back door of the police car, but as Gage turned, Hancock blocked his way. Hancock looked right past Gage; it was Peter he was after.

"I wanted to see what a traitor looked like," Hancock said. "Up close."

The muscles around Peter's mouth seemed to freeze. Hancock came forward a step and spat in Peter's face.

Gage raised his fist to take a punch, but felt his arm suddenly yanked back, nearly pulled out of its socket. Peter, manacled to him with three inches of chain, had checked the blow. Gage tried again, jabbing at Hancock with his free hand even as he was being dragged away.

"You touch my kid, I'll tear your heart out, you hear me? I don't care how many goddamn medals you're hiding behind. . . ."

Peter and Espinosa both pushed him back. "Okay, okay," Espinosa said, "get 'em in the car."

Peter slid into the backseat and tried to pull Gage in after him, but Gage wasn't done yet.

"This General Patton act doesn't cut it with me, mister. You want a piece of me, we'll take care of that right now."

"Don't test your luck, old man," Espinosa said. "Watch your head." Espinosa stuffed Gage into the car seat with both hands and slammed the door shut. Gage stared up through the crack in the window.

"What do you think you're doing?" Hancock said.

"What am I doing?" Espinosa was riled up now. "These are my arrests, all right? I've been here for six hours and you show up just in time for the pictures. The hell with it. I'm taking them in. All three of them."

Espinosa walked around to the driver's side, shouting instructions to one of the other officers, pointing toward Matín. Hancock might as well have been in a body cast, totally immobilized.

Espinosa threw himself in behind the steering wheel. He glanced back at Peter. "You look like hell." He took a folded white T-shirt off the dash and opened the wire mesh screen that sealed off the back of the car. He leaned across the seat to wipe the spittle from Peter's face.

A teenage girl hopped up on the hood of the car. Espinosa hammered on the window, yelling and waving her off. The girl jumped down, laughing.

As the police car moved forward, some of the kids ran alongside, pressing hands and faces to the windows. Espinosa turned on the siren to clear a path. Once they hit concrete, Espinosa stepped on it, quickly leaving the running kids behind.

They moved up the long hill, came out of the valley and were suddenly in a world of moonlight and jagged rock, reservation land. The police radio crackled in the front seat. Off to their right, set up in the Jemez Mountains, were the lights of Los Alamos. Though they were twenty miles off, the clear night air made them seem almost within arm's reach.

"Your mother loved it when she first came out here," Gage said. Peter's head swiveled; he was startled at the sound of his father's voice. "How could she not have? For her and her father to go from Nazi Germany to northern New Mexico, she said, it seemed like heaven on earth. The mountains, the air, it was freedom. . . ."

The tires squealed as they went around a curve and Peter braced his free hand against the cagelike mesh. "Do you think they know yet? Sandy and Amy?"

"I don't know," Gage said. "We'll call them when we get to the station." Espinosa's headlights flared across three or four cattle grazing just off the shoulder of the highway. They were in open range, not a fence in sight. If you were driving at night out here you had to stay on your toes.

Gage stared at the dark mountains. "Her father bought her a horse. For her fourteenth birthday. She ever tell you that story?"

"Yes," Peter said.

Gage tried to push the handcuff further down on his wrist. "She'd ride that horse everywhere. Up in the mountains, down into the canyons of what's Bandelier now. I don't know if she ever told you this story or not, but one day she was out on one of the mesas and she found an Indian shrine. Stone figures, bits of horn, feathers, little colored bags hanging in the trees. The point was that it was *live*, people were still using it. Here was this little German-Jewish girl scared out of her wits. She didn't know quite what she'd stumbled into, but she was sure that whoever it was was coming back any minute and at the same time it was the most magical thing that had ever happened to her. She was there maybe three, four minutes before she got the hell out. . . ."

Something caught Peter's eye and he turned to look out the back window and Gage turned too. A procession of lights crawled across the plain, maybe a half mile back. It seemed they were going to have a full escort going in. Peter tapped on the wire mesh screen.

"Arturo, what about Matín?"

Espinosa glanced over his shoulder. "There was a doctor taking care of him. Two of the cops I know are driving him in. He's going to be all right."

For a moment the lights of Los Alamos disappeared behind tall, eroded spires of rock. Peter seemed tight as a snare drum. They still had a thirty-mile ride ahead of them. The key was to talk, talk about everything except what lay just ahead. The key was to beat back the silence.

"I always used to tease her about that, tell her she'd probably

270

imagined the whole thing. Then one summer we were back here. It was the summer before you were born, she was maybe a couple months pregnant with you. She was determined that she was going to show me. She was sure she remembered *exactly* where the shrine was. So we rented a couple of horses and we went back in there. And we looked, I'll tell you, all day. We climbed in and out of it must have been ten canyons. You remember how your mother was. Once she made up her mind about something."

Peter laid his forehead against the dark window. Gage tasted blood again at the back of his throat and swallowed. He gazed out at the ghost-ridden landscape, dotted with juniper and stunted piñon. It was a night for predators, coyotes and owls. Anything moving across the hard-packed sand and pale rock would be easy to spot.

"Maybe you'd rather not hear this," Gage said.

"No, I want to hear," Peter said. "I want you to tell me."

Gage paused for a moment before beginning again. The winking lights of Los Alamos had slid around behind them.

"We looked everywhere," Gage said. "But you know how you can get turned around in those canyons. At least a half-dozen times she was sure she had found it . . . it was around the next bend, in the next clump of cedar. In a way it didn't matter. Just being up on those mesas, you could see forever up there. We went through unexcavated ruins, in some places the pottery shards must have been six inches deep, I swear. We scared up three or four deer. When your mother got excited about something, she was one of the most *alive* people. . . ."

Ahead of the car, blinking red lights drifted across the horizon. Gage figured it was the helicopter. Peter, leaning forward to shake dirt from the cuff of one of his socks, missed it.

"In the afternoon there was a thunderstorm and we ducked for cover in one of the caves, sat it out for an hour, eating sandwiches, drinking lemonade, watching the rain pour down on the cottonwoods. It was one of the best goddamn days of my life. She was a beautiful woman, your mother. And I was not such a son of

271

a bitch. Not that day." Gage could feel the tears streaming down his face, but he was not going to give in to it. Peter shifted toward his father. There was enough moonlight through the window for Gage to see his son's stricken face.

"Oh, but don't get me wrong. I kept on teasing her about it. For years. About her make-believe shrine. But you know what I think now? I think it was there. I think we just never did find our way back to it."

JAMES MAGNUSON was born in Madison, Wisconsin, and educated at the University of Wisconsin. He has written a dozen produced plays and six novels, including *Without Barbarians, The Rundown, Orphan Train* (with Dorothea Petrie), *Open Season,* and *Money Mountain.* He has been a Hodder Fellow at Princeton University and has won a National Endowment for the Arts Fellowship for his fiction. He lives in Austin, Texas, with his wife and two children and teaches at the University of Texas.